meantime

Also by Katharine Noel

Halfway House

meantime

KATHARINE NOEL

Black Cat
New York

Published simultaneously in Canada
Printed in the United States of America

First published by Grove Atlantic, November 2016

FIRST EDITION

ISBN 978-0-8021-2549-1
eISBN 978-0-8021-8962-2

Library of Congress Cataloging-in-Publication Data

Names: Noel, Katharine, author.
Title: Meantime : a novel / Katharine Noel.
Description: First edition. | First American paperback edition. | New York : Black Cat, 2016.
Identifiers: LCCN 2016013873 (print) | LCCN 2016021058 (ebook) | ISBN 9780802125491 (softcover) | ISBN 9780802189622 (ebook)
Subjects: LCSH: Self-realization in women—Fiction. | Man-woman relationships—Fiction. | Domestic ficiton. | BISAC: FICTION / Literary.
Classification: LCC PS3614.O387 M43 2016 (print) | LCC PS3614.O387 (ebook) | DDC 813/.6—dc23
LC record available at https://lccn.loc.gov/2016013873

Black Cat
an imprint of Grove Atlantic
154 West 14th Street
New York, NY 10011

Distributed by Publishers Group West

groveatlantic.com

16 17 18 19   10 9 8 7 6 5 4 3 2 1

Eric

meantime

*a*fternoon, March, sky pressing lower and lower. The coming storm meant no one skipped the bus, which meant no chance of getting a seat by myself, which meant the humiliation of watching the humiliation of the ponytailed seventh grader who realized she had to sit next to me.

Outside was dark as evening. We jolted slowly down the school driveway and made the creaking wide turn onto River Road. The black-green rubber seat felt cold even through my jeans; I stuck my hands under my thighs, which didn't help. The warmest places on the bus were over the wheel wells in back, but they were also the most desirable, and no way would I ever try to claim one of those seats. I wasn't the weirdest person in eighth grade: Deborah Roth wore floods and sang to herself. Deborah Roth actually had friends, though. My bizarre home life—people called us the Naked Family—could have mostly been forgiven, the way it was for my stepsister, Nicole, if I hadn't been too skinny, with a sharp nose and pointed chin and very fine, very pale blond hair. And those things might also have been forgiven if I hadn't been a know-it-all.

The seventh grader beside me sat with her back turned, feet sticking into the aisle as far as she dared without the bus driver yelling.

"You know what I'm doing?" I asked her.

She pretended not to hear.

"You know what I'm doing?" I asked louder.

"Shhh," she hissed. "What?"

I waited until finally she had to look at me. I pretended to break an egg, stir with a spoon. "I'm baking a cake, for your pity party."

She rolled her eyes, folding her arms across her chest. I smiled, in case anyone was watching, then leaned my head on the window glass. The bus rocked, knocking around the smell of body odor and gym shoes and Confession, a drugstore spray that smelled like sour Tang. Maybe because of the strange mid-afternoon darkness, there was more shrieking than usual, more grabbing of notebooks and throwing them against the ceiling, where they burst like shot birds.

The bus hit a pothole. The guys in back whooped as they were tossed a few inches into the air; Nicole and the other cheer-leaders giggled. At home, we had a device that switched lights on or off at the sound of a clap. Or at any other loud sound, so that we weren't allowed to let the kitchen door slam, or drop our books on the hall floor, or galumph down the stairs. Nicole and her friends were like that, set off by boy noise.

At Maple Street, Lisa B. and Debbie and Lisa M. stood to get off, books held to their chests. Backpacks had been called out as queer, and almost everyone used a grooved rubber strap around their books instead. I told myself that keeping my backpack showed integrity, but I would have switched in a second if I thought it could make any difference. Jabbering knots of kids got off at Oak, Elm, Hawthorn, and the air lightened, lifting a little with each subtraction. By the time we left the Tree Streets and drove down into the Culvert, it would be just me and Nicole and two sixth graders, and the bus would be so light it would almost levitate.

Even though the storm had been gathering all afternoon, the sky seemed to rupture without warning. A sheet of water crashed over the windows. The world outside vanished.

Our driver jerked the wheel. "Jesus *fuck!*"

Everyone laughed loudly. I didn't, though, and I didn't hear Nicole laugh, either. We thought of ourselves as too jaded for that.

The bus slowed to a crawl, prow breaking through the curtain of water. None of the small lawns were visible, none of the square houses lined up neatly as boxes on the grocery-store shelf. We stopped to let off the seventh grader beside me, the door letting in a blast of rain that hit the front seats. The girl splashed down, began to run, invisible in an instant. The driver swung the door shut again and jammed forward the long stick shift. The bus jerked, coughed, died. Muttering, she turned the ignition off, then back on. The engine whirred, not catching. Off again, on again, *shir shir, shirrrr. Shhhhhhiiiirrrrr. Shhhhh . . . shhhhh . . . sh . . .* click. Click. Click.

I had to pee. I never used the bathroom at school because I'd have to go past the girls reapplying eyeliner at the mirror, knowing they could hear me in the stall. I crossed my legs tightly, which hurt before settling into a pleasant ache.

"This sucks," Nicole said. She dropped down heavily onto the empty seat next to me. "Do you have anything to do?"

I shook my head. "Homework."

"God, you're so . . ." She trailed off, seeming exhausted by the idea of me. If one of her friends had still been on the bus, they could have gone through each other's stuff, or tried on each other's jewelry. Nicole unzipped her purse and shuffled through the contents, then sighed again. She had on electric blue mascara and a skinny tie patterned with piano keys. Her dad was Greek, and she took after him—olive skin, wide mouth.

We'd lived together four years, since we were nine. Nicole wasn't actually my stepsister, but no other word fit any better. My father and her mother had fallen in love on a church committee. Breaking up two families would have caused needless damage, and so the adults decided that all seven of us—me and my parents; Nicole and her older brother, Shawn, and their parents—should move to a new house together. For an embarrassingly long time I had misunderstood the move as being for my benefit: my parents stressed how much I'd appreciate having siblings, especially a sister. When we first toured the house, my dad had announced, "And for the girls," sweeping aside a chattering bead curtain to show fake wood paneling, a gold-flecked mirror above a built-in bar. The smaller basement room—formerly a workroom, pegboard still covering the walls—would be Shawn's.

When everyone else tromped upstairs, I pulled at my mother's sleeve to hold her back. "You didn't say we'd be sharing a room,"

I whispered, panicked. "Nicky and Shawn can be down here. You guys in one bedroom, and then them guys, and then me."

"No, that's—didn't you understand what we were saying? About your dad and Holly?"

"Yeah. They like each other and want to live in the same house and I'll have a sister."

"I thought you . . . Claire, my *sweater*, stop pulling. They like each other like married people like each other."

"Are you and Mr. Kapetanakos—?"

"No!" Then, more evenly, she'd said, "We're friends. We're all friends. You're lucky, getting to live in a group of people who choose each other like that."

While the bus driver tried to reach someone on the CB, I started my world studies homework, a crossword. *Bread line. Ruble. Young Pioneers. Dissident. Siberia. Politburo.* I wouldn't have minded homework if it had been challenging. Voicing this kind of complaint, loudly and often, was what had made me universally beloved by teachers and students alike.

Nicole found a felt-tip pen in her purse and drew another set of Van Halen wings on the white rubber sidewall of her sneaker. She reached over and made a dot on my homework.

"Cut it out."

"Cut what out? Oh, you mean this?" She made another dot.

"Come on, I mean it."

"Come on, I mean it." She reached to dot my paper again.

"So funny I forgot to laugh." I yanked the worksheet away, not quite fast enough, and her pen made a long, stuttering line. "*Ugh*. We should just walk."

"Yeah, right. It's pouring." She lifted her other foot onto the seat, found a blank space on the sneaker's front bumper, and then seemed to run out of interest. "Fine, I guess. At least I won't die of boredom."

"Give me your books, then."

In a high accent supposed to sound British, she mimicked, "Your books, please, spot spot." Even as she said it, I unzipped my backpack and she shoved her stuff inside. We struggled together to get the zipper closed, Nicole calling over her shoulder to the bus driver, "You can just let us out here."

"Only at your home stop, unless I have a note from your parents."

"This *sucks*." Nicole flopped against the seat.

I tilted my head towards the back of the bus.

"What?"

I jerked my head, giving her a Significant Look; jerked again.

"I don't speak Spastic."

"The e-mer-gen-cy ex-it?"

Nicole whipped around. "You're *kidding* me," she whispered.

When we shoved the door handle, there was a moment like an intake of breath, and then the alarm howled. Nicole jumped, muddy water splashing onto her pinstripe jeans. "Cold!" she said, "Cold, cold!"

My knees locked; I couldn't move. "Hey!" yelled the driver. "Girls!" She lumbered out of her seat, a big woman, bracing herself on the bus seats.

I didn't know I'd jumped until I found myself in the air. The jolt hurt my feet, reverberating in my calves. I wasn't prepared for the shock of the icy water. I laughed in surprise. Nicole said, "Run," but I was already running.

The rain seemed to bombard from all sides, like a car wash. I needed to pee so badly that my abdomen ached; it occurred to me I could just do it right then. As soon as I had the thought, it was happening, burning hot. The smell rose up around me, sharp as vinegar, and then it washed away.

"Oh my God. Did you just *go*?" Nicole stopped in her tracks. I braced myself, but to my surprise she burst out in a real, amazed-sounding laugh. "You really don't care what people think, do you?"

I shook my head no, meaning she was wrong, then realized with a thrill she'd think I meant no, I didn't care. I tilted my head back, pretending to wash my hair. "Don't hate me because I'm beautiful."

She bent double with laughter. "Stop, you're making my stomach hurt."

The ground was swampy with mud and drowned grass the color of a paper bag. I could smell Nicole's shampoo, the same brand her friends all used. At sleepovers, they got drunk on wine coolers, and later they held back each other's flowery-smelling hair as they threw up the flowery-smelling drinks. Two advantages of living in a basement rec room, for Nicole at least: the bar had a sink for vomiting, and none of the parents ever came down.

The rain slowed. We had a storm like this almost every spring in Maryland. The roads flooded, tree branches snapped and fell and were carried away, spinning, and then the downpour stopped almost as suddenly as it had begun but less dramatically: a TV dial turned lower, lower, off.

On the walk home, Nicole and I passed stranded cars. The sky was soft, the porous lavender-gray of damp cardboard. We stopped at the Dr. Doughnut by the gas station, scrounging up enough change for one cup of coffee. I'd never drunk it before, but it felt adult, right for the sodden, scraped-raw afternoon. The guy behind the counter went to our same school, but we didn't *know* him know him so we didn't say hi. He asked if we wanted room for cream. When I looked to Nicole, she stuck her hands in her back pockets—"Neg, we're good"—though I could tell she didn't know how she wanted it either. Because I spent way too much energy trying to work out what made people cool or uncool, I'd determined that Nicole was only pretty, not beautiful. Right now, though, she looked beautiful, her brown hair black with water, eyelashes clumped thickly together, skin flushed with cold.

It turned out that coffee tasted like charred wood.

We walked home passing the cup back and forth. Beside us, the storm gutters tumbled and fumed. My backpack pulled heavily at my shoulders, and I knew our books were probably soaked through. But something buzzed in my chest, happiness knocking around: a wasp trapped under a glass.

"Cup," I said, bumping Nicole with my shoulder. I'd never touched her on purpose before.

She handed it over, then a minute later bumped me back: "Cup." Her coat was open and the rain had plastered her T-shirt to her chest. She was very modest—she changed clothes in the bathroom, or under the covers—and in all these years, this was the closest I'd come to seeing her naked.

"You should get wings," she said.

Shrug.

"I'll do it for you if you want."

"Maybe." I felt a moment of the old hope. Feathered hair could be the thing that transformed me. I'd be all, *Yeah, Nicole cut it, so what?*

We reached our back door. She pulled up the key that hung around her neck on one of those glittery silver shoelaces her mom sold at her store.

The kitchen looked like it always did, but for some reason that day I saw it as a collection of its elements: the checked yellow ruffles above the windows, the chicken-and-egg salt and pepper shakers, the counters crowded with appliances. In the merging of households, no one had wanted to argue over which crock pot to keep. I'd gotten used to unplugging a toaster or blender or electric can opener so I could plug in whichever one I liked better.

My mother sat at the table reading one of her cinderblock-thick bestsellers, James Michener or Stephen King. Her long blond braid was pulled over her shoulder and she ran her hands down it as she read. At the counter, Holly stood with her weight on one leg, pouring Prego from a jar into a pot. She turned to see us, already starting to smile. My mother looked up with that underwater expression she got while reading, but clicked into focus at the sight of us drenched, dripping on the floor. It should have been a relief to arrive in the warm, jumbled kitchen: Billy Joel on the radio, steam from the pasta water beading on the wall, fathers not yet home from work to take over with their noise and demands. But I had the strangest sensation, the first time I'd ever had it, that I was inside the room and also still outside it.

One of the moms was saying, "What *happened* to you?"

Nicole and I looked at each other. We'd forgotten to get our story straight.

I let go of the back door. It thwacked shut and the lights cut out. After a second, a mother clapped them back on—but first, for just a moment, it felt like I could be anywhere, that anything might happen now.

part one

true weight

1

a late fall morning, late to meet an old girlfriend of my husband's for brunch. I wrapped a scarf around my neck and took a last glug of coffee, then knelt in the front hallway to scratch our dog behind the ears. He licked me all over my face; slobber went in my nose.

"Ugh, no." I pushed him away, laughing.

Jeremy stood in the open doorway. "Claire, I'm leaving."

"Okay okay okay."

Fortinbras bumped his big, boxy head into me, hard enough that I had to throw my hand back to catch myself against the floor. A year earlier, I'd found him starving under a car. We assumed he was a full-grown, dun-colored mutt, but a bath revealed his coat to be white, irregularly mottled with blue-gray, and the vet said he was still a puppy, a Great Dane. His marled coat was probably why he'd been abandoned: "You can't show dogs like this," she'd said, in her frustration sounding mad at *us*.

Jeremy took another step toward the porch. "I am genuinely leaving you now."

"No no no, I'm there."

We bumped our bikes down the front steps. Outside our house, yellow leaves drifted down from the spindly trees. Air cool and sharp, though not really cold enough for the puffy down coats on the kids hanging out by the Laundromat. As Jeremy crouched on the sidewalk, rolling up his cuff so it wouldn't catch in his bike gears, strands of gray glinted in his dark hair.

At the corner, we swerved around a small shrine marking the place a teenager had been shot dead a week earlier. Maroon chrysanthemums dry as straw were heaped on the sidewalk beside a guttering candle; an exhausted Mylar balloon wobbled a few inches from the pavement. On the wood of the telephone pole, people had written messages in Sharpie: *RIP l'il brother. Love you 4-eva.*

When we stopped for a red light, Jeremy asked, "Are you nervous?"

I shook my head and smiled quizzically. In truth, I was a little annoyed. I didn't like that he imagined it would throw me to meet an ex-girlfriend. "It's been a long time," I said.

"I saw her at that W-K fundraiser last fall."

I'd meant a long time since they'd been together: their last two years of high school, nearly twenty years before.

"Watch how long it takes Gita to work Harvard into the conversation," Jeremy said. Then, "God, what's with this light?"

As usual, our lateness was my fault: it had taken some time to decide what to wear. I'd settled on a nip-waisted tweed jacket from the forties over a T-shirt from the seventies—once black, now foggy gray—with a flaking Star Wars iron-on. Skinny drainpipe jeans, cuffs turned up to show olive green wedge-heel boots that zipped up the back.

"We're *five* minutes late. She might not even be there yet."

Jeremy nodded in that way that didn't mean he agreed or had even really heard. Across the street, a clot of Norteños joked and wrestled outside the corner store, wearing their 49ers jerseys. When I first moved to San Francisco, the zeal for football in this part of the Mission had surprised me, but red and black had turned out to be gang colors. A few blocks from here Sureños slouched around in Dallas Cowboys gear.

The light changed and we kicked off, turning left onto Twenty-Fourth Street. Through the open door of a storefront church came the sound of electric guitar and tambourines; there were more people onstage than in the folding chairs. Past butcher shops with their soft funk of meat, a crater-cheeked man selling spears of mango dredged in chili, an empty nail salon where a woman napped across two of the chairs, paper mask covering her nose and mouth. We passed one of the stores that were just beginning to seep into our part of the neighborhood, the kind that sold the Perfect Cherry-Handled Garden Trowel next to the Perfect White Shirt and the Perfect Walnut Salad Bowl and then always one witty synthetic thing, Pop Rocks or Chinese jacks or action figures, and one utterly bespoke thing, like lipstick blended to exactly match the inside of your cheek, or succulents in tarnished antique sugar bowls.

Outside the restaurant clustered groups of two and three. As we coasted to a stop, Jeremy raised his hand. "Sorry we're late."

A woman stepped from the crowd. She wore a windbreaker and the top of her hair was frizzy. "You're not even late. I put our name on the list. Your name, actually. No one ever knows what to do with Jayaramen." She turned to me to shake hands, then said, "So cold!"

"The ride over, I guess."

"Here." Gita took both my hands and rubbed them between hers for a moment. "Better?"

I pulled away, giving a little hum, smiling in a way that didn't mean yes but could have.

Gita told us in great detail about finding a parking space. She spoke quickly and smiled a lot and tipped forward on the balls of her feet. She projected eagerness, a kind of nonspecific enthusiasm that made her seem young, though she and Jeremy were thirty-seven, five years older than me.

After Goldsmith-party-of-three was called inside, after we squirmed out of our jackets and scarves, after we scooched into one of the high vinyl booths, she pulled their prom picture from her purse and handed it to me: "Can you believe this?"

In the photo, Gita wore bottle-green taffeta, shiny as a beetle, knee-length in front and floor-length in back. Eye makeup, also green, that she'd gobbed on in a way that suggested she didn't usually wear it. Next to her in the photo, Jeremy looked skinny and serious, with an unfortunate mushroom-cloud haircut that made his ears stick out even more. His bright green cummerbund didn't quite match her dress.

"We bought into it so totally. . . ." Gita studied the photo she'd just handed me. "But it was still a really nice night. What about your prom?"

"I had zero interest in going." More precisely, I hadn't been asked. Nicole, of course, had been part of the royal court. Not queen or princess; one of the twelve ladies-in-waiting. Maybe being from the Naked Family kept her from the very top rung of popularity—or maybe it was the simpler fact that she was solidly built and had to bleach the faint dark hair on her arms and upper lip. She dated basketball or soccer players, but the very slightly off-brand ones, boys who were shy or had too-curly hair or took art for elective.

Jeremy put his arm around my shoulder and toyed with my collar. Now that we were here, Jeremy's annoyance at me for making us late had dissolved. As someone with a tendency to nurse grudges, I admired—grudgingly—that he let things go.

"We wanted its theme song to be 'Don't You Forget About Me,' remember?" Gita asked. Was she still talking about prom? "Jeremy was in student gov but he got outvoted for 'We Go Together.'" She used her hands a lot when she talked and then went very still, canted forward, waiting for an answer.

I bumped Jeremy's knee with mine. "Oh shit, it's the Mean Waitress."

Gita said, "You know. From *Grease*."

The Mean Waitress had reached our table. Sighing deeply, she pulled her order pad out of her apron. She didn't say anything, looked away from us.

Gita asked for a salad, no dressing. I'd been about to get just a grilled cheese, but Gita's dieting spurred me to show off, adding fries and a chocolate shake. Jeremy ordered blueberry pancakes, like always. Gita was apparently familiar with this habit, too; she caught his eye and laughed. Then, as the menus were being shuffled up, she turned to me, touching her finger to her nose. "Did that hurt?"

Reflexively, I reached up, mirroring her. The silver ring felt cold beneath my finger. My nose had been pierced so long— since a bored night in college—that most of the time I forgot it. "Not too bad."

"She did it herself," Jeremy offered. "With a safety pin."

"*Yugg*."

I shrugged, secretly pleased. Even after all these years, impressing someone gave me a kick like I used to get when Nicole and I shoplifted in high school: the sense of pulling off a trick.

"We saw a good play last night," I told Gita.

Jeremy said, "I don't think it would be your thing, necessarily."

"I like plays." She sounded defensive.

"This company is putting on Beckett down in one of the warehouses on Cesar Chavez," I said. "It's actually six short plays simultaneously, and you walk around them." I had trouble picturing Gita in that neighborhood, where syringes glinted among the waist-high weeds and the shit on the sidewalk was as likely to be human as dog.

Jeremy said, "Claire's always finding cool stuff no one else knows about," and I had to swallow a very uncool grin.

Our food arrived. There was the negotiation of silverware and ketchup. Jeremy talked about Wilkerson-Kettlewell, the private high school where he and Gita had been students, and where he now taught. My phone buzzed: a text from Nicole. *How is she?*

Squiddish, I typed quickly, holding the phone under the table.

Jeremy was telling Gita about their old English teacher, her probable alcoholism. Gita said, "She's still there? She seemed so old."

"She must have been about forty then, I think."

"Good*night*."

He smiled. "Good*night*."

I asked Gita about moving back to San Francisco. She said she'd loved Boston, where she'd lived for fifteen years—God, such a dull city to declare *love* for—but her parents were getting older, and she was an only child. She'd taken a position here, running a small marine lab that partnered with elementary schools on science education. Her hands jabbed and twisted as she talked. From a distance, I might have thought she was using sign language.

"My salary's like—" She held her palms in the air, a half-inch apart. "I guess I'm one of those anomalous Harvard people who turn out not to be ambitious."

I glanced at Jeremy, then at my watch: she'd gone twelve minutes before mentioning it. With just the tiniest wobble at the edge of his voice, he told me, "Only Gita could head up a nonprofit and think it's not ambitious."

"It's a very tiny nonprofit." Hands rushing together. "And I'm not the head, there's a board." Her hand hit the air, then hit again higher.

"Right," he said. "One of those very, very tiny nonprofits that has a board."

She had a surprisingly great laugh, loud and delighted.

Next we paid our respects to what I did for a living, restoring old furniture. I found myself slipping into that mode of bragging disguised as self-deprecation. The financial precariousness of having my own business, etc. The seeming mismatch of a nice Jewish math teacher and a woman who worked with power tools, etc. I said I hadn't been sure I could even handle a normal relationship, considering how fucked-up my role models had been.

"Her family lived with her dad's girlfriend," explained Jeremy.

"For six years. The girlfriend and her kids and her husband."

"Who was their minister," Jeremy added. He liked to help lay out my gaudy history; his own parents had been stable and a little cold.

Gita looked kind of dazed. "Wait. Your minister?"

"We were Unitarian."

"Ah, *Unitarian*." Gita sipped her tea. "Did you sing 'Kumbaya' at church?"

"Sing what?"

"'Kumbaya?' *Really?* You don't know it?"

Jeremy kicked me under the table. I kept my face blank. "Nope, sorry."

Of course we'd sung "Kumbaya." But people always asked that same exact question in the same exact jolly, self-congratulatory voice.

I said, "Maybe if you sang it? That might jog my memory."

Jeremy interrupted to ask how she liked her new neighborhood.

After we'd gone around the circle a couple more times, filling in our microbiographies, we stood at the register so the Mean Waitress could ring up our bill. Then Jeremy headed back to the table. He'd leave too big a tip, I knew; he always tried to fix unhappy people. From behind me came the gusting of wind and a sound like someone had chucked a handful of gravel at the front window: rain hitting the glass. When I twisted around, the street had gone dim. Cars slowed, wheels slurring, turning on their headlights. It was chilly inside all at once, and damp. The Mean Waitress stared out the wide front window. The top two buttons of her shirt were undone, revealing a beautifully detailed tattoo of a luna moth big as my hand, its pale green wing tips just touching her clavicle on each side.

Gita asked me, "Do you have any tattoos?"

"God, no." I noticed her expression. "Wait, do you?"

"Um." She pulled up her cuff to show a fat orange star about the size of a half-dollar on the inside of her wrist. "Grad school."

"Huh." This was exactly why I wouldn't get a tattoo: even people who wore nylon windbreakers had them.

At our booth, Jeremy took a last sip of tea, then put down bills, using the cup to anchor them. He had a jutting Adam's apple and heavy eyebrows that touched above his nose. Bert-brows, he called them. When I looked over at Gita, she was watching him, too. I could tell part of her still liked him—*liked* him liked him, we would have said in high school. But everyone had a ghost or two. That Gita's seemed to be my husband only made me feel lucky.

A flurry of awkward goodbyes. Gita stepped forward, then back just as Jeremy stepped forward, and they ended up doing one of those one-armed side squeezes. When she turned to me, I stuck out my hand.

I'd convinced Jeremy that instead of biking home we should wait out the rain at the bar across the street. By the time we ducked into Pop's, my hair and jean cuffs were soaked. Blowing off work—I was supposed to be refinishing a bureau, Jeremy should have been grading tests—made me a little giddy. I lifted my T-shirt to dry my face. Jeremy touched my stomach with his cold hand.

We ordered Guinness, shook our heads at the bowl of kibble the bartender offered us, made our way to a table. I sipped my beer. "You know when I first had Guinness? At Santa Cruz. The college I attended for college."

"You didn't like her."

I sighed and tipped back in my chair. "No, I liked her fine. I don't see us becoming great friends but—yeah. She was fine."

He frowned.

"What?"

"Just, you never like my friends."

"I like lots of your friends! I like . . . Steph. I like Pankaj. All I said was I didn't see myself being super close to Gita."

"You call Steph 'The Open Wound.'"

"That doesn't mean I don't *like* her."

Jeremy reached over, gathering my hair, wrapping it around like a boxer taping his hands. He tugged gently, at once reproach and forgiveness.

At the table nearest ours, a man with a strawberry nose had a small green parrot on the shoulder of his worn tweed jacket. He whispered to the bird between slugs of beer. The parrot closed its eyes, cheek pressed against the man's.

"That's so sad," Jeremy said quietly.

I took his hand. Jeremy worried about people. I loved the way he seemed to lack a layer of insulation. If one of his students had a crisis, Jeremy couldn't think or talk about anything else. The man stroked the parrot, murmuring. He didn't seem all that sad to me.

Pop's was one of the last old-man bars that hadn't yet been driven out of the Mission by the rising rents or discovered by twenty-three-year-olds as a quaint walk-in diorama. I'd moved to the city after college because I'd liked it on the handful of weekends I'd come up from Santa Cruz; Nicole had moved here because one of her sorority sisters needed a roommate. Back then, every future had seemed equally plausible: I could just as easily have gone to Seattle, or saved up to travel around the world, or married someone who needed a green card. But once Nicole and I both chose San Francisco, it began to feel obvious, then inevitable, and ten years later we were still here.

Jeremy and I lingered at Pop's, as I'd known we would, one beer turning into a second, one game of pool into *just one more*. In the late afternoon, we came out into cottony damp, the sun wan and low. We crossed the street and unlocked our bikes. I didn't feel drunk, but the world had a pleasant gauziness. Motor oil rainbowed a puddle.

"Race you," I said.

"For what?"

"Doesn't matter, you're not going to win."

Jeremy tilted his head as if considering the offer. I'd turned to admire the bright blue paint of a truck when, out of the corner of my eye, I saw him jump on his bike and begin to race away.

Clambering onto my bike, I stood on my pedals to try to catch him, but he'd gotten too much of a head start. "You cheat!"

The wind caught his laughter, spinning it. He swerved to avoid a pothole and then without slowing swung right at Folsom. His tire skidded, hopping on the pavement. He slid sideways, seemed to right himself.

I yelled, "Ha!"

Then he hit a crack. The bike jumped, twisted. The wheels went up and his body slammed down into the pavement, a sound like a window blowing closed. His bike bounced onto him then clattered to the street, spinning in a half-circle.

"Jesus fuck!" I jerked sharply so I didn't hit him. Kicking into the pavement to stop myself sent a jolt all the way to my hip. "*Fuck*. Are you okay?"

His front wheel still spun, whirring. He pushed himself up, pushed up the ripped sleeve of his oxford to show a wide pale graze. "Ouch."

"Can you bend your arm?"

He tried a few times. "I don't think anything's broken." He pulled open his ripped pant leg: another, deeper scrape, bumpy and maroon like bacon. "*Ouch*."

"You cheat," I said again.

"You're just jealous," he croaked. He put a hand over his heart, then reached out and I helped pull him up. He leaned down to his calf, wincing as he tugged out a couple of the black chips of gravel caught in his leg hair.

I jammed my shaking hands in my pockets to hide them. "Think you'll survive?"

"Touch and go." Taking a couple of gingerly steps into the street, he bent to lift his bike. When he stood, he was outlined against the waterlogged sky, torn plaid sleeve pushed above his elbow. Long, knuckled nose; caterpillar brows. He reached out, unstuck a strand of hair from the corner of my mouth, fingertips grazing my cheek. "Scared?"

I shook my head. "Yeah, right."

2

a woman lurched down Howard Street pushing a stroller overflowing with plastic bags. Her jaw worked back and forth like the carriage on a typewriter. In the week since we'd had brunch with Gita, the fall had gone prickly with frost. I rounded the corner and almost walked into a prostitute shivering in a dingy pink bustier, its elastic garters flapping loose against her thighs. Arms axe-handle thin. She started to mumble "Watch—" before losing focus.

Trash tumbled past on the sidewalk; a gap-toothed string of colored lights flashed in the window of a storefront church. I pushed open the door to Gymfinity, letting out a gust of sudden brightness and warmth. Justin Timberlake thumped from the speakers, the room blurry with activity. Five or six gymnastics classes were going on at once, the littlest kids tubby and graceless in their T-shirts, the older ones straight-backed, buns on the top of their heads like knobs on sugar bowls. The girl coaches were all super-enthusiastic, their faces expressive as Muppets': eyes wide and mouths open for delight; brows furrowed for seriousness. Making my way to Nicole's office, I passed two preteen girls doing tricks on the trampoline with stuffed animals clamped between their knees. One let her legs come apart as she flipped and her stuffed animal, a once-fluffy, once-white cat, spiraled into the air, falling almost at my feet. I stepped around it.

In the office, Nicole stood bent over some paperwork, phone to her ear. She still looked like the cheerleader she'd once been: sturdy legs, brown hair pulled back in a ponytail, a perky, up-turned nose. She lifted a finger, *one second*. I pointed at the ceiling to let her know I'd head to the roof.

Up the clanging ladder, I crossed the asphalt, achy with an irritation I couldn't pinpoint. Sitting against a vent, I pulled my sweater down over my knees. I was probably supposed to observe my breath, or picture waves on a beach or something. Years before, a friend had dragged me to a meditation group where the leader wanted to teach us to visualize healing energy moving through our bodies. Healing energy wouldn't have been my thing no matter what, but because it reminded me of my stepfather, it was so completely not my thing that I'd had to get up and leave. Anyway, I didn't want to summon foaming waves or leaping deer; I just wanted to curl into my bad mood and let it cradle me.

A serrated wind picked up off the Bay, smelling of salt. Nicole and I hung out maybe once a week. We ordered take-out, like tonight, or we did the same things we'd done as teenagers: lie on her bed, eat raw cookie dough, amuse ourselves with dramatic readings from magazines. We talked about people we'd known since childhood—what they were doing now; scandals from twenty years ago. Wearing those old grooves deeper and deeper was at once comforting and claustrophobic. We made homemade facial masks of avocado and honey, and I knew that when the mask dried on my face into scales, Nicole would call me Lizard.

Including each other in group plans wasn't disastrous, but my moodiness clearly made her friends uncomfortable. They were so evangelical about their optimism that it had become a kind of game for me, bringing up the worst news I could think of and watching them find the silver lining. And my friends liked Nicole, just without the admiration necessary for real friendship. The more they wanted her to be ironic about things like managing Gymfinity, or the cop she dated for a while, or her college sorority, the more cheerful and vague she became. Of course, she *could* be ironic about those things; what seemed like cluelessness was actually steely obstinacy.

Nicole's head rose up through the skylight. I'd almost forgotten I was waiting. As manager she dressed in odd combinations of business clothes and sportswear that sometimes worked and sometimes looked as if she'd gotten fatally distracted in the locker room mid-change. Today's wide-legged plaid wool pants and blue Gymfinity hoodie fell into the latter category.

She crossed the asphalt and kicked me lightly in the hip, *scooch*. Neither of us had thought to grab cups and so we passed the wine I'd brought between us, sitting shoulder-to-shoulder. She raised her hood and I reached over, pulling the drawstring tight so that only a saucer of her face showed.

"Ugh," she said, and loosened it. "So—?"

The week had felt hectic, but as I tried to think of things to tell her, they skittered away, cockroaches when the kitchen light goes on. I'd worked; Jeremy had been kind of sick and run-down; we'd had our same argument about the future that we'd had in the past. "Oh, I met Jeremy's ex."

"That's right. Pretty?"

I reached for the wine. "She had on running shoes with khakis. Prom still has a special place in her heart."

"Aha. *Nice*, then."

"Exactly." *Nice* meant bland. *Nice* was what people said when they couldn't come up with anything better. "I'm meeting her for a drink after here."

"Lucky you."

"She suggested like ten different things and that one seemed easiest."

Nicole held out her hand for the wine. In high school, she used to do this amazing thing at parties, turning a handless cartwheel, holding a bottle of something in one hand without spilling a drop. Everyone would whoop. I'd feel envy and pride, a hard shove in my chest.

"So I'm really going to do it," she said. "I've been tracking my cycle."

"Huh, okay." Nicole's relationships never lasted more than a few months: an early flare of infatuation, then the match quickly burnt down to her fingers and she dropped it. After every breakup she'd talk about having a baby on her own.

"For real this time." Taking out her phone, she began to poke at it.

"I still think a sperm bank's safer."

"A sperm bank feels too . . . I don't know. Bureaucratic. Here." She held out her phone.

"Bureaucratic like, will screen for HIV? Because that seems like a good thing." I looked down at her screen, a graph studded with green, yellow, and red dots, presumably for fertile and infertile days. "I don't have any idea what I'm looking at."

"If I'm going to do this, I should do it. I'm almost thirty-three."

I opened my mouth to say I was, too. She cut me off: "You don't even want kids."

"No, I do. I might." Or if maybe I didn't, I still wasn't ready to cede the moral advantage. Jeremy and I had gotten married so quickly after we met that we hadn't figured out right away that we felt differently about children. I blamed the five-year age gap, but privately I worried I'd feel exactly the same five years from now. I didn't exactly *not* want a child; they just didn't exert any pull on me. At parties, it was Jeremy who asked to hold friends' infants. At cafes, sometimes his gaze snagged on something behind me, and from the way his face went simultaneously slack and intent, I'd know he was looking at a baby.

Last night, we'd been fooling around, and when I started to get up to put in my diaphragm, he'd grabbed my wrist. "No, don't."

"Come on." I was half out of bed. "I'm not making the decision like this."

"So when?"

"Would you stop hectoring?"

"I'm—*You're* the one who turned this into a fight."

"You're the one who brought up a huge topic in the middle of something else."

"Fine," he said.

"Fine." I went to put in my diaphragm. By the time I got back to bed Jeremy seemed over it. We had sex and I came, then he came, then I came again, and we'd fallen asleep with his hand on my hip.

I slipped my arms out of my sleeves and under my shirt, hugging them against my chest for warmth. This close up, I could see the downy hair on Nicole's cheek but couldn't read her expression. There were fine lines around her eyes, and she'd gotten ashy highlights that were supposed to look natural. I admired women who had babies on their own, so I didn't know why Nicole talking about it always made me cranky. "You're planning on just picking people up? That's maybe the worst idea I've ever heard."

"It seems, I don't know. Random. In a good way."

"It's definitely random."

"Maybe it won't happen. If it does it's fate."

"God, Nic. If it happens it's because you're ovulating. With some guy too stupid or too odious to use a condom."

"You've been saying 'odious' a lot lately." She made her voice sticky: "Is that your new word?"

Easy, sometimes, to find ourselves sucked into the endless, picky quarrels of nine-year-olds. "You know who you sound like, with that fate stuff? Holly."

Nicole shrugged and started to peel the label from the wine bottle. Holly—her mom—talked about finding her soul mate in my father. What struck me was the word's inarguability. It might be sordid to leave your husband for a taller, younger, handsomer man, but meeting your *soul mate* meant you essentially had an obligation to upend your life. Back when I'd first heard the term, though, I'd imagined it as a moment of recognition so absolute that even if I was on a moving walkway in an airport and my soul mate was on the moving walkway in the other direction, we'd lock eyes and *bam*. I'd work myself into a nervous tizzy because: What if my soul mate lived someplace like Boise, and we never crossed paths? What if my soul mate was in *Mongolia*? And didn't even speak English?

From up on the roof, the city spread out around us, blistered with lights. A siren keened, the sound swelling and then abruptly cutting off mid-wail before I could locate its source. One of the Muppet Girls brought up our food. We always ordered from the Polish place around the corner and we ate without talking much. Steam rose from the cabbage and potato dumplings, which swam in so much butter it was almost like eating soup.

Nicole said, "But that's the part you think is crazy, picking someone up? Not the single-mother part?" Behind her, the lights of the Bay Bridge shimmered, its legs wrapped in fog. She pinched the sweatshirt over her stomach, ballooning it, tilting her head to consider the shape it made. "No one will be able to argue with me about how to parent, at least."

"How much was dinner?" I asked.

"Shut up. Just get next time."

I smiled despite myself: it was so high school to say "shut up" when you did someone a favor. "You'll be great. That thing about fate and Holly came out meaner than I meant it."

"You only meant to be a little mean?"

"Ha, right."

"Okay, then. I'll still be your best friend."

I reached over and took her cold hand. Her bones felt as small as a child's. "Foolish you."

3

*J*eremy and I got up the next morning at six. Pushing back the covers, I walked to the kitchen naked. While the espresso pot heated on the stove, I rummaged through the clean clothes heaped in a basket by the washing machine, fishing out jeans and a Mid-Atlantic Polytechnic sweatshirt my stepbrother, Shawn, had given me, God, probably fifteen or sixteen years ago, back when we were teenagers and still talked. I didn't bother with a bra: on me they were merely decorative, like tying a lacy ribbon around a box. I couldn't find underwear so skipped that, too. Behind me, the espresso popped and sputtered into its pot.

The Wilkerson-Kettlewell Winter Karnival would start at ten. Jeremy had to be there early to help set up and every year I helped, too. He scrambled eggs for himself and Fort. I couldn't eat first thing in the day but I sat with them on the back steps. A cold morning, silver mist rising from the grass.

I leaned against Fort's warm shoulder. "Listen, I've been thinking. I really need to work on those chairs from Nadia. Maybe I should stay here and do that."

Jeremy stopped eating, fork in midair. "Really? I mean . . ."

"I haven't been doing long days because you're the one who wants me to be less binge-and-purge with work stuff."

"I guess that's fine . . ."

"You're doing that *thing*. If it's not actually fine you need to tell me, because otherwise I'm going to assume you mean it." A hint of Maryland tinged my voice: *I'm gurna assume.* Next thing I'd be saying I was from *Marilyn.* "Your eggs."

He put down his fork. "If you need to work, you should work."

I pointed at my face. "This is me taking you at your word." I didn't really mind Karnival—except the clubby way some people called it the Wook-Wook because of its initials—but I actually did need to do the chairs. A few months earlier, I'd relinquished my last bartending shifts at Two Fingers, but it still felt scary. I had trouble trusting the restoration jobs would continue coming. For some reason, I couldn't come up with a name for the business, which made it feel even more provisional: my cards just said *Claire Hood, Repair.*

Jeremy stood up, a little creakily. He'd tucked in his T-shirt the way I hated. With his knobby wrists and coarse hair and angular face, Jeremy's gawkiness could skew either cool or awkward. "I should get going." He put his uneaten eggs down on the ground for Fort to finish.

"Not hungry?"

"Eh. I feel sort of flu-y."

I forced myself not to sigh. Jeremy got sick a lot, and it didn't bring out the best in us: he had a tendency to complain, which made me itchy with impatience. I *knew* all he really needed was sympathy, but it felt almost impossible to bestow. "You're probably overtired."

"Yeah." Taking the licked-clean plate, he went into the kitchen, washed it, stuck it in the dish rack to dry.

I followed him in. "You could skip the fair," I offered without much enthusiasm.

He shook his head. "I'm signed up for booths. Which sucks even more because it hurts to stand too long." Balancing with one hand against the counter, he lifted his pant cuff. The week-old scrape from the bike accident had been healing, but today it looked puffy and hot, beaded with pus the color of eggnog.

"Fuck, Jeremy. That's infected."

He smiled, glad to have ruffled me at last. He poked at the skin around the wound and winced. "Should I see a doctor?"

"I don't know. For a scrape? Do you want Neosporin or something?"

"Nah, I'm good." He gave me a jaunty kiss on the ear, and I took the opportunity to pull his T-shirt out of the waist of his pants.

He said, "That's been killing you, hasn't it?"

Our five-room Victorian cottage always felt lighter when he was gone. I took the espresso pot with me to my studio at the front of the house, stopping at the doorway to push my feet into a pair of clogs. This room had once been the living room; it had a bay window and an elaborate fireplace now filled by a small radiator with chipping silver paint. Shelving I'd built from iron pipe and salvaged maple lined the opposite wall, jammed full of wood scraps and tools and rags and newspaper and jars of wood stain. Finding the cleanest of the cups scattered around the room, I wiped it with the hem of my sweatshirt, poured espresso. I turned the radio to KUSF, which might play punk rock one hour and Sufi music the next. That morning it was Throwing Muses and Scrawl and L7, bands I'd listened to in college when I stayed up all night to write papers I should have started long before. Nostalgia can accumulate on anything far enough in the past: those all-nighters, or the aimless, underemployed first year I lived in San Francisco. Or the windowless factory cafeteria where Nicole and I worked afternoons and weekends in high school, stoned, wearing steel-toed boots, ringing up damp sandwiches, amusing ourselves by throwing balled-up paper napkin bits at each other's hair.

The six chairs stood in a naked huddle, stripped of their old varnish. One needed refinishing and three of the others had loose joints. The last two had broken spindles: clean breaks, almost impossible to fix, though people assumed jagged breaks were the hard ones. I was going to need to make new spindles. A fair number of clients who lived in Pacific Heights or—like Nadia—the Berkeley Hills wanted me to pity them for how much they'd have to pay for my work. In Pacific Heights, this conversation often occurred in a circular driveway, my sun-bleached '71 Toyota pickup crouched behind a satiny Lexus; in the Hills, we were more likely to be drinking tea from hand-thrown mugs in a seven-bedroom Craftsman with flying buttresses and walk-in fireplaces, the whole house meticulously restored to the original except for the kitchen's enormous commercial stove and poured-concrete counters. When someone balked at my bid, I shrugged—hire me or don't. I'd worked with Nadia before, though, and we'd moved beyond the stage where she questioned my judgment or thought she could talk me into a lower price. Lifting the shakiest of the chairs onto my worktable, I used masking tape to label each piece, then swaddled a hammer in a washcloth and began to gently knock out the stretchers. You can't just patch unsound furniture; you have to rebuild from scratch.

Making it to my workroom hours earlier than I'd planned made the morning seem oddly hallowed and tranquil. Fort shuffled in and leaned against my hip. Yesterday, a child had pointed at him, his size and his piebald coat, and shouted, "Cow! Cow! Cow!" I'd meant to tell Jeremy; he'd like it. I scratched behind Fort's ears, then leaned down to cup his chin, looking into his eyes. "Lie down, cowdog." Instead of going over to the bed I'd made him in a corner of the workroom, he settled under my worktable, heavy jowls on my foot.

I began to clean the blind holes that had held the chair's tenons, digging out gunky old glue and dirt. I liked this part. As a kid, I used to volunteer to rub my father's head so I could pick at his dry scalp. I had to disguise the picking with lots of massage and scratching or he'd move out from under my hand, *Quit it.* How good it had felt to use a fingernail to gently prise off a thick flake of dead skin and drag it free up the shaft of a hair.

Through the wide front window, I could see the boarded-up purple Victorian across the street, a man asleep in the doorway, knees to chest. Jeremy had moved here right after college. The other two guys on the original lease eventually moved out but Jeremy stayed, living with a succession of housemates. My first two weeks living with him—which were also the first two weeks of our marriage—I'd painted walls, fixed the ceiling that leaked during rainstorms, torn up layers of buckled kitchen linoleum to get to the wide softwood boards below. We could never have afforded a place to ourselves if not for rent control. I pushed the window up an inch, letting a thin wheeze of cold air into the room.

I was using my teeth to rip masking tape from the roll when my phone buzzed. Lunging to answer it, I banged into the worktable. "Fuck."

"Hello?" a woman said.

I'd hit my pelvic bone so hard it still hummed. "Yes, hi, what."

"Claire? Um, it's Gita Jayaramen."

"Oh. Hey." I'd had drinks with her just the night before. I wanted to show Jeremy that I didn't dismiss his friends. Also, Gita had been very intent on making plans, and I couldn't help being kind of fascinated by her fascination with me. We'd sat at the bar at Two Fingers, the place I used to work, Gita taking tiny hummingbird sips of her gin and tonic. She drank so slowly that in forty-five minutes, the drink's level had actually risen from the ice melting.

Over my second Scotch, I found myself doing the same thing I'd done at brunch, playing up the eccentricity of my life in a fake-bored way I'd mostly outgrown. I told her about the subscriptions our parents got for us kids to *Playgirl* and *Penthouse*. How for a while my stepfather got really into reincarnation, trying to goad the rest of us to remember our past lives. In college, I'd talked too much about those years, and with Gita I felt that old pleasure of watching a version of myself come clear, like a photograph surfacing through the wash: brave and offhand, ironic and intimidating. Today, though, the memory of showing off made me a little disgusted with myself. I wedged the

phone against my shoulder, pulling down the waist of my jeans
to see my hip where I'd bumped it.

"I'm not trying to haunt you or anything—" She laughed un-
comfortably. "It's just I remembered how you said you wish you
got outside more."

Had I said that? I put my hand over my other ear: some kids
had moved from the corner to our front steps, *nigga nigga nigga*.

"And I lead Wednesday's low-tide walk. I can pick you up,
even, if you want."

"Shit. I'm meeting with a client that morning."

"No, it's afternoon."

"Oh." I couldn't claim another appointment, and I wanted to
get off the phone. "Sure, great." Maybe I could find an excuse. Or
maybe having my husband's sweet but slightly dull ex-girlfriend
take me on a nature walk would sound better to me in a few days.

It took a few more minutes to disentangle. I said Jeremy was
at the Winter Karnival and she said, *Oh, right, Wook-Wook's
today, I should stop by.* After we hung up, I felt irritated and
thrown off, like someone had stroked the hair on my arms the
wrong way. The teenagers were still shouting to each other. I
pushed the window further open and leaned out.

"Hey." I made myself smile. The three of them had wispy
mustaches; the sides of their heads were shaved, the tops and
backs left long. Over his parka, one of them wore a gold me-
dallion that from a distance reminded me of the flaming chal-
ice pendant my stepfather used to wear over a turtleneck. "I'm
sorry to ask this, but my baby's sleeping. Do you mind moving
down a couple houses?"

The teenagers nodded—the one with the longest hair, nearly
to the small of his back, even said, "Hey, sorry about that,

Mama." It was touching, their respect for babies; I probably shouldn't have taken advantage of it.

While the glued joints set on the first chair, I lifted another onto the table. This one needed new spindles. I'd have to use the lathe, which I wasn't great at and so would require focus. I liked how restoration lent itself to all-or-nothingness. Working at the bar had been good on weekend nights, but on slow afternoons—pouring a drink every ten minutes, fruit flies circling the sink drain—I'd felt my life leeching away. Freelancing meant I could put in a run of twelve- or fifteen-hour days, and then for the rest of the week not go into my workroom at all but instead help Nicole out at Gymfinity, see three movies in a row, drive up to the redwood forest with Fort. Jeremy said it drove him crazy, though, not knowing if I'd be there when he got home from work—and if I were there, not knowing if I'd be so absorbed in a job I'd barely grunt when he poked his head in. For his sake I tried to keep a more regular schedule, which made me a little resentful: just because Jeremy loved routine didn't mean everyone should.

Gita's call had chopped into my momentum. I went to the kitchen and found a green apple and some sharp cheese, hoping food would help. Back in the studio I poured the last of the espresso, cold and silty, into a cup and forced myself to finish labeling the parts of the second chair and start knocking it apart. Maybe forty-five minutes in, I'd finally found the place where the boundaries between the work and myself dissolved when my phone rang again.

Gita. When I picked up she was talking so fast I barely understood, her voice shaking.

4

*h*alf a dozen people were working on him at the ER, such tumult that I couldn't get close. Tubes, machines beeping, people barking numbers like stockbrokers. Sixty over thirty. Six packed blood cells on standby, gram-positive febrile tachy subclavian. Decel. Fifty-five over twenty. He threw up, the retching coming from so deep inside it sounded inhuman, like the grinding of gears. One leg of his khakis had been cut off and his leg looked swollen and red. The nurse by his head asked for another bedpan and passed off the full one. As it came by me, I glimpsed the vomit inside, thick and black. What in your body could even *be* black? Someone asked, *Are you the wife?* Each of the words made sense to me, but I didn't know what she was asking. Was I the wife? Different people shouted across the room or pulled me out into the hallway to ask for his insurance, any allergies, any major surgeries. *He was fine this morning*, I said. *Septic shock*, someone told me, and I shook my head to show I didn't know what that meant. *Major infection, his body's gone into shock, we're trying to prevent his organs shutting down.* The beeping of one of the machines flattened into an insistent shrill. *He's coding,* someone said, no hysteria in her voice, but low urgency. Something was being slid under Jeremy's body and something else was being stuck to his chest, and a recorded voice over the address system *Code Blue two-eleven, Code Blue two-eleven. Intubate,* someone said, and a minute later someone else said, *intubated. Clear,* said a woman in raspberry scrubs, and then she was pivoting towards the bed, towards Jeremy. His body jumped. A black bag covered his mouth and nose. A rush of footsteps down the hall, people pushing past me, someone asking who was running the code. The raspberry-scrubs woman, quiet and fast, said, *Thirty-seven-year-old Caucasian male brought in by ambulance at fifteen-oh-four complaining of light-headedness and nausea. Gram stain of blood smear positive for cocci. Ohgodohgodohgod,* I said, covering my mouth so the words backed up into my head. *Clear!* someone said again, and Jeremy's body jumped, and then the insistent beeping slowed and the people around the bed sighed, shoulders relaxing, and someone gave a short bark of laughter and the woman in raspberry lifted her hand for a tired high-five. "We don't like when we lose someone," a nurse explained to me, his voice almost merry. I bent over, so dizzy I thought I might fall. In my hands was a clear plastic bag I didn't remember having been given. Jeremy's clothes. I pulled out the T-shirt, remembering how I'd untucked it from his pants that morning, Jeremy's crooked grin. The shirt flapped open like a wing, and then apart. I stood there looking stupidly from the half in my hands to the half that had fallen on the floor. It took a minute to understand that I hadn't somehow broken it: to get the shirt off his body they'd cut the seams.

5

*a*n Indian woman in street clothes knocked at the door of our hospital room. For just a second, I thought she was a doctor—but her clothes were wrong, and so was the way her face went through a series of microadjustments as she registered my appearance. Gita, I realized; and apparently I looked horrible.

"Are you okay?" she asked. "No, don't answer, sorry. Stupid question."

"Don't you—you're not at work."

"Sunday."

"Oh. Right." So we'd been here over a week. "You don't have to whisper; he's out."

"I tried calling—"

"Cell phones don't work in here." Though of course, whenever I left the unit, I'd seen that she'd called. I'd deleted her voicemails without listening to them. At Winter Karnival, after

Jeremy collapsed, his colleagues had thought he should rest under a tree and sip water. Gita had been the one to call 911. She'd quite possibly saved his life. I felt sick with gratitude, and also sick with jealousy that it hadn't been me. And then guilty about the pettiness of feeling jealous.

She walked over to the bed where Jeremy slept then pulled up short, looking suddenly winded. I was used to his face and body being swollen, his eyes nearly invisible, tubes running into his arms and neck and under his hospital gown. He slept most of the day, and because he was intubated he couldn't talk during the brief times he woke.

"I wanted to come earlier. They said just family."

"Yeah, he . . . There were four days in a coma." I swallowed and finished lamely, "Anyway, you're here now."

"Is it okay to touch him?" Gita asked. "My hands are washed."

"Yeah."

She started to reach out, then stopped. "Sorry, I should—" She ducked into the bathroom to wash her hands again, then rubbed in sanitizing gel for good measure. I understood the need to overdo it: eight days in, my hands were chapped, scored with cracks. I'd said to Jeremy that Lady Macbeth probably couldn't get her hands clean because the more she washed them, the more they bled. He'd stared at me, then shut his eyes. I didn't know if he hadn't understood or didn't care.

Gita lifted Jeremy's hand. "Hey, J.," she said, then stopped. I heard her swallow, hard. "Hey, J., I don't want to wake you. I just want. . ."

She trailed off. Quickly, she dipped down and kissed his forehead once, twice. Her khakis and oxford shirt looked strange and stiff. Most people in the ICU wore scrubs or sweats—a big

pajama party, a troop of outsized babies. In normal life, my rule
was to wear at least one feminine piece, one masculine, one vintage, one new. In the hospital, though, I wore Jeremy's clothes.
That afternoon I had on his Cornell sweatshirt and an old pair
of his jeans washed soft as flannel. I used his Speed Stick, too, so
I could smell him. The idea of an engagement ring—he'd given
me his grandmother's, with a little lentil of a diamond—had
before always seemed too conventional and fussy. Now I wore it
on a fine silver chain beneath my shirt, pawing at it through the
cloth probably a hundred times a day.

Jeremy lay on top of the covers, which bothered me—it
seemed so vulnerable. The ventilator pump sighed *ka-pow, ka-
pow*. He was pale, except for one foot that looked like a tree
fungus, puffy and scalloped and black. I saw Gita notice it, her
shoulders jerking up a bit.

"The blood vessels constricted when he was in shock." I
couldn't bring myself to say gangrene, or amputate. I couldn't
bring myself to say that amputation wasn't even an option unless he got stronger.

"He's going to make it?" she asked.

"*Yes.*" Actually, no one had been able to say definitely. His organs had begun to fail in the ER; we were still waiting to see if
the damage would reverse. If Jeremy died, he'd take with him the
country songs we liked to make up. The way he made fun of me for
putting the peanut butter back in the fridge when only the barest
scrapings were left. The way we said "knock around" to mean
sex; the way in front of other people we could ask, *Do you want to
stay out, or should we go home and knock around?* Our secret language,
gone. The way when he was grading at home he'd absentmind-
edly rub the dry soles of his feet together, like a fly, until I'd say,

"You've got to stop that right now or I'm leaving you forever," trying to make the words sound light and affectionate but really, really about to lose my mind, and how he laughed, recognizing it. The way his penis hooked slightly to the left, and as a teenager he'd worried this terrible deformity would mean he'd die a virgin. The way he sectioned oranges and left the pieces on the plate for ten or fifteen minutes, just long enough for the outsides to dry out, becoming slightly crisp. He listened to NPR, even the *pledge drive*, during which he groaned and cheered and muttered *come on, come on* like someone listening to a football game.

Gita blew out a long shuddery breath. "Okay, it's okay, it's okay." Another long breath. She turned. "Have you eaten lunch yet?"

I cast my mind back. I hadn't even eaten breakfast yet.

The basement cafeteria didn't have windows. It was maybe two in the afternoon but felt like midnight. I must have looked as close to catatonic as I felt because she told me to sit down. I didn't move, processing *sit down*. She pulled out a chair for me. "Should I just choose something?"

"No meat." Exhaustion lapped against me. Officially you weren't supposed to stay over in the ICU, so there were no beds, but visiting hours were unlimited and the nurses had been nice about letting me sleep in the chair in our room. Still, it meant waking and half-waking all night as various people came to check vitals or adjust meds.

"Here," Gita said, startling me. She slid a plate onto the table. Something orange, something green. "You're vegetarian?"

"Since I was eleven." Not a story I wanted to tell. "I worked in a cafeteria like this in high school, at a factory. Practically everyone in my class worked for them at some point, either on the floor or doing deliveries or something. Dr. Doughnut. Technically I guess it was a bakery, but no one called it that. . . . Anyway. What about you? Did you do an internship?" All Jeremy's students seemed to have them, as he had.

She shook her head. "I worked at my parents' store, from the time I was about seven. Not paid or anything." The fluorescent lights made her lavender under-eye pouches look brown. "I was supposed to get my homework done between customers."

"Your parents had a store."

"A corner store, in Western Addition. You know, cigarettes and beer; some groceries. Lotto tickets."

I'd assumed that she came from the same background as Jeremy, which I called upper-class and he insisted on calling middle-class for reasons like: over winter break his family skied in the Rockies, not the Alps. Or: his family didn't sit in the expensive reserved seats on High Holidays. I tried to remember what had made me think Gita's parents were engineers or professors. Jeremy had said that they worked long hours and lived "downtown," which I'd taken to mean Nob Hill. The immigrant parents with a corner store made Gita seem scrappier and more complicated. Her eagerness and enthusiasm, which I'd taken as easy responses to an easy life, might in fact be harder-won.

"I had almost a full scholarship at W-K. It was my idea to apply to private schools; my parents wouldn't have thought of it," she said. "And W-K turned out to be a great place for me, though my first year was pretty bad. Everyone else knew all about things I'd never even *heard* of. I remember listening to an argument about whether *Blue Velvet* was better than *Eraserhead* and I was trying to figure out if they were talking about a band or what. And no one else seemed to notice money. There's something so . . ."

"Insulating," I suggested.

"Right! Something so insulating about not even having to think about it."

"People at Santa Cruz would sometimes ask things like *why* I had a work-study job."

"Exactly! Exactly! My friends knew my parents' store, but still they were always suggesting we do things that cost money, and I made up excuses why I couldn't, until I realized I probably sounded snobby. So I started admitting I couldn't afford things, and people were nice about it, which—you know, whew, big relief. But then they'd suggest something else that didn't cost quite as much, but to me it might as well have." She shook her head, as though resetting. "So if you worked at a factory and then a bar, how did you get into furniture repair?"

"I did set design in college. And there was hardly any budget, so I'd find things that needed fixing and figure out how to fix them."

For a week, I had seen almost no one but Ruth and David, Jeremy's parents. They lived in Sebastopol, about an hour up the coast, where they'd moved when his dad retired. Ruth was one of those disorganized people who wasted time trying to be organized. Usually this trait didn't bother me, but when they'd burst into the ER—urgent and flustered, three hours after I called but sure they'd gotten there the very first second they could—I'd felt hatred unfold in me, dark and opulent.

I was, I realized, ravenous for someone I could actually talk to. I told Gita about the all-women's theater troupe I helped found at Santa Cruz, how I'd taught myself to upholster but hated it, how I'd figured out restoration techniques from trial-and-error and the single book that the university library had on the subject. I didn't mention, though, that I'd fallen in love with a version of myself, one who pulled back her pale, silky hair before bending over the rip saw. I'd gotten a little obsessed with trying to see myself from outside, and sometimes (no; often) as I strode across campus, I catalogued: heavy, square-toed harness boots, a delicate silk dress I'd constructed by cutting apart and re-piecing a vintage kimono. No makeup except a slash of dark red lipstick. A man's watch rattling on my narrow wrist. I suddenly had lovers, seemingly anyone I wanted, though I was careful never to want too much from them. I convinced myself I was Renaissance-Italy beautiful and so sometimes it was a shock to see myself in the mirror: same long nose and quartz-white skin, same jutting chin, not changed at all.

"You haven't touched your food."

In my fatigue, I'd forgotten. I took a bite of the macaroni and cheese. After not eating all day, the taste nauseated me. Then, like a trapdoor sliding open, I was hungrier than I could remember ever having been.

6

*f*or a while, my stepfather was into past life regression, which he called Going Back. Costa and I didn't get along. He used to lock me out of the house even in winter over any perceived disrespect, like if he called me to dinner and I finished the page I was reading before coming upstairs. He took everything I said as a complaint. I might ask, "We're stopping at the hardware store?" and he'd mock, *Poor me, poor me.*

Nicole and Shawn had each tried Going Back once and thought it was bullshit. I was good at it, though. Or rather: good at pretending. Costa believed that our past selves existed inside us, walled off. He'd have me lie down on the living room carpet while he ran through a series of you-are-getting-very-heavy exercises and then I'd describe things lifted from my World Studies textbook. I was an Ashanti girl grinding groundnuts. I was in London during the Plague, under quarantine. What I liked about

Going Back was its sense of privacy and respectful attention, the way Costa closed doors and drew curtains and afterward treated me gently, like I needed time to recover my strength.

I was fond now of some parts of my life that hadn't been particularly great at the time—to make our shifts at Dr. Doughnut less interminable, Nicole and I would get stoned in the walk-in freezer, teeth chattering—but I had pretty much zero nostalgia for the Naked Family years. Just thinking of that time made me feel stifled, like I'd sweat through my clothes and had to keep my arms pinned to my sides to hide the reek.

There was this one afternoon, about a year and a half into all of us living together, when my father and Costa carried a dead goat into the backyard, slung between them by its hooves. Its coat was pale tan, with a black necklace of dried blood. When their feet slipped around on the wet grass and the goat swayed between them, Costa sang *swing low, sweet chariot* in his bass voice to make my father laugh.

Nicole came out the screen door, which sighed behind her, then bounced hard in its frame; sighed again and bounced again: softer, softest. She still went by *Nicky* then, up until the year Prince released *Purple Rain* and boys in the school hallways would sing at her the lyrics about masturbating in a hotel lobby. Though I didn't like Nicky, I was so envious of her style that I tried to memorize every detail of her clothes and music and favorite movies. I knew I couldn't copy what she'd already claimed, but what if I could get out in front, identify the next desirable thing before she did?

Nicky pulled up short at the sight of our fathers kneeling by the dead goat on the grass. Costa, short with a dark beard and barrel chest, held the goat's horns so that my tall, fair father could saw off its head with a serrated bread knife. He sawed and sawed at the pelt of the neck, without effect. "Pull tighter," he said, and finally the blade began to stutter through. I was surprised to see no blood. I don't know where they bought a goat in suburban Maryland; they must have driven to a farm somewhere past Rockville. Costa yanked to rip through the last little tag of hide, and lifted the head away.

"Oh my God," Nicky said softly. "Like people don't already hate us."

Holding a horn, Costa moved the chin with his other hand, opening and closing the goat's mouth: "Nobody haaaaaates us."

My dad laughed. "I think you're doing sheep."

Costa twisted the head left and right. "Niiiiiicccce baaaaackyard."

"What we *really need* is for the neighbors to think we *sacrifice animals*," said Nicky. She turned and flounced into the house in a way meant to look mad but also meant to not look *actually* mad. The back door slammed and the fathers laughed.

With the tip of his shoe, Costa flipped back the edge of a towel on the grass to show a glinting pile of tools—knives, the garden shears, a little hatchet that usually lived on the back porch by the firewood. Without looking at me, he asked, "Don't you want to run away, too?"

I shook my head.

"We're gurna need to skin it," my father told me, apologetic. He'd grown up in western Maryland and still had a faint accent that dulled some of his words: *ruf* for roof, *kin* for can, *wadder* for water.

Costa turned the goat's head towards me. With his thumb, he lifted the eyelid to show its yellow iris, black pupil like a keyhole. "That's why people associate them with devils." The eye had a soapy film. Then he dropped his thumb and jammed the head into the V of one of our small trees. Taking off his Orioles hat, he stuck it on the goat at a jaunty angle, then stepped back to admire the effect.

A pelt of dense black hair covered Costa's chest and arms but stopped in a sudden line across the top of his shoulders: he shaved his back. Actually, Holly shaved it for him after his shower at night, a ritual so ingrained that they seemed to regard it as no more remarkable or intimate than her folding his laundry or making his dentist appointments, both of which she also still did.

My father lifted the goat's legs up and apart. Costa squatted and began to cut the coat free at the ankle, peeling it slowly to show the lavender fascia beneath. "Hold still, you bastard."

Karin stepped out the back door, carrying a case of Cragmont sodas, the Safeway brand. My mother was a tall woman, her blond hair pulled into a braid that lay straight down her back. She was as pale as me, except she had a ruddiness high on her cheeks, as if the bones rubbed the skin raw from beneath. She glanced at the men kneeling on the grass above the half-skinned goat, and then up at the tree and stopped in her tracks. "No. Nope. You're not giving some poor kid nightmares."

Costa stood and grabbed a soda from her cooler, rolling the cold can up the side of his neck, over his wide jaw, across his forehead. In his goat voice: "Relax, baaaaabe. It's the circle of liiiiiiifffffe."

My mother turned to my father. "Jim."

He smiled and shrugged, testing if that would suffice. My mother's expression didn't change, the same smile she would have used at the library asking a kid to clean up his mess. Jim shrugged again, this time at Costa, and jerked the head free of the tree. Carrying it by the horns, he started towards the house. Costa made an exasperated sound and pitched his unopened can back into the cooler.

"And please don't let me find that at the foot of my bed," Karin called.

My father opened the metal trash can by the back door, dropped in the head, then turned and bowed elaborately. "Happy?"

"Delirious."

As families arrived, the men took turns at digging the pit, joking and drinking beer from cans. It was September but very warm, and many of the men took off their shirts to dig and then left them off, stomachs spilling white as batter over the waistbands of their shorts.

Greer, our town, wasn't big, and a lot of people knew or kind-of-knew about our family's living arrangement, but my father and Holly were usually discreet in public. Occasionally, I'd see a flicker of the effort it took them not to touch—she'd start to reach for his wrist to check the time; he'd almost put his hand on the small of her back. Here, though, among friends, he had his arm around her shoulders. Holly, delicate and dark-haired, had both arms around my father's waist.

Everyone had been drinking on near-empty stomachs—for now, the only food on offer was potato chips, which made people drink more. They seemed a little giddy. Or else a little too serious, like the woman I found grasping Karin's arm. "How are you holding up?" she asked, voice soft and eyes sharp.

My mother smiled politely. "Good. We're finally done with

the Read-a-Thon; things always calm down after that."

"No, but, how are *you* doing?"

My mother tilted her head, frowning as though confused. "Well, like I said. I'm good. The Read-a-Thon takes so much time that afterwards it feels like I have twice as many hours in the day. Claire, do you want to help me carry the cooler around?"

I followed her down the yard. "Vulture," she said quietly. "Never let them know they've gotten to you." She passed her palm over my hair. I froze, trying to hold on to her touch.

My mother and I limped sideways through the party, the cooler slung between us banging our shins. There was a loud pop from the roasting goat. A delicious and terrible smell of burning fat itched at the back of my throat. The volume of laughter crested, crashed, began to build again. At the far end of the yard, Nicky tumbled with her friends.

My mom and I reached Costa, sitting with the church's choir director. Donna was overweight and pretty, with long, graying blond hair and huge breasts visible down the neck of her Guatemalan blouse. Costa's hand almost touched Donna's on the grass. In the low light, the space between them vibrated.

We continued around the lawn, coming closer to my father and Holly. My mother didn't act any more aware of them than of anyone else, but to me they were like the eye of the storm, the quiet center around which everything else revolved. He reclined on his elbows in the grass and she sat between his legs, leaning back against him, forearms resting on his thighs. I didn't think my mother and father had touched very much—certainly not like this, melted together—but they'd always seemed friendly, very much in the way they still did.

My father was listening to Holly with an expression of

alertness, half-smiling, occasionally throwing out a comment. He and I had the same sharp features, but somehow they made him strikingly handsome and made me look like a snapping turtle. My dad had the ability—I only half-recognized it back then, and certainly didn't understand its rarity—to make people feel special and seen. He listened closely and laughed easily, with unforced delight. He could turn from one mode to the other in an instant, shifting his weight to stay perfectly balanced on the conversation's crest. Holly—fine-edged, dark-haired, very quiet except with my dad—picked at a fray in the knee of his jeans as she talked. Ache swelled in my legs and arms, almost a physical need to kick, or run, or throw the cooler.

"Coke?" I blurted when we were still six or seven feet away. I cleared my throat. "Um, Jim?"

My father looked up. His smile had two stages: mild and general, and after a few seconds, a deeper smile of recognition. "Bear. What?"

"I said, do you want a Coke?" For some reason, it felt like I needed to ask this in a silly, dramatic voice.

Holly tilted her head back, looking up at my dad from below his chin. "Babe, maybe you should bring out the doughnuts?"

"I thought the doughnuts were for dessert," said my mother, also to my father. "Babe." Her voice stayed casual and light. Whenever she talked about Holly, she said how great she was, how much she liked Holly's store, Cherish. It didn't occur to me that she was being ironic: I thought Cherish was the bomb. Holly sold stickers by the yard, stuffed Pegasi with gold lamé wings, Lucite boxes you could personalize and fill with rainbow layers of jelly beans.

Holly shot her a quick, distracted smile. "People are getting hungry."

Faintly from across the lawn, I could hear Nicky horsing around with her friends. Costa called to my father. "Meat's done."

Jim leaned forward to kiss Holly's shoulder, and then pushed her gently to the side so he could get to his feet. He ambled toward the fire. He was one of the only men there wearing a shirt. Costa had cut open a flap in the goat's side; with the tip of the knife, he held it open.

Jim shook his head. "Needs a little more time."

"We have lift-off!" Costa shouted toward the party. A few people heard, sending up a weak cheer.

"It's looking pretty purple. . . ."

"People only cook the hell out of meat if they're covering up poor quality."

My father seemed doubtful but shrugged and grabbed the other end of the thick tree branch. They counted three and hoisted. Legs bent, they carried the goat's corpse heavily between them, swinging it onto the table with a loud thump.

Costa wore heavy oven mitts printed with crab claws and an apron, also with a crab on it. He carved into the goat's side, flakes of charred skin floating down to the table like black snow. Hoisting up a thick, magenta slice of meat, he asked, "Who likes rare?" He swung the meat onto a paper plate, which buckled under its weight. "Claire! Put some hair on your chest."

I took the plate. The outside of the meat was as black as a hunk of volcanic rock. Inside, it was dark red and almost gelid.

"Go ahead," Costa said. He sawed a corner off the meat and speared it with a fork, which I took, lifting it to my lips. In my mouth, the meat was slippery and still cold, resistant to my teeth. My jaw started to ache as I tried to chew. I could feel the threat of tears rising in my throat. With effort, I gulped, swallowing the piece whole. I managed to nod and give the thumbs-up sign.

"Keep going," Costa said. I hesitated and he reached over, carving another piece. He held the fork out towards me, and when I didn't take it, touched the meat to my lips. "Open." He pressed gently but firmly. "Wider."

Nausea rose scratchily in my throat. I twisted my head away, but Costa pushed the fork into my mouth. He put his palm under my chin, clicking my teeth together through the slimy, uncooked meat. I retched. He let go of my jaw just enough for the raw goat to slide a little further back before pushing my mouth closed again and there was a grating noise in my throat. I jerked from his grasp and spit the meat into my hands and then bent over, gulping to swallow the vomit that had risen. My stomach ached as if I'd been kicked.

"I should have known," said Costa, throwing the fork hard into the yard.

"No, it's fine, I'm fine." A prickly sweat had broken out across my forehead. I fought down another surge of nausea, sounds clotting together, everything going black at the edges.

When my vision cleared, two men were helping Jim lift the spitted goat over the fire. The roaring in my ears fell back, breaking apart again into party chatter, the high chant of insects. From next door, the buzz of a lawn mower sent up the sweet green smell of grass twisting around the darker reek of gasoline.

7

"Okay," said the resident, readying her grip on his ventilator tube. "Cough."

Jeremy coughed, a polite throat-clearing, and then kept coughing, roughly, after she pulled the tube from his throat. "Finally," he croaked.

My own throat pinched closed for a moment. It had been more than a week since I'd heard his voice. What I missed most acutely was the way we filled each other in on things we'd observed. We'd always had almost too much to say. *We need to go to sleep*, one of us would try to insist, and then an hour later we'd still be talking.

I'm going to be a wreck tomorrow.

I know. We need to sleep. I mean it this time.

I know. I know. Just one more thing.

Now that his tube was out, I tried to interest him in conversation. About the nurse who over-explained everything, super-gently, like Mr. Rogers. About how Jeremy's mother couldn't check the voicemail on her phone, even though I'd shown her twice. About the way the residents flirted with each other during rounds. "I mean, it makes total sense. It's their job, and they're young, and they're smart, and they come into the room all serious, and then out in the hall they're cracking jokes. It kind of makes me want to kill them, and at the same time, I get it."

"My foot hurts," he said.

"I can get Todd in."

"Todd."

"Your nurse. I—" had just talked about Todd for a long time, but it seemed whiny to point it out. "Never mind, I'll page him." Jeremy and I waited until Todd came through the curtained door, pudgy and smiling, twisting towards the hand sanitizer. I reported that Jeremy's foot hurt.

"Let's see what's going on with us," Todd said.

I didn't like watching when Jeremy's dressings were changed, but I would have amputated my own toe with a pair of manicure scissors before I admitted it. Jeremy didn't watch. His foot still wasn't recognizable as a foot: swollen, pale, almost as wide as it was long. Hanging off like withered grapes, his toes were wizened and purple-black.

Todd seemed pleased, though. "I think we have good news here." With his blue-gloved hands, he bent the toes this way and that. "We might only lose one of these. The big one, so that's not the best news. But see how these others aren't as inky as they were? We should feel really good about this."

I waited for Jeremy to catch my eye. *We should feel really good about this.* But he just shifted irritably in the bed, pushing at the rumpled sheets. "Is it time for my meds yet?"

★   ★   ★

While Jeremy passed in and out of sleep, Nicole and I played a game we'd made up long ago, half basketball and half darts. We threw balled-up flyers at the GIVE A HAND FOR HAND WASHING! poster, trying to hit the stern-looking bar of soap (ten points) or the jolly cartoon germ (five). As kids, we'd aimed for the back of the door of our bedroom, which was on Nicole's side of the room. She'd had a poster from her mom's store of a unicorn, tendons straining in its neck; replaced in junior high by Kevin Bacon; replaced in ninth grade by Bernard Sumner, the lead singer of New Order. Despite having been on the basketball team in high school, I kind of sucked at this game. Nicole did a much better job of correcting for the paper balls' lightness, the way they always veered off course.

Beside the hand-washing poster hung a whiteboard with Jeremy's counts and various nurses' pager numbers. The whiteboard felt like the thing that most gave shape to our days. In the bottom right corner, I kept another, private tally of each time someone said that none of us knew when we might die. *I could get hit by a bus tomorrow!* Always that same demon bus; never *I could choke to death on a carrot tomorrow*, or *Tomorrow I could be brutally stabbed in the head in a dispute over a parking space*, as had happened recently in our neighborhood.

Nicole bent to scoop up the paper ball, saying something muffled. "What?"

"I, said, 'So, no, baby, this, month.'"

"Oh." It startled me that she'd gone ahead with the idea, like everything in my world should be suspended until I was ready to pay attention again.

"I mean, I guess I knew it wouldn't happen right away."

"How many people—"

"Just one. But what you said about lying? It did feel weird. Maybe I might do a donor after all."

"So you really . . . He didn't mind not using condoms?"

"Yeah, right." Now she was bouncing the crumpled paper off her palm. "Can we talk about something else?"

"*I* didn't bring it up."

She threw the paper ball hard and it caromed off the back of the door. "So, who else visited?"

"Steph—"

"The Open Wound?"

Clearly a mistake to have called her that. When I'd first met Steph, she'd been going through a bad divorce with three young kids and everything made her cry: breaking a mug, seeing a homeless woman on the sidewalk, hearing the Nationwide Insurance jingle on the radio. "Yeah. Just her and his parents and Gita. I told people to wait for his tube to come out. Now I should get in touch but I kind of can't deal."

"Gita as in old *girlfriend* Gita?"

"She's nice. And I'm constantly back and forth for work or Fort. It's better if someone's here when I'm not."

Nicole raised her eyebrows. "I thought you thought she's still into him."

"Yeah, maybe, but. I don't know. Anyway, she's not—" The accepted San Francisco phrasing would be *not conventionally beautiful*, but I hated that kind of euphemism, which didn't actually soften the blow, just drew attention to your own delicacy of feeling. "She's not someone you'd lust after."

The truth was, I did think Gita had some kind of hangover

crush on Jeremy, but it didn't make me like her less. If anything, it maybe made me like her more.

Nicole lifted her arms and tilted her chin towards the ceiling, arching backwards until her palms rested on the floor, a backbend. Her Gymfinity T-shirt fell over her face and she batted it away. "What about Hal?"

"Visiting?" I shook my head. Hal had been my boyfriend for almost two years at Santa Cruz. We'd broken up junior year but both of us moved to San Francisco after college, along with half our graduating class. For a few years, we had been the kind of friends who sort of hated each other and then sometimes ended up sleeping together. Jeremy, who found Hal obnoxious, had never understood why I'd dated him. I said his obnoxiousness was a medium-range missile, not aimed at the people closest to him. Then I made the mistake of pointing out the obvious, Hal's extreme beauty, which Jeremy had simultaneously disputed and scorned: Hal was "normal looking," and why would I care about something like that anyway?

"You know who would have fantastic genes," Nicole said.

"Ugh. Don't sleep with Hal. Besides, it's only physical good genes. His soul is like steel wool."

Still in her backbend, she lifted one leg up towards the ceiling. "He's from a *million years* ago. I didn't think you'd care."

"I don't care. Not like that." Though right that minute, I did. Once, he'd told me, *I finally figured out that you look like a good witch* and *a bad witch*. "You're freakishly limber. You know that?"

"I do, in fact." She lowered her leg and lifted the other.

"Anyways, isn't the plan supposed to be that the guy never knows? It's not like Hal wouldn't put the pieces together."

"Oh, right." Nicole unfurled herself in one quick, graceful wave back to standing. She dug her phone from her bag and bent over it, tapping and swiping. "Here. Here's their website, the sperm bank."

I really didn't want to talk about babies right now. "I forgot, I have—I'm supposed to meet the occupational therapist. She's Baha'i. You know, with the turban." People usually got vague when they lied; I always made sure to be detailed. "I totally— I'm sorry. I totally forgot."

"God, no, that's fine." She started to slide the phone back into her purse, then hesitated. "Let me just show you this one profile. I'm kind of in love with this guy."

"Sure, quickly." I came to stand next to her. If she thought it was okay to come to the hospital to talk about stupid normal shit, it was largely because I'd insisted that I was fine, that I *wanted* to talk about stupid normal shit. But now it made me want to jump out of my skin.

I stepped back. "Actually, I am so late to meet her. Maybe like email it to me?"

"No, yeah, that's fine. Sorry."

"No, *I'm* sorry. I've got to—"

"Yeah, go, go." She opened her arms to give me a quick hug goodbye, and I forced myself to duck in towards her before I ducked away.

When Jeremy's white blood cell count fell below twelve thousand, it finally seemed okay to sleep at home. That evening, walking up our porch stairs felt like incredible freedom: I didn't have to charge around, grabbing things we needed, stuffing the mail in my bag, taking Fort on a rushed walk that would baffle him. I didn't have to race back to a room where the smell of bleach and chirp of machines made my skull ache. No one was going to ask anything of me. How had I not noticed before the luckiness of just regular life?

I laughed out loud, then felt guilty. Without taking off my jacket or putting down my keys, I called Jeremy's room. We talked for a minute about the little that had happened in the half-hour since we'd seen each other, and then I held the phone up so Fort could hear his voice. Fort went absolutely still, trembling with concentration.

I hadn't actually intended to get work done, but now I felt like I should. I had a pedestal table I'd been putting off that a woman from Pac Heights wanted me to crackle-glaze white, with gold showing through. I applied sizing and, while it dried, sat cross-legged on the floor to go through a box of old hinges and bin pulls, separating brass from chrome from nickel. I'd meant to sort them for a while but I didn't actually *need* to, and it felt decadent to do something by choice. Once the sizing was just barely tacky, I used a dry brush to lift one sheet of gold leaf at a time and transfer it to the table, pressing down. The window between too wet and not wet enough was brief; I had to work in stages. I brushed on the next swath of sizing, then took Fort for a walk. I didn't notice I still had on my particulate mask until the third or fourth person looked at me strangely, this one a pregnant-looking guy who strutted down the street, coat open, no shirt underneath.

Sometime over the last two years, I'd stopped noticing where we lived, everything gone blurry with familiarity. The mediocre Thai place, filled at lunch with doctors from S.F. General, but empty now, the owner asleep on his feet behind the counter. The Laundromat with its warring television shows, both full-blast, one in Spanish and one in English. A guy ran out of St. Francis, the diner where we'd had breakfast with Gita. He squatted quickly in the street—Jeremy and I called it the Urban Crouch—to check his tires for the DPW chalk mark.

Despite its ugliness, the table was absorbing. I ended up working too late and then I woke at four, conditioned to the nurses' intrusions. They'd be checking Jeremy's vitals around now: apparently, at 4 AM you were at your truest weight.

I lay there for half an hour, trying so strenuously to sleep that I only woke myself up completely. Finally, I got up and made espresso. In my workroom, I dragged one of Nadia's still-unfinished chairs into the bay window and sat in it, warming my hands around the little cup. I realized that for all the thousands of hours I'd spent in that room, I'd never had the lights off. Someone had painted an intricate constellation map on the ceiling with glow-in-the-dark paint.

Once I'd challenged Jeremy to count the people he'd lived with in this house before me; he got to eighteen but thought he might be forgetting a couple. One of them must have painted the stars. For just a second, it felt like a communication. I hadn't known the true weight of my loneliness until that moment when it eased, then settled back in.

Pulling my knees up to my chin, I watched through the window as the darkness in the street slowly loosened and broke apart. The lines of the tall, purple Victorian opposite ours sharpened, emerging from the gloom. A woman crawled out through a gap in the boarded-up front door and then straightened, swaying. She was ruinously thin, a cotton bandana over her hair and neon-yellow jellies on her feet. Her eyes fluttered shut and she began to tip forward; then she jerked upright and took a staggering step back. My fingertips itched, and I looked down at them. The whorls glittered with gold dust.

8

*t*he morning of the amputation, a father and a bald, puffy-faced toddler got into the hospital elevator with me. The girl wore a mask, the plastic tubing of her central line showing above the neck of her flowered T-shirt. "Is it okay if she pushes the buttons?" he asked as we got on.

"Sure. Eleventh door. Floor, I mean, eleventh floor."

"ICU," he said.

"Yeah, my husband. Are you fourteen?" The fourteenth floor was pediatric oncology.

"Yup." He squatted down, lifting the girl under the armpits. She leaned forward, pushing the control panel with both palms, so that nearly all the buttons lit up. "Whoops, sorry."

We rode up a floor, waited while the doors opened and shut, then rode up another floor. Maybe behind his polite demeanor, this father was thinking that I had nothing to complain about: a sick toddler was worse than a sick husband. Or maybe this dad was nicer than me, not comparing us at all. But if he were nicer, he'd deserve for his daughter to get better more than I deserved for Jeremy to get better. And she probably did deserve it more. She'd have a sudden and miraculous recovery, and Jeremy would have a sudden, unexpected swoop down and I'd arrive at his room to solemn faces saying, *There was nothing we could do*, and it would be my fault for having slept at home two nights in a row.

The father told me that the cancer was in her marrow; they needed a donor. I told him that Jeremy was having surgery to amputate the two toes that had died when he was in shock, except I didn't say "toes," just amputation, trying to make it sound less minor in comparison. I'd had a dozen of these conversations over the last two and a half weeks, trading intimate details with people whose names I never knew.

The little girl was fussing. The elevator doors opened again and she shrieked *No!* flapping her hand in the air as though waving someone away. "Terrible twos," said the dad, and I gave one of those laughs you give not because something's funny but because you want to respond.

I knelt down. "I'll tell you what. You want to see something cool?" I dug in my bag, not knowing what I had in there, and found a level. "Look at this. If you tilt it, the bubble goes . . . see, like that. But if it's perfectly flat . . . there. The bubble stays right between those lines."

She took the tool from me, tipping it back and forth, then looked up and smiled. Maybe I actually wasn't bad with kids. We rose past the ninth floor, the psych unit, where the elevator wouldn't stop without a key, and came to a stop at the tenth. The doors opened to the empty hallway, waited obediently, sighed closed.

"Next floor's mine," I chirped, holding out my hand.

"Mine," said the girl, jerking the level to her chest, twisting at the waist.

I looked at the dad. "I actually need it for work."

"Yeah, sorry." He talked quietly to his daughter. The doors dinged open; I stuck my boot onto the threshold. The girl was embracing the level with both arms, shaking and shaking her bald head. The doors dinged, began to close, sprang back when they hit my foot. He worked the level out of her grasp. As I walked down the hall I could hear her wailing until the elevator doors shut.

Someone was already in Jeremy's room when I got there, sitting on my chair. Gita, looking rumpled. She must have gotten there really early. I felt a strange, juddering anxiety. Why hadn't I just let the little girl have my stupid level?

"I know we didn't talk about me coming, but I realized I have a ton of overtime banked," Gita said.

"Right. Me too."

She looked confused.

"Joke."

His parents were late, of course. Doctors and nurses came and went. Dr. Bayh, the surgeon, came to check in. Apparently the anesthesiologist had already stopped by. Jeremy told me, "I felt ridiculous, but I asked her to tell me I wasn't going to die during surgery."

"What did she say?"

Gita said, "She goes, 'Let me put it this way. When you go out to get your mail, have you ever been hit by a truck?' And Jeremy—" she started to laugh.

"And being super-literal, I was all, 'Well, my mail comes in through a slot in the front door.'"

I picked up the ball of crumpled paper from my game with Nicole and bounced it off my hand: front, back, front. I couldn't sit down. I kept walking the perimeter of the room, a circle in one direction and then the other.

"Tell us something interesting," Jeremy said to me.

I looked around the room, trying to think: cards, TV, magazines. "Did you know *National Geographic* used to have a rule about how dark a woman's skin had to be before they'd show her bare-breasted?"

"Did you learn that at *Santa Cruz*?" he asked, in the same tone people used for *Oh, Unitarian*.

"Well, but it's true. Your turn."

"Okay." He closed his eyes for a minute, until I thought he might have fallen asleep. "'Algebra' comes from Arabic, *al-jabr*. It means the reunion of broken parts."

"That's a good one." I didn't turn to Gita next: it didn't seem like her kind of game, and I didn't want to put her on the spot.

She said, "Do you know what it means to be decimated?"

I nodded, feeling awkward for her.

She went on, "It's not what you think, though; it means reduce by one-tenth. *Dec*-imate. It was a way that conquering armies showed their power. They killed one person in ten to show they could, and also to show they didn't have to."

Jeremy's face was pale as talcum powder, which made his eyes look startlingly dark. "That's good," he said, faintly.

After a minute, Gita said, "I brought Scrabble? It's a brand-new set, so germs shouldn't be. . ."

Jeremy nodded. "But Claire sucks at Scrabble."

I'd been about to say I sucked at Scrabble, so I wasn't sure why it annoyed me.

Dr. Bayh came in again to tell us that the OR was ready. Just before he left, he put his hand lightly on Jeremy's sheet-covered knee. "As Shakespeare said, 'Screw your courage to the sticking-place, and we'll not fail.'"

I was pretty sure Shakespeare hadn't intended Lady Macbeth as a motivational speaker. I glanced at Jeremy, but he just nodded at the doctor, his lips pressed together.

After Jeremy was wheeled away for surgery, Gita and I went out to wait in the family lounge. A talk show jabbered just loud enough I couldn't ignore it and just softly enough I couldn't quite make out the words. When Ruth and David came in— flushed, rushing, sure they'd gotten there as fast as they could— I said, "You remember Gita, right?"

"Hi, Mr. and Mrs. Goldsmith."

"Oh," said Ruth, vaguely. And then to me: "You still have that in?"

My nose ring. I matched her mournful tone: "I'm afraid so."

Gita swallowed a smile. I'd be glad when it was just the two of us again, with Jeremy. Hard to believe that only a couple of weeks ago I'd barely recognized her when she came to the room; now I felt like I'd know her anywhere.

Nearby, a Latino family was eating a huge picnic, maybe four buckets of fried chicken. The idea of eating dead bodies made me sick at the same time that the smell made me salivate. I was scared and bored; hungry and nauseated; exhausted and wired.

On TV, a beautiful Indian actress in a pink silk dress was being interviewed. Gita said quietly, "When I was born, some people sent my parents condolence cards."

"*What*?"

"One: girl." She flashed her hand at me. "Two: dark skin." "Jesus." I felt like I should touch her but didn't know how. I bumped my forehead down against her shoulder, just for a second.

Ruth worked on one of the pastel acrylic baby blankets she made for charity. Convinced she'd catch something in the hospital, she insisted on wearing a paper mask and blue latex gloves; as her hands flashed over her knitting, they almost seemed to leave vapor trails in the air. Jeremy's father perched awkwardly on the narrow windowsill and tried to work a sudoku puzzle. Gita and I had our mystery novels, a habit she'd gotten me into. I'd never understood before why someone would read mysteries— why would I want to read about made-up violence?—but now I felt the comfort of repetition: order destroyed, order restored; order destroyed and restored.

Jeremy's father shifted. "So, Claire, any more thoughts on a name?"

I shook my head. "I'd kind of forgotten about it. Why, do you have anything?"

"Did you get my email?"

"Probably? I haven't been checking regularly."

"Nothing specific, I was thinking: maybe there's a tool you use that would work for a name? A plane, or a compass?"

"Oh, huh. Yeah. I'll think if there's something like that."

About a year before, Jeremy had mentioned to his parents that I was having trouble naming my business. He thought my ideas—Homefront, Domestic Science, Second Sight—didn't communicate anything. And his suggestion, On the Mend, seemed corny and second-rate to me. Ruth had said to use Hood Repairs, and when I pointed out it sounded like an auto shop, she shrugged, done.

David enjoyed the challenge of coming up with a name, though, and it gave us a shared topic. He pulled out the notebook he kept in his breast pocket. "So, for example—" He wrote a few words and then with surprising skill quickly sketched in a compass, the kind with a sharp point on one end and a pencil on the other. Ripping out the page, he handed it to me.

Claire Hood. Compass Repairs.

Mistaking my silence for consternation, he said, "I know that's not it, yet," and tried to take back the sheet of paper.

"No." I jerked the page away. "I mean, no, it's good." It wasn't the business name I couldn't stop looking at, but my own. Claire Hood, the words at once intimately mine and entirely strange.

For three days, his post-surgery meds made Jeremy vomit so much that blood vessels burst in his eyes, starring them red. The skin on his face was flaking off. I grasped his bony hand in mine; he barely had strength to grip back. Revulsion wriggled in my chest. I said, "I love you I love you I love you."

And then a moment later, I did feel that love, so absolute I couldn't imagine how I'd felt disgust. He looked naked and bleary as a fledgling, his beak opening towards me. I leaned forward, and put my cheek down on the mattress beside him. The meds made his skin smell of sulfur, like egg yolks overcooked to gray. Closing my eyes, I breathed him in. The shush of machines. Blood shushing in my head. *This.*

This. Sometimes I said it to myself when I touched Jeremy, trying to memorize the feel of the back of his head, the soft hollow at the base of his skull. I tried to store him up, an animal stockpiling for winter. When I was a kid in Greer, a family down the street kept their dining room packed with emergency supplies: boxes of canned soup, plastic barrels of water, canned beans, all stacked higher than my head, the windows entirely blocked. A chemical toilet. Blue box on top of blue box on top of blue box of generic tampons. A family that seemed, in its private way, as crazy as ours.

And now that was me, trying to store up against disaster. Jeremy's right foot was bandaged, so I studied his other foot, the way his long second toe curved and rested on the big toe, like someone resting their chin on someone else's shoulder. His hands with their wide, flat nails. Thinking he might not survive made me feel guilty, like I wasn't putting enough trust in him. And simultaneously, I felt guilty because if he did die, I would have wasted part of our time together on being unhappy.

Jeremy's throat was still raw from being intubated, and the vomiting irritated it even more. When talking hurt too much, he began writing on a whiteboard. Dr. Wu wrote an order to up his morphine but said it might constipate him. If he needed, a nurse could give him a suppository in his anus. At the word "anus," Jeremy glanced at me; I tried to keep my face still.

After she left, Jeremy scrawled on his whiteboard, *I guess nothing's mysterious between us anymore.*

"It's not like the mystery of your anus was ever what I stuck around for."

He smeared away the old ink from the whiteboard with the little sponge and wrote, *Country song. "The Mystery of Your Anus."*

"That one's going to race up the charts."

The morphine had begun to tug at him. Jeremy's eyes were closed, but he raised his eyebrows, an attempt at wiggling them. And then his face went slack as the drug took him.

I got the front-desk person to buzz me off the unit and made my way down the hall to the Family Kitchen, which had cheap, white laminate cabinets, all the doors hanging askew. I kept a stack of identical rice bowls from Trader Joe's in the freezer—tofu, broccoli, not really my thing but nothing about the hospital was my thing anyway. *Poor me, poor me.*

Someone had left behind an ancient *Us Weekly*, back from when Brad and Angelina had been adopting a girl from Ethiopia. A survey asked if they should have a biological child, too. Which was more disturbing, that people thought their opinions on this mattered, or that they had opinions about it in the first place? I'd read the magazine before; now I went through it again, picking clean the bones.

A husband I'd seen around came into the kitchen a few minutes later. He was shorter than me, with blue-black stubble and a bit of a belly. He nodded at my rice bowl. "How original of you."

"And you'll be having—?"

He reached into the freezer, paused for effect, and then pulled out one of the frozen Trader Joe's chicken burritos he kept stacked there like firewood.

"Equally original."

"It's like my taste buds got zapped," he said. "You have that?" I shook my head. "More like I just don't care."

"Well yeah, that too."

He and his wife were on the oncology unit. Over the couple weeks we'd been here I'd learned slowly that she worked as a bookkeeper for a chain of grocery stores. That she really loved Bikram and fantasized about leaving her job to become an instructor. Honestly, he wasn't sure she would have had the guts to do it before, but now he thought she actually would, after. He said more than once that maybe this whole thing would turn out to be worth it if it meant a chance at a new life.

She'd been in and out of the hospital for nearly a year, and their kid had been "weirdly mostly okay" but apparently his preschool teacher had gone on maternity leave a few days ago and Jack had completely lost his shit with the substitute. Now he was on probation for biting.

"Probation? In preschool?"

"But even more absurd? My wife's brother—have you seen him? Tall guy, shaved head. He shaved it the day she was diagnosed, "in solidarity," even though she hadn't started chemo yet. He used to be an addict, and he's been clean for six years, and I know I should respect that—I do respect that. And he works with at-risk teenagers, etcetera etcetera. But he's the kind of person who makes everything about him, so you just know he's working with those teens because he loves getting to tell his story to them, and he loves getting to tell everyone else that's his job, and how what he can teach them is nothing compared to what they've taught him, and how humbled he is. Anytime anyone says something humbles them, they basically mean the opposite. So Amanda's diagnosed, and like an *hour* later her brother shows up at our door, sobbing, with his head shaved. I wanted to fucking slam the door in his face. *Into* his face." The microwave dinged and he opened it, looking at the burrito like he had no idea what it was. His dark business suit showed through the thin, blue paper suit he wore over it. "But that's not the thing I was going to tell you, the worst thing. He got this tattoo of Mandy on his bicep, from a photo, very realistic. Or at least it looks like it's of a real person, but not necessarily like her. The eyes are—I don't even know, they're wrong. Too intense. Like—" he pointed to his chin, his cheek, his eyes: "normal face, normal face, Charles Manson." He started to laugh and laugh, a high barking noise. Finally, watery-eyed, he got enough breath back to say, "And there's a banner over her picture that says '1975' and then a dash, and the other side is blank."

"Nineteen seventy-five? Wait, is that—?"

He was laughing so hard he could barely even nod.

"Like on a *headstone*?"

Tears coursed down the sides of his nose. I started laughing, too, mostly at the sight of him. A nurse I didn't know peered in, shook her head and withdrew. Presumably, hysterical laughter in the Family Kitchen was nothing new to her, which made us laugh harder.

When finally we wound down, I said, "It could be worse. It could be on his ass."

The husband didn't laugh. He was staring in the general direction of the dripping sink faucet. "I really hate him."

9

*V*an Ness was darkening as I drove my pickup towards our house with Gita. We were feeling aimless. Jeremy's naps lasted hours: no reason to hang around, but so much togetherness had worn a deep groove into the day. Once we'd dragged ourselves out of the room, dragging apart from each other had seemed like too much effort.

In Maryland, winter evenings used to descend like a pulled shade, but in San Francisco dusk drifted into corners and along the edges of buildings, accumulating from all sides. I parked at the curb. Mr. Makarov, the landlord, hadn't done any work on the house in a million years and its pale-gray paint had cracked into a scalloped pattern like fish scales.

Jaxon sat on our porch, hunched sleepily. He sometimes shot up there, probably because we didn't hassle him about it. He was less handsome than he'd been even a year before. His hands were in his windbreaker's pockets and he listed to one side, but when I said hi, he stirred himself and moved over so we could pass. The light from the streetlamp showed a half-crusted wound the size of a quarter above his eyebrow.

"What happened?"

He looked puzzled. I put my hand to my own head.

"Ah." He mirrored me, gingerly. "No idea."

"Let me . . . Just a sec." I went back to the car and grabbed the first-aid kit Jeremy made me keep in the glove compartment. Climbing the stairs to the porch, I dug out alcohol wipes, a tube of antibiotic cream, and a bandage. I dabbed at his cut, aware of performing a little for Gita. If I'd been alone, I would probably have done the same thing, but I wouldn't *necessarily* have done the same thing. It wasn't a performance of look-how-kind-I-am—I'd never had any interest in that—but look-how-matter-of-fact-I-am-about-patching-up-the-heroin-addict-on-my-stairs.

When we went inside, Fort came galumphing in from the kitchen, then stopped at the sight of Gita, setting his feet.

"It's okay," I said to them both—she had frozen too. I put my hand on Gita's shoulder. "Look, Fort. It's a friend."

In the living room, Gita seemed like she didn't quite know how to arrange her limbs. Her awkwardness made me feel suddenly awkward. We'd never actually been alone together without a clear purpose. She said, "The house looks different."

Having a stranger there made me see the room again in its component pieces. I'd painted the walls a deep green-blue and had done some free restoration work for my friend Meara's shop in exchange for a beautifully worn red Persian rug. Nearly everything else I'd salvaged from the street or from a stage set—velvet couch from *Streetcar*, fireplace mantel from *Extremities*—and then repaired. "I didn't know you'd been here."

"Not in years. After we broke up—I mean, you probably know this but he cheated on me at Cornell, like two weeks into the year."

I nodded, although it didn't seem like he'd cheated on her exactly; they'd agreed to see other people. According to him, she wouldn't have had a problem with it if she'd been the one to find someone else first.

"Anyway, we've kind of tried being friends a couple times since then, but this is the first time it's actually worked. But maybe five years ago I was here? He was dating one of his housemates."

"Right, the writer?"

"Ugh," said Gita. "Helena. So pretentious. He's much better off with you."

I could imagine Gita and Jeremy together as teenagers getting along in much the same friendly way that they did now, two people with similar interests and mild temperaments. It was harder for me to imagine her as very passionate—though of course, that I didn't find her sexy didn't mean she wasn't sexual. Did she have orgasms? She hadn't with Jeremy (this was the kind of thing he and I discussed our first months together), but I hadn't with my high school boyfriend, either. All my talk about sex back then really just meant I knew the names for things— fisting, rimming—that I couldn't imagine wanting to do.

On the coffee table were listing stacks of bills and coupons. A condolence card from someone who'd heard that Jeremy had died, which had been an unsettling thing to open: *I'm so sorry for your loss.* Half-hidden by the mail, a rigid old leather catcher's mitt cupped in its palm a two-yen coin from Jeremy's junior year abroad, an orange Chance card, a little glass jar, a broken blue eggshell. Gita slipped the Monopoly card out from under the other objects and turned it over: Get Out of Jail Free. Drifts of dust and hair gathered like dusk in the corners and along the baseboards.

"What's this?" she asked, picking up the jar.

I pointed to the hand-written label, CANNABINOID SALVE, block letters almost as small and neat as type. "A friend of mine has a prescription."

"Wait; so—it's, um, pot?"

"She got it for period cramps, I think."

"My mother has her nose pierced." She touched her left nostril. "It's supposed to help with cramps. Also childbirth."

"Huh. Does it work?"

Gita shrugged. "No way to know."

"Anyway, you should see this dispensary. It's on Eighteenth and Guerrero, and inside's all white, with floor-to-ceiling glass cases. Everyone working there is hip but in this incredibly clean way, like they're carved out of soap, you know?"

She shook her head, still turning the jar in her hands. "Want to hear a secret? Not exactly a secret. Just, I don't broadcast it or anything."

I waited. When she didn't go on, I realized she was actually holding off until I said okay. "Okay."

"I've never tried—*done*, I guess?—drugs, of any kind. In high school, I didn't even get drunk until senior year. And then marijuana wasn't really a thing at Harvard when I was there."

I felt pretty confident that marijuana had been a thing at Harvard when she was there. "Are you saying you want to try?"

"Oh. I guess—I wasn't at all thinking that—but, yeah, I guess, I mean sure. What the hey." She wasn't a good actor; the faked surprise in her voice made clear she *had* been hinting at exactly this. It didn't bother me, though: I didn't trust anyone who didn't lie a little.

"Here." I took the jar and twisted off the top. With my finger I dug up some salve—gritty, like sand in Vaseline.

"*Now*, you mean?"

"Where else do you need to be?" I turned up my wrist. "Do this."

Obediently she held out her arm, the one with the blobby, orange star tattoo, and I rubbed the glob into her skin. Then I did the same for myself.

Gita was studying her wrist.

"Nothing's going to happen for a few minutes."

She nodded and turned the Chance card over and over in her fingers, not looking at me. "How are things with Jeremy?" Her voice had a false casualness I didn't understand.

"Well, you saw. His counts are up."

"No, I mean, I meant, you know, between you." She stumbled over the words. I realized that for all her questions about what I did and had done, she didn't usually ask what it felt like. "You said you guys aren't always such a great match. That must make this . . ."

"What? No. When did I say that?"

She was blushing so much that I could see it even in the dimness and despite her dark skin. It turned out that very first morning at brunch, when I'd talked about how different Jeremy and I were, Gita had heard it not as boast but lament.

She said, "Maybe it's just you don't really seem like a 'wife.'"

"Oh. Thank you?" I lay back against the carpet and closed my eyes. For a long time, neither of us said anything. Maybe the salve was too old to be any good. I opened my eyes, and the world flattened and tipped up. I was about to say, *I think it's working* when Gita laughed.

She pulled her hand slowly through the air. "Look. Bioluminescence."

"I think it's working."

"Yeah, you said."

"I did?"

"What?"

"What?"

"Never mind." She fanned her hand in the air like someone batting away smoke. "Did you know my thesis was on starfish?"

"Are a lot of fish named after other things? It seems like a lot of fish are named after other things. Jellyfish. Starfish. Horse . . . Wait. Horsefish? Is that . . . ? Horsefish?"

"Seahorse?"

"Seahorse!"

"Swordfish," she said. "Clown fish."

"I mean, birds get their own names, right?" Medical marijuana patients probably weren't supposed to get this high. When my friend had given me the salve, she'd said something about a quarter-sized dab. I'd gone more oyster-sized.

"My thesis was on pink starfish. They're like—" she held her hand up, slightly clawed.

"Wait," I said. "Is that why your tattoo is?"

"And they extrude their stomachs. So they can eat something bigger than their mouths because they can digest it outside themselves. They only have to get a clam open like a millimeter and then they can slip their stomach in."

"That would be a great horror movie. 'Starfish'?"

She was sitting cross-legged, swaying a little. "They can't really move on land."

My laugh sounded choppy to my ears. "Um, Gita? I wasn't actually serious that a horror movie about starfish was a good idea."

She lay back and closed her eyes.

Sour-cream-and-onion potato chips. Canned chocolate frosting. Those candy dots that always still had a bit of white paper after you peeled them from their backing. Only when I was stoned did I want the foods I'd fetishized in childhood. "We need to go to the corner store."

Gita was running her palms back and forth lightly over the carpet. "They'd like to meet you. I'll take you sometime. But don't say 'fuck' in front of them."

"Gita?"

She opened her eyes, which were very dark brown. I couldn't tell where the pupil ended and the iris began. "I'm so . . . so . . ."

"High?"

"*High*. It's freaking me out a little."

I decided not to pursue *freaking me out*, words that made her sound about fourteen. It also probably wasn't the time to tell her the interesting fact that people with brown eyes were seen as warmer than gray-eyed people like me for just this reason: the pupil looked bigger. "Here. Try this."

She put her hand to her chest. "Do people ever have heart attacks from pot?"

"No. Try this." I sat the same way she was sitting, cross-legged, my knees touching hers. "Look at me. Okay. Deep breath."

"Is this a, what? Past-life thing?"

I shook my head. "It's a theater game. Do something."

"Do—?"

"It's okay. Just anything."

Hesitantly, she raised her hand to her head, patting it, and I copied her. She moved her arm out to the side and I moved mine at the same angle and speed. She was staring at me; I could see her getting drawn in, calming down. We windmilled our arms to the other side, like semaphorists or cheerleaders, but very, very slowly, and I bent down towards the floor on the right and then slowly, slowly straightened and bent to the other side, and then back to center and we shook our heads no, yes, no, yes, and I didn't know anymore which of us was going first and which was following.

On our way back to the hospital, we stopped by Lost Weekend Video, where I trolled for something to take back with us. Our room had maybe fifty channels plus the hospital's special programming—the Cardiac Health channel, the Newborn channel, the Relax! channel with an endless loop of waves foaming onto a beach—and yet rarely was anything good on. And watching random junk felt particularly depressing in the hospital, where it was hard to forget that you had a finite and irretrievable number of minutes on earth. I flicked through Lost Weekend's documentaries. Normally, Jeremy liked difficult foreign films with almost no dialogue, or else endless dialogue and no action. But his attention span was short these days, and subtitles hurt his eyes.

"What do you think?" I asked Gita, holding up two boxes.

"I don't know." She looked a little sick. I'd felt great affection for her when we were high but now I felt itchy, tired of her, ready to be left alone.

I wanted a documentary that would be educational enough not to feel like a waste of time but entertaining enough to hold Jeremy's fractured interest. I was still trying to decide when Hal came into the store.

Hal lived in the Mission and frequented the same kinds of places I did, so we ran into each other from time to time. The girl with him was, unsurprisingly, stunning: tall and lanky, with a crew cut dyed the bright blue of antifreeze.

Hal looked up with his wide, generous smile, reaching us in three quick strides. "Claire!"

I smiled back, a mistake: his hand went immediately to the corner of my eye. "I love your laugh lines," he said.

I twisted my head away. "Thanks." This was the second time he'd told me he loved my laugh lines. A few years ago, his favorite refrain had been, "It's so cool you're still tending bar. The other bartenders I used to know have all moved on."

Hal hadn't introduced the woman he was with, so I stuck my hand out towards her: "Claire Hood."

"Liv." She held her hand—cool and light as paper—against mine for a brief moment. Of course she'd have a name like Liv.

"Hi, Liz," I said. "This is Gita, Jeremy's high school sweetheart."

"It's Liv, actually."

"But then I went off to Harvard, and he went off to Cornell, so . . ."

Hal nodded, checking out my baggy sweatshirt and not-recently-washed hair. Before he could compliment me for looking like shit, I held up the videos: "We've got to go, great to see you."

"Movie night?"

I held his gaze long enough to let him know this wasn't a question worth answering. "Pleasure meeting you, Liz."

After I'd paid and we were on the sidewalk—crowds of chattering twenty-somethings; a man passed out in a pool of urine by the wall—Gita whispered, "Who *was* that?"

"My ex from college." Even irritated with Hal, I felt a little crackle of pleasure claiming him. "He does Internet stuff now. Like everyone."

"Was that his girlfriend?"

So Gita had been attracted to Hal; I supposed there was no reason it should surprise me. "Well, probably not 'girlfriend.' He goes through women pretty fast these days. Actually, our relationship was his longest by a lot."

"Why'd you break up?"

"Why does anyone? We were, like, twenty-one."

The driver's side door of my truck sometimes stuck. Clamping the movies under my chin, I yanked on the handle. "Are you okay to drive?" she asked.

"I wouldn't drive if I wasn't."

We were quiet most of the way to the hospital. At Santa Cruz, even if Hal hadn't been so beautiful, he would still have been famous for two things. One: our first year, an RA had been fired for sleeping with him. And two: he'd grown up in Humboldt County on a commune, an actual hordes-of-naked-kids-crashing-through-the-trees-faces-painted-with-berry-juice kind. Comparing notes was how we'd become friends. At some point, he made what seemed like a reflexive pass at me, and I laughed at him and he seemed relieved and we went back to being friends—best friends, we sometimes called ourselves—until the night I pierced my nose. We drank whiskey together, and then I got embarrassingly shaky when I tried to jam the safety pin into cartilage. "Here," Hal said, and pushed it through. Instead of moving back, he very gently ran his finger over my eyebrow, down my cheek. He said my name.

I usually thought wryly of this moment. Did my only perfect first kiss have to have been with *Hal*? With a blood-smeared safety pin hanging from my nostril? Though sometimes the memory caught me unawares and I felt a longing that had nothing to do with him, but with a sense of possibility. A surge of joy like a door banging open in a gust of wind. I felt the same way remembering the Christmas vacation that Nicole and I agreed to work a week of graveyard shifts at Dr. Doughnut, taking our breaks outside at 3 AM beneath a vast sky prickling with stars, drinking thin cafeteria coffee and eating line rejects, still faintly warm, the sugar sticking to the wool of our gloves.

I parked at the hospital and we took the stairs up to the eleventh floor. Gita, who was trying to lose weight, had a no-elevator rule. We blew into the room unwrapping scarves, talking over each other, dropping our bags on the chair.

"We brought mail," I said.

"And movies."

I danced the documentaries in the air, singing, "Penguins or fast food, penguins or fast food."

Jeremy pressed his hand to his throat and whisper-croaked, "Are you *high*?"

Gita and I went still.

"Wait, you actually are?"

"A little?" she said.

Jeremy rolled his eyes, reaching for his whiteboard. *You are such a bad influence,* he wrote to me.

Gita dropped into my chair, pulling her knees to her chest. "We ran into Claire's ex-boyfriend at the video store."

Jeremy scribbled, *H?*

I nodded.

That guy is such a douche, Jeremy wrote. Practically overnight, he'd gone from being puffy with drugs to being very gaunt, cheeks sunken, as though someone had pressed them in with tongs. He sat up in bed—almost upright!—wearing the black cashmere cap I'd given him.

"It's not like I sought him out," I said. "We ran into each other."

"He seemed nice," Gita said.

Jeremy erased the whiteboard and wrote, *Maybe you can resolve this for us. He's not that good-looking, right?* He turned it towards her.

Gita glanced at me, startled. After a moment, we both began to laugh.

Jeremy grimaced. Then he shook his head and smiled a little. "Shit," he croaked, then winced and put his hand to his throat. It had never occurred to me he might be jealous of Hal. I loved him so much right then, I wanted him to die. I wanted to never feel anything less pure than this.

10

*j*eremy moved from the ICU to the step-down unit, where you didn't need to be buzzed in. When I realized I could come and go as I pleased, it felt wrong, like there should at least be a sign-in sheet, or a card scan, *something* to keep track.

Unlike the ICU, the step-down unit was set up to actually allow overnight visitors, with a bench that could be made into a narrow bed. Even so, the lights of his machines and the noises of the hall and the vitals checks every few hours made for not-great sleep. At his urging, I began spending the nights at home. And he was right: it was amazing how much better I felt about everything when I'd actually slept. One of those totally obvious lessons I somehow kept having to relearn.

We knew he'd be able to leave the hospital when his counts were high enough, but still it shocked us both when Dr. Wu, his internist, declared, "So it looks like we'll be discharging you the day after tomorrow." She said it so casually that at first I thought *discharge* was a medical procedure—flushing some tube, filtering some bodily fluid.

The OT came by in the late afternoon to make a mold of Jeremy's foot for a prosthetic. She had him put both feet on silicone pads—he held onto the bedrail, unused to balancing without a toe. To my surprise, it was his intact left foot she rubbed with petroleum jelly and glopped with plaster. She told us that the big toe bore forty percent of your body weight. Jeremy looked glazed. When things were too much for him, he became the guy in the backseat, separated from the driver by soundproof glass.

I said, "I don't get how that's possible, forty percent."

"It's why guys shot off their toes in Vietnam. You can't be in the military without both big toes."

His right foot had fewer bandages now: the stitches where he'd lost toes were covered but not the remaining three, which stuck out, still dusky gray. They might or might not ever change back.

The OT said, "You have big plans for tonight?"

"Tonight?"

"New Year's?"

"It's not—" I glanced at our whiteboard: 12/31. "*Oh*. It's New Year's." Christmas on the ICU had barely registered. Jeremy and I didn't celebrate anyway: Christmases had been stressful and unhappy for me as a kid—even distance hadn't burnished the memory—and I'd been happy enough to switch to Hanukkah. Of course, we hadn't celebrated Hanukkah this year, either.

Jeremy stirred himself. "Are Bella and Heather having their thing? You should go."

"To a *party*?"

"Okay, I think that's set." The mold had hardened. The OT worked her fingers around his ankle, as if under the cuff of a sock. Then, gently, she rocked Jeremy's foot up out of the plaster mold. He'd need two more fittings; she said she'd work with his coordinator to schedule them.

After she'd gone he brought up New Year's again. "Why don't you see what Nicole's doing?"

I hadn't been spending a lot of time with Nicole lately. I couldn't stand having another person who needed anything—even basic interest—from me.

I said, "I'm not going to a party when you're in the hospital."

"Ambien," he pointed out. "I'll be sleeping like the dead. Just go so I don't feel like I'm ruining your life."

There was no way I was up for a party. I supposed I could catch up on work, though. At midnight, I could drink some Scotch and go to bed.

On my way through the lobby, I passed a knot of people crying: my friend from the Family Kitchen whose name I didn't know, a guy clutching his shaved head—presumably the brother with the awful tattoo—and a little kid in a T. rex shirt. Oh no, I thought—a pressing against my chest that made it hard to take a full breath—and then I had to stop myself from thinking.

At home, I ran hot water into our claw-foot tub. Some ex-housemate of Jeremy's had painted its toenails red, which I found annoyingly cutesy, though I was also aware that they might delight me if I'd painted them myself. I carried the warped table leaf I needed to fix down the hall from my workroom to the bathroom, slipped it into the water and held it under.

The wood desperately wanted to shoot up to the surface; I forced it down, my forearms fish-belly white in the bathwater.

From outside, the competing strains of music from different parties. I held the table leaf underwater, my arms shaking, and then in shifting my grip I let up the tiniest bit and it sprang up. "Fuck. *Fuck* it." I sat on the edge of the tub, using my feet to hold the board against the bottom, my jeans wet to the knees, and then I changed my mind and knelt on the board, water sloshing out onto the floor. The wood bobbed beneath me, trying to rise up like a surfboard. I held onto the lip of the tub, gritting my teeth.

Suddenly I saw myself from the outside: fully dressed in the bathtub on New Year's Eve. I started laughing. The table leaf slid out from under me and shot, sideways, to the surface. I left it bobbing there and went to change my clothes.

Bella and Heather lived in Oakland, about five minutes' walk from the Lake Merritt station. The night breeze was warm, discarded papers cartwheeling like tumbleweeds up the sidewalk. I felt giddy with recklessness; then the second I walked in the apartment door, I wanted to leave.

Bella had already seen me, though. "You came!" She squeezed through the crowd. In college she'd been spiky and boyish, with short hair dyed purple. She was softer now but she still wore cargo pants and ancient T-shirts. "Did you BART or drive?"

"What? Oh. BART."

She handed me her cup. "See if you like it. Ginger lemonade and whiskey. We're calling it 'The Click.'" She kept her eyebrows raised: I was supposed to get the reference, so probably a play. We'd met sophomore year when she had the lead in an all-female *Macbeth* and I'd built the sets.

I shook my head.

"*Cat on a Hot Tin Roof.* Brick drinks until he feels the click in his head."

I took a sip: the drink was hot, and better than it sounded.

"We thought about buying tin mugs, but too expensive. Are you okay?" Bella asked.

I nodded.

"I shouldn't even ask. You always say you're okay."

At Santa Cruz, Bella and I had been friends, then briefly and disastrously lovers. I'd turned out to be not so much attracted to Bella as to some idea of myself as cool and adventurous. I made sure our plans always included other friends; when she tried to get me off on my own, I acted like she was the one being weird about it. Hence "disastrous."

I said, "He's getting out of the hospital in like two days."

"Oh! That's great. You actually are okay, then." She jerked her chin at the drink. "Keep that, I'll get another."

She introduced me to some guy who lived in an Airstream parked in a field in Half Moon Bay, a topic I would normally have found interesting but could barely follow. I tried to talk to Heather, Bella's girlfriend, an earnest social worker. Our conversations always limped a little, but tonight it felt like in order to understand her I had to do simultaneous translation. Apparently I didn't do it all that well: the frown groove between her eyebrows deepened until it looked like a coin slot.

Throwing back the last of the Click, I said, "I'm going to get another drink—" just as she said, "How is your work going?"

She said, "Good, I'll let you do that," at the same time that I said, "Fine, fine, it's going well." We gave weak laughs. I missed Jeremy terribly.

At the drinks table was a woman I'd met several times. She had one of those late-seventies head-cheerleader names like Kim or Jill. Around her neck she wore a leather cord with a raw blue sapphire. She touched it when she saw me looking. Her husband had given it to her for Christmas, she said.

She dropped her voice to a merry whisper: "What do you think? Does he deserve a BJ?"

"Whether or not you suck your husband's cock is going to have to be between you and your god." I hadn't heard someone say *BJ* since high school.

"Well, no, I wasn't actually—I mean, I didn't really mean—" She flushed dark red.

Shame rose in my throat. I'd somehow gotten drunk. I turned and left without saying goodbye to anyone. When midnight struck, I was still on BART. My new year began along with the new years of some drunk, shrieking high schoolers and one exhausted-looking Asian woman who'd rubber-banded plastic bags over her shoes. She leaned her head against the grimy window, eyes squinched shut. I couldn't tell if she was sleeping or crying. The extravagant script of one of her footbags read *Thank You for Your P*—and then it tucked underneath. I'd seen those bags thousands of times, but I couldn't remember the last word. *Thank you for your patience? Thank you for your participation? Thank you for your presence?*

11

We'd seen patients get their "celebration dinner" and a big production was made of it: tablecloth, vase with fake red roses. After nearly a month, it felt strange to sit opposite each other at a table as if on some awkward first date we'd never had. Everything I could think to say felt either too banal or too portentous: *Your renewal notice for the* Times *came,* and *Did you ever do that living will thing?*

A nurse took our picture. When she handed my phone back, I saw that we'd made that unconscious move of tilting our temples as far towards each other as possible, so it looked like we had magnets in our heads. I'd always thought of myself as deathly pale, but in the picture I looked hale. You could see there was blood beneath my skin, whereas Jeremy might have been in whiteface.

"What were your resolutions?" I asked. He always made them.

"I'm planning to stay alive."

"How's your chicken?"

He pushed away the plate. "Tastes dead."

I had trouble leaving after dinner. Instead, I prattled on, waiting for something I said to catch. Our Internet was sucking more than usual, maybe we should change companies, and I'd tried to get the Darjeeling he liked at Rainbow but they were out. I wanted to tell him about the crying family, but bringing up death seemed cruel. Anyway, what would I have said? *Something, I don't know exactly what, happened to some people I don't exactly know.*

He looked at the clock. "I'm sorry, I'm just tired. Can we deal with this stuff later?"

"Yeah, right, okay." I looked around for my bag but didn't get up. "Did you see the cleaning guidelines they gave us? I bought three gallons of bleach this afternoon, which of course Rainbow doesn't carry, they were all, 'You should try vinegar.' I ended up at Walgreens, behind this kid shoplifting batteries. It was so depressing."

"God, Claire. There are babies dying in Darfur." He looked at the clock again.

"Am I *keep*ing you from something?"

"It's bad enough to have no privacy! Can I not even move my eyeballs?"

I grabbed my bag. "Move your eyeballs all you want. Have a fucking eyeball discothon."

I hadn't maybe almost died, I hadn't lost any *toes*, but could he really not even acknowledge that what I dealt with might still have meaning? I was on my way home to spend half the night cleaning—not for my sake, for *his*. And yes, I knew there were babies dying in Darfur. I stomped furiously down the hall, into the elevator, across the lobby. A cold wind rattled the tree branches above the parking lot. I threw myself into the truck and slammed the door. All at once, my anger was gone, as if shut outside.

I lay down on the front seat. Through the windshield, dark branches framed a couple of sparse, frayed clouds scudding across the moon. I must have lain there for twenty minutes, my breath slowing, time sliding open beneath me. I remembered lying in the station wagon's way way back as we drove out to western Maryland to see my father's parents. This was the first spring we'd lived with the Kapetanakoses, so I was nine. My dad told me that Bappa and Bama knew about the new house but not "the other part."

I pushed myself up, hooking my chin over the back seat. "Other part?"

"About Holly and all of them," he said. "Bama's not in good health. Bappa either. I don't want to tell them something that's going to make them unhappy."

My father, the youngest of six children, had not just been the first person in his family who went to college but one of the first people in his *whole town* ever to go. Even with a full ride at Maryland, even with his work-study job as a janitor, the cost of books and housing and even the bus ticket home for breaks had required real sacrifice by his parents. He was fiercely protective of them. If he thought I should lie, I would lie.

I wasn't ready to show I'd give in, though. "You told them about church."

"Which was when he decided not to do anything like that again," said my mother. My Catholic grandparents saw Unitarianism as barely more than a cult. It was true that during his sermons, Costa found ways to say God without saying God— "life force," "spirit," "higher consciousness"—and it probably hadn't helped that I'd enthusiastically described some of his more interesting experiments to Bama and Bappa. There had been the congregation doing creative movement together on Easter morning out in the grassy courtyard of the church. There had been the morning Costa had washed his parishioners' feet. Then there had been Costa eating a whole apple, including core, stem, and seeds, to illustrate a sermon about examining our biases. The next day I'd repeated this feat in the school lunchroom. The core scratched up my throat more than I'd anticipated, and though the performance had provoked satisfying reactions, it had mysteriously failed to make me popular.

The weekend with Bama and Bappa felt at first like a game: how happy could we seem to be? And then Saturday afternoon at the soda fountain my grandparents owned, we shifted into a lower, smoother gear. My parents leaned together over the jukebox, my father's arm around my mother. He reached up and pulled the elastic off the bottom of her braid, running his fingers through the long blond strands. You could tell he loved the feel. The jukebox whirred, a record dropping, a moment of staticky whisper and then Janis Joplin's deep scrape of a voice, which opened me up and filled me in all at once.

In the car Sunday, we waved and smiled as my father backed out of the driveway. As soon as he'd turned the corner, he pulled to the side of the road. "You're amazing," he said to my mother.

"I love your parents."

"No, I mean it. I don't think one woman in a thousand would . . ."

"We make a good team," my mother said. My father reached over and squeezed her hand and then didn't let go, using their joined hands to shift the car into gear, steering one-handed back onto the road.

I hadn't let myself admit that I'd known all along the arrangement with the Kapetanakoses couldn't last. This was it, though. My dad was going to break up with Holly. I hadn't known I'd been waiting for it. By the time we entered the house, my hands were shaking with excitement and dread. Holly came down the stairs two at a time. She wore a white sweater and her long dark hair flew behind her, a banner. She seemed almost incandescent with happiness. *I know and you don't*, I thought wonderingly. *I know and you*—and then my father stepped forward and wrapped her in his arms, a hug that almost swallowed her, rocking her from side to side. He gave a great sigh, relief collapsing the lines of his back.

My mother watched them with a strange smile, one side of her mouth pulled up. She started to turn towards me. I couldn't bear to return her ironic merriment; I didn't even know if the mockery in it was directed at my father or at herself or me. I pivoted and walked with perfect posture through the living room, through the dining room, and out the glass doors, gliding them closed behind me. For a second, I stood poised on the small wooden deck, barely bigger than a shipping pallet, and then I started to run, the blood in my head pounding *stupid, stupid, stupid*. I ran until my lungs burned and I collapsed gasping in some stranger's front yard. The trees in our subdivision were short and spindly, two per house, as if someone had jammed broomsticks into the ground. With my eyes watering, they blurred into looking almost like full trees above me.

I shifted on the sticky vinyl seat of the truck. Through the windshield, the full trees above me thrashed noiselessly against the sky. So, okay, Jeremy wasn't at this moment tripping over his own feet in his hurry to thank me. So okay, we'd argued. I needed to get a grip.

Sometimes it wasn't clear where I left off and Jeremy began. Since we'd been together, he'd started drinking bourbon, stopped going to Starbucks, let me throw out his stonewashed T-shirts. Moved beyond CCR and, ugh, Van Morrison, and ugh, ugh, ugh, Steely Dan. Stopped referring to his friends as "the gang" because I threw gang signs when he did. Stopped using the phrase "making love" because my dad and Holly had used it and it made me gag.

He liked to sit in the old armchair in the bay window of my studio and grade tests while I worked. I found it harder to lose myself with him there, but I'd learned I could get nearly as much work done when I faked absorption as I did when actually absorbed. Once he'd pointed to his ear and then mine. I came over to his chair and we switched earbuds, though he recoiled quickly and yanked them out. I'd been listening to something loud and screamy—Sonic Youth, or maybe L7. "How can you work with that?"

"How can you work listening to hold music?"

"It's Beethoven."

"Like I said."

He'd groaned, hitting his forehead gently against my thigh. "*Why* did I marry you again?"

"Because I'm amazing?"

"Ah. Right."

Now I let myself out of the truck, a little shakily, and walked back across the warm, diesel-smelling lot. I could see the exact expression Jeremy would have when I came into the room. He'd say, *You wanted to see how the eyeball discothon's going?*

I'd laugh. *I'm so sorry. It's just stress.*

No, I'm sorry, I know. Me too.

Across the bright, deserted lobby. I didn't want to wait for the elevator and so ran up the flights of fire stairs to the fifth floor, where the step-down unit was. Brianna G. looked up from the nurses' station and waved. I pushed open our door and pulled back the curtain.

Gita perched on the end of the bed. She'd been in the middle of saying something; she turned, mouth snapping shut like a coin purse. They stared at me.

After a moment, Jeremy said, "Gita just stopped by."

"Oh." It seemed imperative not to seem thrown. I couldn't think what to say. "Right."

She jumped up and pushed her feet into her sneakers. "Just, I stopped in, just for a minute—"

Jeremy said to me, "It totally surprised me, I didn't—"

"Anyway, I should probably—"

"Yeah, and—"

"You should—" She reached down to pull the back of her sneaker out from under her heel, hopping off balance. To Jeremy: "You must be—"

"—wiped, yeah, I should get some sleep—"

They hadn't been touching. Still, I felt that old sick drop in my stomach, the one that said *something's wrong.* The one that said *run.*

part two

house arrest

12

*N*othing was safe. I'd never even heard of septic shock, and now it suddenly seemed like everyone knew someone who'd died from it after the smallest, most ordinary of events. You could cut yourself shaving and die, you could have a bad cold and die, you could get an infected hemorrhoid and die. You could finish a marathon Sunday and be dead Wednesday *from the chafing of your running shorts.* I'd been desperate for Jeremy to come home but as I pulled up to the curb, I wished I could rewind and want it less, as though wanting it less would somehow lower the stakes of everything that could still go wrong.

Stooped and pale, he bumped up the front stairs of the house. Veins shone blue through his translucent skin. Leaning heavily on his crutches, he waited passively for me to find my keys. They'd left his central line in—he'd be getting IV antibiotics for another week, outpatient—and I bumped it accidentally with my elbow as I swung open the door. "Oh, shit! Your cath."

He winced, pain edging his voice: "No, it's okay." Taking a step inside, he croaked, "Fort!" He cleared his throat and called louder, "Fort! Here boy!"

"He's at Hal's." Despite the prickliness between us, I knew I could count on Hal when needed. I had the sickening feeling I'd forgotten to tell Jeremy. But no: we'd discussed it. "Bella was going to but their landlord nixed it."

"Right, I remember."

"We can call Fort later."

He had a blue mask over his nose and mouth, but I could see by lines around his eyes that he was smiling. "How weird is Hal going to think we are if we call him and ask to talk to our dog?"

"Well, since he lived in a tree house, and since he ate a hash brownie by mistake when he was five . . ."

Jeremy frowned. "Yeah, I know."

"And since his real name is Halcyon . . ."

"Why are you telling me all this again?"

"Just, nothing we could do is going to faze him."

Jeremy nodded, looking away. "I guess I can take this off now." He lifted his hand to the paper mask but then paused. "You didn't feel weird about, you know, last night, did you?"

"No, it's fine. It was totally—yeah, nothing. Fine." I took a breath, pushing down a swell of dizziness. Crushes happened. Long ago, I'd worked out they were like the headlines scrolling across the bottom of the screen while you watched the news. You might glance down; you might follow along for a little while, but those distractions weren't the real story. Jeremy couldn't be seriously attracted to Gita, with her pyramid-shaped hair and a wardrobe that looked like the spoils of a heroic assault on the Lands' End outlet.

"She was just driving by and decided to stop in. I didn't know she was coming."

"So not an issue for me," I said.

"Good. Because it's—well, like you said. Not an issue." He reached up to the mask again and pulled it off, fast, the way he might have yanked away a Band-Aid.

My mother flew out from Maryland for the first few days Jeremy was home. She refused to let me pick her up at the airport and so I tried to use that time to get work done. If I missed any more deadlines I might never get back on track. But starting about five minutes after her plane landed, I began going to the window, looking for the shuttle.

I decided to finish uglifying the table I'd gold-leafed. I found the tube of sizing to do the white crackle glaze but then found myself walking around the workroom, collecting espresso cups, straightening towers of newspaper, slotting CDs into their cases. The idea of the business failing filled me with panic—not a stimulating panic, but the kind that made me fuzzy and tired.

I went into the hall and dug out my old steel-toed boots from the closet. To be hired at the Dr. Doughnut cafeteria I'd had to buy them with my own money, even though I wasn't on the factory floor. What might have fallen on my foot? A tuna sandwich? Usually, just putting on the heavy boots made me feel purposeful, but today I stomped back into the studio still blurry, as if I'd just woken from a bad nap. I picked up the sizing, unscrewed the top, and looked at it. Was there a next step? Find a brush. I checked the window, flicked through the coffee can of brushes,

pulled one out, checked the window again. Apparently, the purple Victorian crack house across the street had changed hands:
two white guys in their twenties were ripping the boards off
the windows. One of them had on work gloves; the other—his
thin mustache, shaped like a croquet wicket, reached halfway
down his neck—seemed to be wearing yellow dishwashing
gloves. They passed a thermos between them, laughing, swollen
with self-regard. I despised them, and I also longed to be them,
wresting out nails, flapping sawdust from their T-shirts, drinking coffee or spiked coffee or who knows, fermented yak butter,
but at least not trapped in my loop of stupid thoughts. When
the airport van turned the corner, a blue so electric it seemed
to vibrate against the dingy street, it shocked me: I'd forgotten
what I was looking for.

I went onto the porch. A damp January afternoon, bleary and
colorless as pre-dawn. My mother wore her fair hair—streaked
with gray now—as she always had, in a long braid tight and
straight as a second spine. Her suitcase bumped up the cratered
sidewalk, teetering from side to side but not quite tipping.

"Karin," I said. I'd never been able to go back to "Mom"
without the word feeling strange and mushy in my mouth.

"Bear." She reached to hug me.

At her touch, something in me cracked. I swayed; a harsh,
grating noise came from my throat. I didn't understand at first
what it was. I never cried in front of anyone, least of all my
mother: for almost as long as I could remember, we'd bubble-
wrapped everything in irony. I clapped my hands to my mouth,
trying to stop, but the very act of trying to stop brought on a
new wave of self-pity.

"Is it that bad?"

I took a step away, pulling my sleeve down over my hand to scrub at my face. "He's . . . Sorry. No, it's good. He's sleeping. Since—" I reached for her wrist to check the time. "Like three hours now. Sorry, I'm fine."

"Of course you're not fine."

On a nearby stoop, a teenager in short-shorts and a 49ers jersey, bangs shellacked up into a claw above her forehead, listlessly dry-shaved her legs. "No, really. I'm good, we're good. This has made us—we've always been incredibly close, but even more so, you know? . . . Why are you looking at me like that?"

"I wasn't looking at you like anything."

"You seem, I don't know. Skeptical."

She shook her head. "So let me put this down. Let me take a quick shower, and then you can put me to work."

"Not tired?" I said.

"I'm good. You?"

"Fine." Around Karin's practicality, I began stripping down my own sentences, until sometimes we all but spoke Morse code. Actually I was exhausted. The night before, I'd kept getting halfway through something like scrubbing the stove burners when I realized what I really needed to do was the bedroom. I'd find myself with an armload of papers, turning circles because: should I spend the time to file them or should I just dump them somewhere? As long as I was cleaning, shouldn't I do it well?

I got Karin a towel and carried her suitcase into Jeremy's study at the front of the house. Before I moved in, this room had been a bedroom, and despite its smallness there had always been a wait list of friends-of-friends who wanted to move in. Now it held the tanker desk I'd found in an alley and refinished to give Jeremy for our first Hanukkah, plus shelves that held his books and four orange shoeboxes of memorabilia—two for college, two for high school—and there was just enough room for us to unfold a double futon when guests stayed.

Even though I knew my mother was in the shower and Jeremy asleep, I glanced over my shoulder before kneeling and opening the first high school box. Inside: his varsity letter from cross-country. Some report cards. A green Rolling Rock bottle from a long-ago party, back when the mere fact of drinking was exciting enough to commemorate. Certificates from the Center for Talented Youth, the summer camp where he spent six hours a day in math classes and first kissed a girl.

I knew the kiss had happened during a slow dance. I even knew the song had been "American Pie."

I'd snooped in the boxes before, but the high school stuff usually just got a cursory glance. It had always been one of his Cornell girlfriends—Allegra, a painter—whose photo I occasionally pulled out to study. In it, she hugged herself, smiling unhappily. She was depressed and they fought a lot and had, I imagined, passionate reconciliations. Leaning against the back of our hall closet was a nude she'd done of Jeremy, his scrotum all lurid magentas and yellows. Allegra with her moods and heavy black glasses and ragged sweaters seemed cool enough to inspire jealousy, but I'd never been jealous of Gita. They'd gone to prom together! *He'd* broken *her* heart when he hooked up with that girl in his freshman dorm.

Second high school box. The spent green canister of a whip-it. A picture of his graduating class—boys in dark suits, girls wearing white dresses and carrying roses, like some cultish mass wedding. From the same day, Jeremy and Gita sitting together on a bench in front of the school. She'd had fuzzy hair nearly to her waist; he had a few spots of acne on his forehead. How awkwardly Jeremy's arm lay across her shoulders, how young they looked. The camera had clicked a moment too early, so that Gita's eyes were half-closed, blurry hand raised to push back her bangs.

Before Jeremy, I'd dated a violinist who played in a punk band; before that, a rangy craft brewer of small-batch nonalcoholic beer, his bathroom strung with plastic tubing. The guys I got involved with all had in-the-meantime jobs pulling espresso at Ritual, or stocking shelves at Rainbow Grocery, or modeling for life-drawing classes at the art institute, or bartending someplace divey. They were the same kind of people I liked as friends—quick, funny, a little mean in their judgments. I hadn't been drawn to kindness or reliability until I'd fallen in love with exactly those things in Jeremy.

A button—Go for the Gold(smith)!—from Jeremy's successful campaign for senior-class president. If they'd gone to Greer High, Gita would have been deemed a Squid, a studier, and Jeremy would have been Squid or else S-Gay, Student Government Association. We'd also had Jockhallers, so named because athletes hung out in West Hall, and Quaddies, and JAPs. Shawn was a Hobbit. I was a Drama Fag, even though I had a bigger role on the basketball team than in plays, and Nicole was a Jockhaller, even though she smoked in the quad between classes and had silver rings all the way up the rims of both ears. But Wilkerson-Kettlewell hadn't had the same rigid distinctions and Jeremy had been both brainy and popular.

Transcript from the advanced classes he took at State. Another beer bottle. A cassette tape labeled ♥ JG/GJ! Mix♥, with Bob Dylan, Fleetwood Mac, Modern English, James Taylor.

Even if I discovered that they'd considered themselves madly in love during high school, so what? In high school, I had only one boyfriend, junior year. Steve and I used to imagine what it would be like when we got married: we'd live in Manhattan, and he'd drive a Porsche-some-letter-some-numbers, and we'd go to plays and art openings. One afternoon during a break in dress rehearsal, we sat on the edge of the stage—Steve in his Harold Hill costume with the gold braid on the shoulders; me in my Pick-a-Little Lady #3 high-necked blouse and long skirt—telling each other stories about our future apartment. We didn't know anyone else who talked about Central Park views and so assumed they were ours for the asking. The thought made me smile. Dropping the pictures and cassette back in the box and shoving the whole thing back on the shelf, I stood too quickly and had to hold onto the bookcase for a moment until the floor righted.

I found my mother in the kitchen. She had braided her hair damp, and her shirt stuck to her back in places where it had gotten wet.

I said, "I'm not even going to try in my workroom. But in here, and the living room . . ." I unscrewed the bottom of the old espresso pot and filled it with water. "Coffee?"

"I have some." Instant, she meant: she dug through the outer pocket of her suitcase, coming up with a baggie of brownish-red crystals.

"I'm making real."

"This is fine."

That she always contented herself with the barely adequate drove me nuts. She must have seen it on my face: "Claire. Why do you care?"

"I *don't*." I blew out a hard breath.

"Spoon," she said, not a question, opening drawers until she found what she needed. She dumped some of her sawdust into a cup and ran tap water over it. "Microwave."

"Jeremy doesn't believe in them," I reminded her.

"Well, I'm pretty *sure* they're real. Though I can see how it might seem like magic." Reaching for a small saucepan, she poured in the sludge from her cup and then lit a burner on the stove. My mother didn't waste a second on things she couldn't change. "Sugar," she muttered, heading for the pantry. "Wow, it's a mess in here."

"Hence . . ."

"Right, hence." After some clanking, she emerged bearing the sugar jar, which she put on the counter. Then she ducked towards the stove, tucking her hand into the hem of her shirt.

"Karin, we have pot holders. Never mind."

Still using her shirt to protect her hand, she poured the hissing coffee into a mug. Then she swung open the fridge. It was crowded without having any actual food, just sticky condiment bottles and jam freckled blue with mold. "Trash bags," she said, again not a question.

After a moment of hesitation—just like that?—I followed her lead, going into the pantry and beginning to move things off the shelves. Jeremy bought from the bulk bins at Rainbow, and there was a comfort to wiping clean each glass jar with bleach and steaming hot water, though the fumes made my eyes water. In an unmarked tin, I found expired prescription medicine for someone named Rebecca. With so many former housemates, I occasionally still came across a cookbook with an unfamiliar name written on the flyleaf or someone's lipstick that had rolled all the way under our claw-foot tub. There was nothing good among the meds, not that we didn't have plenty of painkillers and Ativan anyway. It looked like Rebecca had suffered from allergies and yeast infections. Oh, wait: Becky. She'd been one of the two housemates still living with Jeremy when I met him. I'd actually known she had yeast infections because some naturopath had told her to put yogurt in her vagina and so there was often a cup of the stuff sitting on the bathroom counter with tampons soaking in it, tails hanging out like a little clutch of drowned white mice.

Apparently the white mice hadn't worked, because Becky had progressed onto Flagyl; I threw the packaging into the trash. I wiped down the shelves and then replaced the jars. Through the door of the pantry, I could see Karin lying on her side, using a spatula to get something from under the fridge. I started to say we didn't need to be *that* clean, but she would have just ignored me. With a small grunt, she extracted a faded carrot and grinned in triumph: "Ta-da!"

Back when I was about twelve, she tried dating for a few months. One time I sat on the floor of her room while she got dressed; my father lay on what had long ago been his side of the bed.

"What about this?" Karin held up a blouse patterned with dark green leaves on a white background.

Jim said, "Try it."

Karin raised her eyebrows, then shrugged—"Nothing you haven't seen"—and pulled her T-shirt off over her head. She didn't wear a bra underneath: she was small-breasted, with long nipples like thimbles, and I was relieved when she pulled on the blouse, covering them. "Ta-da."

"That's nice," I offered from the floor.

"What about that other shirt?" said Jim. "That stripy thing."

"Stripy thing?" My mother turned to the closet and began to hunt and peck among the hanging shirts. The closet was crammed full of clothing; many of the hangers held two different shirts, or two pairs of pants, one over the other. She never got rid of anything. She managed to work out from the crush a silky polyester blouse, black with red stripes and a tie at the neck. "This one?" she asked.

"Try that. . . . Yeah. Now undo one more button."

Her pink Nordic complexion flushed even pinker.

"Good," my father said. "That's foxy."

Karin rolled her eyes but she smiled a little. She twisted right, then left, in front of the mirror.

"Wait, I have an idea," Jim said. My mother had just unbuttoned her green cords and begun to pull them down. Violet nosegays of varicose veins bloomed on her thighs.

My father left the room. From the top shelf of the closet, my mom found a pair of silky black slacks. She flicked to unfold them, then swatted at the material a few times with her hand. "I could iron them, I guess." She held the pants against her waist.

"Who's your date with?"

"Hmm? Oh." She came close, putting the pants under my nose. "Do these smell?"

"Gross."

She held them up and sniffed the crotch. "They're okay." With her thumb and forefinger, she pinched off a pill of fabric.

I frowned at her. "Your date?"

"Someone a girl at work knows. Restaurant manager, I think—or no, that's Wednesday. Something in government."

My dad returned, carrying another shirt: cotton, with diagonal gray and purple stripes. My mother turned, smiling, but then she froze at the sight of the top. "She's six inches shorter than me."

"Just try it." He danced the shirt on its hanger up and down. It was one of Holly's favorites—sleeves puffed from shoulder to elbow, and then tight down the forearm. Holly sometimes wore it with a matching headband around her forehead.

My mother began pulling on the black pants with jerky motions. They were tight, and when her foot caught in the long leg, she stumbled, caught herself by throwing her hand against the closet doorjamb. She must have hit hard because she winced and her mouth stretched wide and ugly for a second.

But her voice was light as she said to me, "*Men*." And to my father, laughter tapping against the underside of the words: "That would never fit. We're not built even remotely alike."

Now she pushed herself up from the kitchen floor, holding the wizened carrot out towards me like a relay baton. I took it automatically. "Why did you stay with Jim?"

Karin gave me an odd look and tilted her head. Of course, she knew I already knew: they'd thought it was best for me.

"Well, I was in love with him," said my mother.

I wouldn't have been more shocked if she'd reached out and tweaked my nipple.

She began to laugh. "Your *face*."

"Sorry. Just. I mean—*really*?"

"Yes, really. You don't think I stayed six years for some philosophical belief in open marriage? Soap."

"Under the—yeah, there."

She turned on the sink. Matter-of-factly, she said, "I thought that the thing with Holly would run its course. Infatuations do. I mean, obviously I got it wrong. I thought when that part wore out, the excitement of being adored, he'd realize that there wasn't a deep friendship underneath to fall back on, like there had been . . . I wanted to keep our bond right there in front of him, so he'd have it to compare—What? Are you okay?"

"No, I'm fine, I'm good, I'm fine."

"And with Jeremy? Things are okay?"

"We're *great*," I said, too emphatically. I realized I was still holding onto the limp carrot; I couldn't think what to do with it. Trying to sound more casual: "We're . . . Everything's been hard, the hospital . . . But it's better now. Why do you keep giving me that look?"

"I'm not giving you any look," she said. "I'm glad things are better."

"They *are*."

"That's what I said." She hefted the trash from the can and then, ignoring the drawstring, pulled the sides of the bag into bunny ears and tied them tightly. I always tied bags the same way—Jeremy made fun of me for it—because I hated how drawstrings left an ugly little sphincter. But I'd forgotten that the habit was one I'd learned from my mother. She'd taught me to wash jeans with vinegar, to signal turns with an arm out the truck window, to rub potatoes with olive oil and sea salt before baking them. And of course to never let anyone see they'd gotten under my skin.

13

i spent most of my thirty-third birthday in my studio, trying to finish the ugly crackle-glaze table. My mother had left that morning. Every half-hour or so Jeremy needed something and would call out my name.

I pressed my lips together, holding back a sigh, before calling, "Minute!"

Of course I got it. I mean, of *course*. In his place, I would have wanted to do the same thing. But still, I felt his need physically, a spiderweb with him crouched at its center.

I stopped in the bathroom to scrub in, singing "Happy Birthday" under my breath twice to time myself. When I turned, I saw a dark coil in the toilet. At the hospital, where they'd needed to check every micron that left his body, Jeremy had fallen out of the habit of flushing. I pressed the handle and the shit slithered backwards down its hole, a malevolent eel. I bent over, putting my head for a moment on the sink edge. It seemed too much to deal with, even though I'd dealt with it.

He lay in our bed, propped up on pillows. Raising his arm, he pointed the remote at the TV to mute it. "I talked to Delfina." He was too tired to cook so had decided to order fancy pizza for my birthday. Bella and her girlfriend were doing some kind of silent multi-day retreat at Spirit Rock, but Steph was coming, and Nicole. "We're supposed to get the pizzas at six, so you could grab wine at Bi-Rite at the same time?"

"Ah, yes, the I'm-throwing-you-a-party-you-just-have-to-do-the-work." I was smiling as I said it; I thought Jeremy would smile.

He squinted. "Why do you always have to be so bitter?"

"It was a *joke*."

He looked at me, intense and puzzled, as if he needed to read my lips to be sure what I said. He'd gained back a little weight, his cheeks no longer squeezed-by-forceps hollow but his T-shirt still hanging from his shoulders. He reached for his phone and began to tap at it.

"You hate texting."

"Well, but it's . . ." He frowned, poking. "Okay. I asked Gita to swing by Delfina on her way."

"Oh." He'd invited Gita? "Do you want me to change your dressings, since I'm here?"

He turned the clock towards himself. I usually changed his bandages later in the day; I could tell he was wavering between wanting me to stay and not wanting to use up the chance to have me back. "I'll do it now," I said, and went to wash my hands again, scrubbing under my nails. I put a clean towel under his foot before I unwrapped it. The foot looked strange, but in a way that made me aware how strange feet were anyway. Toes in particular, hanging there like those little strips with a phone number that you rip off the bottom of a flyer. I asked how they felt. He said the missing ones hurt.

"Dr. Bayh said there's not usually phantom pain, with toes."

"Well, then I guess they must not hurt."

"I didn't mean it that way." I swabbed his sutures with hydrogen peroxide. Keeping my voice casual, I said, "It's interesting, I thought Gita's job was kind of serious, from her description. But it seems like she's never there, practically."

"What are you talking about? She's there every day."

"It just seems she can leave whenever she wants. I mean, it's great for her, it's lucky to have that kind of job. I think they pay her kind of a lot."

He pointed the remote at the TV and its chatter resumed. I glanced over my shoulder: white coats, a steel table. Hospital. No, a cooking competition.

Was I always bitter? And even if so, hadn't he liked that quality? He wanted the criticism voiced without having to voice it; he wanted to have his virtue and eat it too.

I figure-eighted the elastic bandage over his foot, pulled on a clean compression sock. Then I scooted up the bed, next to him. I couldn't believe I felt nostalgia for the awful time in the hospital. He didn't put his arm around my shoulder.

The chefs even wore the same Dansko clogs as doctors. I said, "You'd think this show wouldn't work at all. I mean, you can't have any sense for yourself of whether they're successful."

"That's true, actually."

The relief of snagging his attention. I'd never had to feel it before.

He said, "You trust the judges, though."

"But do you? I mean, everything's *incredible* or else *terrible*, no middle ground. It's like in high school, when if something wasn't 'cool' it was 'queer.'"

He said, "I always hate that one of them gets sent home. It seems so sadistic, the whole slow revelation."

"Mr. Nice Guy."

He looked up quickly. "Boring, you mean."

"No! No. Boring people get called nice a lot. But *genuine* niceness isn't boring."

"Sometimes I think the only interesting things I've ever done are marry you and almost die."

I took his hand, feeling a tentative happiness. On-screen, someone scraped out the insides of—could those be Fig Newtons?

Jeremy said, "They have to make something with an ingredient out of . . . what are those things? You put in money and pull a lever?" He'd been struggling with vocabulary; I didn't know if it was exhaustion, or a temporary aftereffect of the coma, or something more lasting.

"You mean vending machine?" Under the pretense of grabbing a pillow, I brushed my hand across his temple. His doctors had emphasized we should come in at the first sign of infection—*Right now, there's no such thing as an overreaction*—but his temperature seemed fine. I settled back. "Remember how cigarette vending machines had those signs on them not to buy cigarettes if you were underage?"

"I bet that totally stopped you."

"Totally."

A woman with a magenta mohawk crumbled Doritos on top of a slab of fish that looked like a chunk of raw marble. Jeremy's phone bubbled: a text. He picked it up. "Okay, Gita's getting them." He started jabbing buttons with his index finger, then paused. "What?"

"Nothing."

He finished his text, then tossed the phone onto the bed beside him. Almost immediately it bubbled. I held very still, not letting myself check his expression as he grabbed for it.

There was an exact moment when I knew Jeremy was falling in love with me. I used to live on the top floor of a Victorian in Dogpatch, a studio apartment with blue walls. From the tiny window above the sink, I could glimpse a narrow gray slice of the Bay between the hunched shoulders of two warehouses. My downstairs neighbor hated that I made noise. If I turned on my stereo, or wore *shoes*, she'd pound on her ceiling with a broomstick.

A cold June morning, sky a dull aluminum. Jeremy and I had woken and "made love"—I hadn't broken him of that phrase yet. Unshowered, musky, wrapped in bulky sweaters, we kept bumping into each other as we came down the narrow staircase on our way out to breakfast. We'd been together about six weeks, that stage when you feel giddy with luck, like you're getting away with something every minute. Just as we went out the front, someone behind us called "Hello!"

Jeremy reached back one lanky arm, catching the door before it closed. My neighbor had come out of her apartment and jogged down the hall. She was in maybe her early forties, with stylish glasses. "You know I don't mind a reasonable amount of noise . . ." Then she listed my most recent infractions, beginning with a teakettle I'd left to whistle for a minute and ending with what she called the "knocking around" this morning. Jeremy and I glanced at each other, biting back smiles.

She said, "I tapped on the ceiling again. Maybe you didn't hear me? Because of the noise."

I gave her my flattest look. "I don't speak Broomstick."

Half a block later, Jeremy burst out laughing. "I don't speak Broomstick! You're brilliant."

The doorbell rang. Jeremy said, "That's her."

Gita's actual presence was shockingly normal. Little wings of hair escaping from her ponytail; waxy crow's-feet. She held a stack of pizza boxes against her chest and a grocery bag by its handles.

"Oh, hey, thanks." I took the boxes from her. Something had leaked through one, leaving a dark, oily spot on her pink sweater. Following my gaze, Gita looked down: "Uck, of course, the first time I wore this." She smiled, trying to catch my eye. "Happy Birthday, though!"

"Yeah, okay." I led the way back to the kitchen, where Jeremy was retrieving a bottle of wine from the pantry, his movements as slow as an old man's.

She called out, "Hey, you!" in a hearty voice I didn't quite recognize.

"How was work?"

"Good! How was your day?"

"Good, too."

"Good! I brought lemon cake."

He said, "A woman after my own heart."

The bell rang again. "Nicole," I said, unnecessarily.

In January, dusk fell around now, four-thirty. The air was the purple-gray of dryer lint. Nicole grinned at me. "You're thirty-three!"

"Gita's already here. Steph's babysitter flaked, so."

"How do I look?" Stepping back, Nicole spread her arms with a merry expression on her face. She wore one of her hybrid outfits—stiff oxford shirt, yoga pants, flat boots.

"Like you didn't have time to change after work."

"So . . ." she said.

"What?" I started for the kitchen, calling over my shoulder, "Come *on*."

We dragged the kitchen table into the living room so we could all fit. Jeremy had ordered my favorite pizza, the one with chard and a fried egg on top. I took a piece, then offered him the box. Gita said, "He doesn't like soft eggs."

"Yes he does."

We both turned to Jeremy. He glanced between us. "They're okay."

"But we always get this one." I hated that the words came out almost a whine.

"Because I know you like it."

"Oh." It should have been nice, but it made me feel like a selfish bitch. Worse: it made me feel that I came across as a selfish bitch in front of Gita. I held up the wine bottle towards Nicole, who shook her head: "Little bit of a headache." She glanced at Gita and Jeremy, to make sure their attention was elsewhere, then raised her eyebrows at me: *Really? That's her?*

We could have had a whole conversation that way, eyebrows and shrugs, winces, half-smiles, but instead I looked at Gita.

Through Nicole's eyes, I could see her as I first had: eager and frumpy. I tried to fix the image in my mind, as if I could fix it that way for Jeremy, too.

She was saying to him, "I remember once in high school, you pointed out eggs were chicken period. So you actually turned me off from eggs pretty much forever."

Jeremy smiled. "Sorry."

"No, you're not."

"No," he said with teasing mock-sincerity. "I'm *really sorry*. If you want to eat chicken period, you should feel free to eat chicken period."

She laughed. "Yugg, gross, stop."

Everything felt off-kilter, out of sync, a movie where the sound and the picture weren't matching up. My voice seemed to come out overloud: "I don't get why people think eating one body part is worse than eating another. I mean, is eating something's tongue actually worse than eating its flank?"

"*Please*," said Nicole.

Jeremy said, "She wasn't talking about tongues."

I flashed him a look: was I really *always so bitter* that he needed to defend Gita from me? "Here, give me your plate," I said to Nicole.

"Mmm. I'm not really eating eggs."

"You're not eating eggs?"

"I'm not eating soft-cooked eggs." She had a weird smile, like someone had snagged the side of her mouth with a fishhook and she was trying to resist its tug.

I tilted my head at her. She gave an infinitesimal nod.

"I think we need napkins," I said, standing.

She jumped up. "I'll help."

I grabbed her wrist and pulled her through the kitchen, into the pantry. I raised my eyebrows and she grinned so hard it looked painful. There were tears at the corners of her eyes. I hugged her, and we jumped up and down, silently, a few times. We might have been teenagers ordering hash browns and milkshakes at Roy Rogers during what should have been third period, the day I whispered in her ear that Steve and I had *done it*.

In the pantry, she whispered, "I just found out. I don't even know how to count how many weeks I am." And then in a rush, both hands on her stomach: she was beginning to feel sick sometimes, no actual throwing up but, and when did I think she'd start to show?, and also she did this calendar thing online, this gender-predictor thing that said *boy*, and maybe Griffin as a name?, and today someone had brought fried food into the staff meeting and she'd sent him out of the room—

"One of the *gymnasts* was eating fried food?"

"The boys will eat anything. Well, Ryan's anorexic, but the rest of them, you should see it, they can put away fifteen hundred calories in a sitting."

"So you chose a donor." The exhilaration of the news was shrinking back, leaving an oily residue.

"It just happened."

"Oh, like, spontaneously?"

She reached for her purse on the kitchen counter and fished out her wallet. With a finger, she dragged another driver's license from behind hers. In high school, we'd stored our fake licenses behind our real ones this same way, and when she handed it to me, I half-expected to see Nicole at fifteen, wearing one of my mother's library blouses.

Instead: someone named Dirk Hertzberg two years younger than us, dark red hair. He was one of those men you could tell had put on weight since his frat-house days. His features had stayed bunched together rather than spreading, so that he still had a small, handsome face, cupped on each side by a flange of new flesh.

"Dirk? You slept with someone called *Dirk?*"

"Plenty of people are called Dirk. Anyway, people's names aren't their fault." She took the license back. "He has a girl-friend, which . . . Well, two things: he's not going to be look-ing for a relationship, and he's never cheated before, so he's not going to have an STD."

"Right, that's not sordid at all. You can totally trust guys who cheat on their girlfriends and say they never cheat. You stole that?"

"When he was in the shower, I just, you know, in case. I had this feeling."

"Fate?" I asked.

She frowned. "I thought you'd be happy for me." We were still in the pantry, still whispering. "Don't say sordid, it wasn't *sordid.*"

"I just thought you were going to tell me if anything hap-pened." It felt almost like she'd cheated on me.

"I'm *telling* you."

I grabbed the napkins and led the way back out to the living room, calling, "Guess what?"

Jeremy looked between us. Cautiously, he said, "Okay, what?"

Nicole rolled her eyes at me. "I'm . . ." She pointed to her stomach, words catching in her throat. "I—"

"She's with child."

"What? You did it?" He stood, grinning, took a step with-out remembering his foot and stumbled. "*Shit*, ouch. Wow, you did it!"

"I did!" Nicole was laughing, teary.

Jeremy wrapped her in a hug. "I can't believe it."

"Me neither."

"How old are you?" Gita asked.

"Almost thirty-three." Nicole pointed at me: "We're two weeks apart."

The smallest wince under Gita's eyes. So she wanted kids.

"What's with all the pointing?" I asked Nicole. She gave me a look, so I enumerated: "At me, at your stomach . . ."

"That's twice. What's your damage?"

Outside a morose, desultory rain had begun. Jeremy said, "Ugh, *again?*"

Gita laughed. "You're such a California boy."

I said, "Except it rains all the time in San Francisco." A moment late, I remembered to smile; its suddenness probably looked strange and leering. "In the winter, at least."

Gita tipped her head to the side, a question. I clarified: "Rain can be Californian."

"Well, but 'all the time'? I wouldn't call it—"

"*In the winter*, I said."

And so it went through the meal. I name-dropped constantly: *Jeremy likes . . . Jeremy thinks . . . Jeremy and I . . . We don't . . .* I answered for him. I interrupted. I probably made myself thoroughly obnoxious. When Nicole asked how much longer house arrest would last and Jeremy said another week, I corrected, "*At least* another week."

I had on thick-ribbed black tights (new) with a Victorian slip of heavy white cotton (vintage), a sheer black cardigan (feminine), and Frye engineer boots (masculine). I found myself looking down at my clothes every time I needed steadying: yes, *this* is who I am. Silver wedding ring, bought for eleven dollars from a street vendor. The old, heavy Swiss Army watch that had taken nearly half a year of Dr. Doughnut afternoons and weekends to afford. Maybe Jeremy enjoyed Gita's attention, but he couldn't really leave me for someone in a pink sweater, could he? She was the kind of person who got *left*.

Nicole stood and crossed to the windows, shoving one open. Cold mist poured into the room. She sighed, leaning towards it, then sprang upright and clapped her hand to her mouth. "Oh sorry! I'm just—I'm always hot. Is that okay?"

Jeremy said, "Air isn't going to make me sick."

Nicole put her head out the window, sighing. Our living room overlooked the backyard with its three different fences—the splintering wood of the neighbors' to the right, the sagging, green chain-link of the house directly behind us, and, to the left, the smooth, ultra-modern concrete wall erected by the architect couple with their smug Prius and their smug cloth grocery bags and their fat, smug baby that they carried so smugly in that front-purse-thing. Previously, their place had been rented to a sprawling Latino family who'd been Ellis Acted to make way for rich buyers. Sometimes I hated San Francisco.

"That's nice," Gita said, and went to join Nicole at the window. "Ahh," she said. I looked over at Jeremy, trying to read his expression.

"What?" he said.

"No, nothing."

In the past, I'd always made sure I broke up with people before they could break up with me. When I'd ended things with Hal, he'd protested, "That fight was barely *anything*." But why waste time? I thought that once a relationship started to slip there was only one way it could go, just as a house in a mudslide wouldn't suddenly reverse direction and clamber back up the hill.

I wasn't twenty anymore, poised to flounce off at the first waver in attention. I loved Jeremy. I knew he loved me. Still, I didn't think I'd be able to stand it if I touched him and he pulled away. I put my hand on the table, kind of near him, so that maybe it would occur to him to take my hand but not occur to him that I hoped for it. I wanted Jeremy to find me exceptional, irreplaceable, and yet that very desire made me feel appalling and dull.

I'd been calling myself a feminist since age twelve, except for the years at Santa Cruz when I said womanist instead. Babies were dying in Darfur; every day at SFMC, I'd seen kids facing death. We were at war in two countries. And now Jeremy's hand on the table filled my entire vision.

Please, I thought. Please please please touch me.

He was looking towards the windows. "Does that feel good?" He stood, crossing the room, and Gita said, "Here," and stepped back so that he could lean out. He grinned at her over his shoulder. "Wooo!" When he pulled his head in, droplets of water shone on his short dark hair.

14

*t*he salvage yard sprawled just off Third Street, not far from the warehouse where Jeremy and I had seen the Beckett plays a million years ago. Wild fennel grew by the fence; under the flat hand of the afternoon heat, its sharp chartreuse smell was everywhere.

Jeremy's niece, Kaylyn, didn't move to unfasten her seatbelt. "We're at a junkyard?"

"It's cool."

"Ohhh-*kkay*," Kaylyn said, as though placating a madwoman. Her big glasses—they had lightning bolts for stems, probably supposed to be "fun" but mostly just looking left over from 1983—reflected the sunlight so that I couldn't see her eyes. I wondered if she felt that her dramatic skills were being wasted without an audience of her peers. But with her peers, she probably *was* the audience, trying to laugh enough to be part of things but not so much that one of them might spin around to snap, *Who asked you?*

Not that I knew anything about that.

I'd offered to bring Kaylyn with me to give Jeremy some time alone with his older sister. When we'd left, he and Janice had been lying on the living room floor. "I still can't believe about your toes," Janice had said, chopping the side of her hand against her own foot. She liked to take Jeremy's painkillers with him; it was her way of commiserating.

"They actually didn't cut my toes off with a cleaver," Jeremy told Kaylyn. He, too, was on serious Vicodin, but he was used to it. "Despite your mother's highly scientific demonstration of the process."

Janice giggled. She wore primary colors and Statement Jewelry, big hammered-metal pieces that looked like plates of armor. She was an attorney—never *lawyer*—who lived in San Carlos, a celery-green suburb forty-five minutes south of us, in a house so bland it made my jaw hurt. Janice's ex-husband, also an attorney, lived in an almost identical house two doors down. I'd met him a few times, and they in fact seemed like a perfect match, two people who saw injustice everywhere: a neighbor's barking dog, the steak that came medium when he'd ordered medium-well, an idiot principal at Kaylyn's supposed-to-be-so-excellent public junior high, the pebbles from the driveway that flew onto the lawn. Always in a joking tone, meant to show that they weren't *complaining*, they just thought it was funny how nothing ever worked out for them.

I swung myself down from the truck's cab and headed for the salvage yard gate. Kaylyn could hang out in the pickup if she really wanted. After a minute, though, I heard her door open and close behind me.

The salvage yard was one of my favorite places in the city. To the right of the entrance were hundreds of old doors; further on, bathtubs rested on their bellies like sea lions basking in the sun. There were windows, cabinets, rust-speckled stoves. Kaylyn came up to stand at my elbow. I asked, "Don't you love this place?"

She rolled her eyes, saying with what was probably meant to be withering irony, "Not ex-aaact-tally."

"Is it still here?" I called to Eddie, who knelt on the pavement, helping a customer go through a dusty box of doorknobs. He nodded. I told Kaylyn, "Come on, I'll show you my favorite thing."

I led her to the metal building that served as an office. Inside was a beautiful, old wooden phone booth with a hinged folding door. The wood looked like it was probably walnut, the grain almost burled. In the corner was a little triangular shelf with a fluted edge so earnest it broke my heart.

"A *phone*?" said Kaylyn.

"Wouldn't this make a cool bar? You could put up shelves." The phone booth was priced at eight hundred dollars. I couldn't justify buying it, but about once a week I came to look at it. Actually, I *could* have justified buying it because I was pretty sure that it could sell for a lot more upcycled into a bar. But I also knew that I could never bring myself to let it go, and that I'd end up with a bar we didn't need and couldn't afford.

Kaylyn shrugged at the phone booth and walked away to check out an elaborately carved mantelpiece, then the boxes of blue and green sea glass by the door, the shelves of old brass faucets. I started towards the bins of wood scraps: I needed something to make a new apron for a table. The table was cherry, but if I found the right poplar or even pine, I could grain it to match. Off to the right was a life-sized skeleton.

I reached out to touch the leg bone, which swung away from my finger. They must have gotten a shipment of stuff from a school: behind the skeleton were high lab stools, some boxes that held beakers, and a rolled-up periodic table printed on canvas. I sometimes sold things through my friend Meara's store on Valencia; her mark-ups were so high that even paying a commission, I came out ahead.

Kaylyn, back from wandering around the edges of the space, made a big show of looking at her wristwatch, then folding her arms and doing that foot-tapping thing that drove me crazy. When I ignored her, she flopped down almost on top of my feet and opened her joke book. It seemed much too young a thing for a twelve-year-old to be toting around. "What kind of room has no windows and no doors?"

Did any of our cards have credit left? Jeremy's insurance covered eighty percent of hospitalizations, but twenty percent of a nearly three-week stay was still a staggering amount that we'd had to spread out across three credit cards.

"Claaaairrrre. What kind of room?"

I spun towards her. "*Christ*. Let me deal with this for one *minute*."

Eddie helped me tie the periodic table to the top of the cab and load the skeleton into the truck bed. I'd had to pass up the stools and beakers, but maybe I could figure out a way by next week. Eddie threw in the wood and hardware I needed without charge—probably fifteen dollars' worth of free stuff, but it made me happy nonetheless.

I drove home, the skeleton clicking happily behind us. I'd paid seventy dollars for it, forty for the chart. Meara would sell them for ten times that much: the higher you valued a thing, the more people wanted it. Feeling cheerful, I said, "A mushroom."

Kaylyn didn't respond.

"A room with no windows or doors. A mushroom, right?"

She watched the passing scenery, humming a little tune as if I weren't there.

"You want to go by Bi-Rite? It's pretty much the best ice cream in San Francisco."

She shrugged and mouthed something at the window that looked suspiciously like "Big whoop."

I parked in the red zone in front of a hydrant. Bi-Rite lines could be around the block, but it was cold and gray, midday and midweek. From inside, I kept one eye on the truck—we could hardly afford a parking ticket—then jogged out with Kaylyn's cone. She liked plain vanilla, which seemed an admirably austere choice for a kid. "Here," I said, holding it through her open window.

I could see her struggling. I said, "You can still be mad at me if you take it. Otherwise it's going to melt."

She took the cone from my hand. I kept my face blank, not showing triumph: I'd lied about getting to stay just as angry. Costa had always been good at sensing the moment I reached my limit of exasperation and right then offering something I wanted too much to turn down: a Benetton sweatshirt. My ears pierced. A small compliment so specific that it bowled me over: I'd been seen.

I let myself into the driver's side. Kaylyn was quiet, licking her cone. She looked so sad, sitting there in the passenger seat in her horrible glasses. I searched my mind for a joke, but all I could think of was the one about why Southern girls don't like orgies. (Too many thank-you notes.)

I said, "So, you're in junior high now. That's exciting."

"Yeah, real-ly ex-cit-ing."

Someone honked to see if I was leaving the space. When I glanced over my shoulder, shaking my head no, Kaylyn blurted, "You know what this girl did?"

"What girl?"

"This girl who used to be my friend, but she got popular." With the hand that didn't hold her ice cream, Kaylyn clicked the glove compartment open and closed, open and closed. "She told this guy that if he would go with her for a week, she'd . . ." Click. Bump. Click.

Go with: that's what we'd said in junior high, too. "She'd what?"

"You know." Bump. Click.

I grabbed the little door. "You're going to break that, Kaylyn, and I *don't* know. Either tell me or don't."

She blushed a blotchy dark red that mottled even her eyelids. "Make a baby without making a baby."

I gaped at her. "Did she do it?"

Kaylyn shrugged and nodded at the same time. She looked embarrassed almost to the point of tears.

"She's *twelve*?"

"Never mind, it's no big—"

"It *is* big. It's fucked up."

Kaylyn's hand went to her mouth, as though she'd been the one to let the word slip.

"Sorry," I said.

"No. You're right, it's . . . um, what you said."

I swallowed a smile; her dorkiness was kind of sweet.

She started to reach for her seatbelt, then said, "Can you—my hands are sticky—"

"Oh, right, sure." I stretched across her to pull the belt down. She had that little-kid sweat smell, like a penny clutched in a warm hand.

We were quiet on the way home. I couldn't tell if she was embarrassed now by confiding in me. By Kaylyn's age, I'd already learned to act out knowledgeable weariness. Scorn had been the first—for a long time, the only—way Nicole and I were united: "God, it's only *sex*, what's your *problem*, do you think maybe you're *gay*?" At the time, I thought it came naturally to Nicole, that she was so cool it left no space for someone to find her uncool, but later I realized she'd been faking almost as hard as me. After a while, people stopped trying to get under our skin with Naked Family stuff. They still used the term, but just as an easy reference point.

Actually, no one in the family ever walked around naked. There was other frankness, though: Holly and Jim might be tired in the morning after a night of "lovemaking;" we had those subscriptions to *Playgirl* and *Penthouse*. Our parents reasoned that we would find our way to porn anyway, and why should it be a big secret that people enjoyed thinking about sex? On syrupy, hypnotic summer afternoons Nicole and Shawn and I would end up in Shawn's bedroom, cool and dim, the thin band of sunshine visible above the window wells only making the room feel darker. Sometimes I'd do dramatic readings from *Penthouse Forum*. "Listen to this one. This guy has a relationship with a pillow."

"Like a *doll*?" Nicole asked from the floor.

"A regular pillow." I began reading from the middle of the letter in a deep voice: "I like to buy her sexy lingerie. I'll dress her in a black silk slip, and by the time I've gotten it on her, my nine-inch cock is rock hard."

"My two-inch cock," Shawn said.

"That would be yours." Nicole opened and closed her arms and legs, as though making a snow angel on the rug. Shawn's walls still had pegboard—the fathers' brief, cheerful attempt at removal had sputtered out when they found it was rubber-cemented in place. On three sides of the room, the outlines where hammers and T squares had hung showed in the spaces between his posters of busty warrior maidens. A photo of the Maryland state seal covered the fourth wall: Shawn had a business making fake IDs on his computer, forty dollars each, no price breaks for family or friends. Jockhallers and Quaddies and Drama Fags—even the occasional S-Gay or Squid—came to the house asking for him, then clumped downstairs to have their picture taken in front of the state seal. As far as I knew, none of our parents had ever questioned his popularity. DC's drinking age was eighteen then but Shawn made everyone at least twenty, on the theory it looked less suspicious than just barely clearing the hurdle.

"I love the feeling of silk around my manhood," I read. "But I force myself to hold back and go slow."

"What I have to wonder is why you're always reading a guys' magazine." Shawn stroked his chin in mock contemplation. His faint mustache made him look not older but younger, like he hadn't wiped his mouth after drinking cocoa.

"It's *funny*," I snapped, though he was right. The girls' half-closed eyes and half-open mouths reminded me of a cat I'd once seen in labor, panting shallowly, her eyes slitted. The girls had that same broken, semi-conscious look, as if they'd been picked up and flung hard across the room. If I stared for long enough, I might finally riddle out what made them so important. "Listen. He says she's the perfect woman, because with girlfriends you have to buy them meals and go to movies and talk to them and they still might not put out."

Shawn hung his head backwards over the edge of the bed, shoulder-length hair almost brushing the dirty linoleum floor. "You know how they always start, 'I thought your letters were made up, until . . . '? I don't think that one's made up."

I found Jeremy in the bathroom, washing his hands before dinner. I shut the door behind us to tell him about the girl who might or might not have made a baby without making a baby.

"Did she?"

"Kaylyn says so. Who knows. That's the kind of thing kids would insist happened even if they only think it might have."

"God. In seventh grade, I'd never even kissed someone."

Me either, but with him I kept that kind of detail a little blurry. "Why would Kaylyn tell *me*, though?"

"Are you kidding? She worships you." Jeremy turned off the water and reached automatically towards the towel rack. He'd made me remove the cloth hand towels though, because damp might breed Bad Things. We both knew it was stupid, but still. Even stupid action at least made me feel less powerless.

I ripped off a paper towel and held it out: "She doesn't worship me."

"*Complete* worship."

"Then only because I'm mean to her."

"That's one of your very junior-high theories." Jeremy still made fun of me for how standoffish I'd been when we'd first begun dating, a strategy he said people should outgrow after about eighth grade.

I put my arms around his waist, burying my nose in the front of his sweater. I whispered, "Kaylyn's *in* junior high."

He said, "Interesting point." The paper towel in his hand crinkled against the back of my shirt. He rested his head against mine. *This.*

15

a few days later Diane Winter, the woman whose table I'd ug-lified, called to ask if I uglified walls, too. I found myself say-ing yes. She wanted her "powder room" done in trompe l'oeil marble. It sounded ghastly, like the walls of a tourist restaurant in North Beach, but I just said, "I'll bring my samples." When we hung up, I'd have to figure out how to make samples. The only trompe l'oeil experience I actually had came from mak-ing stage sets in college. For a lesbian musical version of *Romeo and Juliet*, I'd done a church with stone walls and stained-glass windows. Kneeling by the dead Romy, Juliet toasted with the empty poison bottle and sang an angry ballad ("So Here's to You, Montague"). At the play's end—dead lovers lying entan-gled, families pledging new tolerance—the colors had slowly dimmed from the stained-glass windows until only pink trian-gles remained. I didn't mention lesbian musical theater to Diane

Winter, just said that I did trompe l'oeil *all the time*, and that if she liked my work, I'd write out an estimate. I'd have to figure out how to write an estimate, too, once we got off the phone. Gita would probably know but no fucking way would I ask.

Accepting the job was profoundly impractical. First of all, I hadn't yet caught up on past projects. In the hospital, Gita had mapped out for me a careful grid of dates after she'd seen the pile of scrap paper that I used for keeping track. Now I had a neat notebook with a page for each job and one page showing all the jobs together. Every story Jeremy and I had heard about life-threatening illness seemed to be about the awesome gift bestowed in its wake: gratitude, perspective, a renewed appreciation of family. Better record keeping seemed pretty trivial in comparison. Second reason it was impractical to accept the job: I'd have to learn how to do faux marble. And third, I'd gritted my teeth with distaste the whole way through gold-leafing and crackle-glazing Diane Winter's table.

A new project, though, after weeks of dutifully plodding through work that had gone stale from sitting in my workroom. Energized, I found pictures of marble online and spent the afternoon making samples on squares of wood. The first ones were disasters—in trying to smudge the lines, I made them thick and blotchy—but after a couple hours of experimentation, I learned how to smear the right amount for the veins in the marble to look organic. The world tapered to the work before me.

A key in the front door: Gita. I felt my shoulders tense but I forced myself to keep my eyes on my painting. Behind me, she paused in the doorway. Pretending absorption, I hummed a little under my breath. I dunked my brush into a jar of paint thinner, the color twisting away in a translucent ribbon. A wisp of playground rhyme floated through my mind—*turpentine, wine*—but I didn't try to catch it. After a moment, Gita continued down the hall.

Since my birthday, I'd split in half. If I showed that I saw Gita as a threat, it reinforced that she was a threat. I invited her to stay for meals, I asked her about her job, I left her alone with Jeremy and went to work in my studio. *Sure, sure, give her a key, that makes sense.* I made sure not to watch them with any kind of intensity because it was fine for them to hang out, fine, totally fine.

And then the other half of me actually did think it was fine, and that Gita was great, and marveled that I was having a hard time. Friendships *were* exciting. That day in the rain with Nicole when we were thirteen had been the purest falling in love I'd ever experienced. I'd felt like my head might explode with joy.

I labeled the back of each sample with the name of the marble I'd copied. Marquina, black with splotchy feathers of white. Verde Alpi, black tornadoing through deep green. Rosso Francia, pink veined with lighter pink. I felt on edge now that Gita was there, like I had a deadline to meet.

I could go in and see Jeremy. Some of the pressure eased in my chest. It wouldn't seem jealous, or like I thought I needed to check up. I could show him—them—the samples.

When I came into the bedroom, they were leaning towards each other, Jeremy on the bed and Gita perched on the cold radiator. They said hello but didn't pause.

Jeremy said, "But if the mainframe went down . . ."

"There'd have to be back-up. Also, would they even think of it as deaths if it did crash?"

"Well, would the simulations *experience* it as death?"

"I don't think so," she said. "It would just be like, Pop. Like pulling a plug. One second you're there and the next second, you're nothing and there's nothing."

"Would that be better or worse? Having no idea you're about to die and not even a second to be afraid? Or to say goodbye?"

"Saying goodbye, though—that only matters for the people remaining, so they remember it. And here no one is left, right?"

They were flushed and excited, their words practically tripping over each other's, *virtual nervous system, astronomical resources*. It took me awhile to work out that they were discussing whether the world—no, the universe—might be an elaborate computer simulation. I stood there, my hands full of the wooden samples for Mrs. Powder Room.

I said slowly, "So when I get a zit, it's because some person on a computer has nothing better to do than give me a zit?"

"By then people would have evolved so much that we'd no longer be able to classify them as Homo sapiens, they'd be post-human." Jeremy slept so much of the day that he'd stopped wearing contacts; he had on his old glasses he never wore anymore, with the heavy brown frames.

"Wait," I said to him. "Wait, you really believe this? If we're part of someone's game, then why don't people just disappear sometimes when their creator gets bored?"

Not boredom! they said. Parameters might be adjusted, though. Maybe people did disappear, and the program was designed to erase all traces of them. They seemed to be saying that the theory had to do with our computers developing so fast that one could reasonably imagine they'd be able to create entirely realistic simulations not long from now. Jeremy said that once you accepted that idea, then the chance of our being in the one "real" universe was a lot lower than the chance of being in a simulated universe, of which there might be millions, billions. My head hurt, right between the eyebrows, and then the needle hopped on the record and I thought that *Gita* didn't get headaches over this stuff.

No. I wasn't going to start that again.

"I might have a new job." I lifted my hands, filled with the wooden samples. "This woman wants me to marbleize her bathroom."

Gita said, "I hope you quoted her a higher rate."

"Here," I said to Jeremy. "This turned out kind of well, even though the background still doesn't have enough depth. But then this one's pretty good, I think."

In his hands, the samples suddenly looked real, like marble and not like streaky paint on blocks of wood. My mood steadied for a moment.

"These are great," Jeremy said. "You just did these, just now?"

I hid my pleasure. "It's such fussy work. I feel like my eyes are crossing."

"They're great."

Gita had on a silky rose-colored shirt I hadn't seen before. She held out her hand for the samples, turning them over. In a strangely wistful voice, she said, "I don't do anything creative. There's literally not one thing I can do."

I said, "The first time Jeremy asked me out, I almost said no because I wanted to get work done." I paused to let him take up the story. We had a little performance piece about our meeting. He said I was sexy and intimidating and that he drank too much because he couldn't think how else to talk to me other than ordering more drinks. I said that I was happy he kept coming back to the bar, even though he wasn't my usual type. As if we hadn't heard these details dozens of times before, we'd ask each other, *I wasn't your type? You thought I was intimidating? You were happy I came back*? "Have you told Gita how we met? Jeremy thought I was scary." I looked over; he was studying two DVDs Gita must have brought over. "Do you still think I'm scary?"

"You're nicer now."

Next he would say, *But that's my doing, of course.*

After a minute, I said, "That's your doing."

Gita took the movies from Jeremy, holding them up for me to see. "Which one?"

"I should keep working."

"You know," said Jeremy slowly. "If you're not going to watch anyway, maybe we should get out of the house. Go to an actual theater."

He'd said it so casually, so reasonably, that as quickly as I doubted him, it doubled back into doubting myself. And in fact, his doctors had told him he didn't need to be so paranoid about germs; it *was* reasonable to go out. "Well, but you've been really tired."

"I'm so fucking sick of this house!" Jeremy said. "I can't keep living my life like this. Like my *feet* are bound."

"Just one of them," I pointed out. He didn't smile.

"It's a Monday night," Gita said. "It shouldn't be crowded, so not a huge germ risk. And we can come home if he gets too tired."

"I'll wear my mask."

They looked at me, kids waiting for their mother's permission to go play in the backyard.

"Sure," I said. "Great."

★ ★ ★

Seven o'clock; eight; nine. I'd never felt more awake, every part of me vibrating. Once in ninth grade, Nicole and I snorted ground-up NoDoz, and it had felt something like this—a high-pitched, fluted-edged nausea. But then at least, I'd known it would be over eventually.

I can't keep living like this.

I was the one who'd gone for years without health insurance, the one who drove the cranky old truck, the one who worked with power tools. The one who brought home music by bands Jeremy had never heard of. I'd done more drugs, had sex with more people. I'd pierced my own fucking nose with a fucking safety pin. When I was twenty-one and broken-hearted over Hal (for which I blamed him entirely, even though I'd been the one to end things), I'd dyed my hair black and then spent a whole summer pretending I was fine, even though the matte-black hair plus my pointy nose and chin meant I actually scared children. How had our roles gotten tangled? Why did Jeremy get to be the reckless one now? Whether he was actually interested in Gita or just interested in her interest, was he reckless enough to see where things might lead?

Into the kitchen to put water on for tea, then out to the living room, where I picked up the top *New Yorker* from the stack. What were they doing right now? Were they still at the movie theater? Was Jeremy tensely attuned to the exact placement of Gita's arm on the armrest, the exact sprawl of their knees? Or were they not even pretending? Had they gone to Gita's car? Were they groping frantically? Or—and this seemed somehow worse—what if Jeremy just had Gita's hand in both of his?

I slung the magazine back at the table—it overshot, but I didn't pick it up—and banged into our bedroom, turning circles in place. What was I looking for, what had I come in here for? A high whine rose: teakettle. I ran to turn it off, flinging open the cabinet to look at our teas, then slamming the door shut without choosing one. Tea might calm me, but the thought of bringing myself down made me feel worse, not better. Maybe I could use this energy to get some work done. I stomped to the studio, knowing it wasn't a good idea to use tools in this jagged, erratic mood, and yet an accident actually seemed appealing. I imagined Jeremy returning home to find my blood all over everything and a note that I'd driven myself to the hospital.

Because, yes: what my mother's example so clearly showed was the irresistible draw of competence. Jeremy had always liked that I could take care of myself—but didn't it also let him off the hook? I turned around in place again. There was this table I'd had forever, one I'd found at the curb. It had beautiful lines, but someone had inflicted a succession of artistic delusions on its surfaces, painting the wood with a forest of lumpy trees, then covering the top with a pottery-shard mosaic. I needed to find a chisel and some safety goggles. What if Jeremy was an hour late? Two? What if he didn't come home? Why wasn't he back yet? Why weren't they back?

And then yellow light slid, watery, across the ceiling, and stopped: headlights. When I pulled back the curtain, Gita's Honda Civic idled in front of the house. The passenger-side door opened and the inside light came on. Jeremy put his crutches onto the curb but stayed sitting, turned to talk to Gita. My heart began to pound: suddenly, I wasn't ready for him to be home. I had to say something, and what on earth would I say?

I ran to the bedroom, shucking off my clothes—I always slept naked—and got under the covers, opening some random book I could pretend to read. Even though I'd only run down the hall, I was out of breath. God, get a hold of yourself, get a *hold* of yourself. What had actually happened? He'd come back from a movie a little later than I'd expected, but I didn't even know what they'd seen, or how far away. I cupped my hands over my mouth, trying to breathe slowly, willing him not to come in quite yet. Until finally I was calmer and thought, why hadn't he come in yet?

In my workroom, I pulled the curtain just enough to see that he'd gotten out of the car but stood, leaning in. Something made him laugh and he stepped back, pinching one crutch to his chest with his elbow so he could raise his hand in farewell.

For a brief time, early in the Naked Family era, Costa had wanted me as an ally. He'd been the one who woke me in the middle of the night to watch the stray cat give birth under our back porch, panting and slit-eyed. Another time, he showed me how to make a hole in construction paper to watch a solar eclipse. I thought of that day now, how it felt to see something framed by the tiniest hole. And then not even the thing itself, but the shadow it cast.

Jeremy watched the car even after she'd gone around the corner and out of sight. I stood there, breath caught in my throat. What would show on his face when he turned? But when finally he did, he just looked like himself. Halfway up the front stairs, he pulled out his phone, checking something—the time, maybe. It wasn't until the lock turned in the door that I remembered I had no clothes on. I began to skitter down the hall but he was already inside, and I froze midmovement.

"Hi," he said, sounding confused. "You're naked."

"I was just . . . I got up. To go to the bathroom." I reached for a towel from the back of the bathroom door but we didn't reuse towels these days—germs—and the hook was empty. I shivered. Turning away, keeping my voice casual, I asked, "How was the movie?"

"Okay. It totally wiped me out, though."

"What did you see?"

"Some stupid action thing." He pressed his hands to his eyes.

"You don't remember which one? It will say on the ticket stub."

"I don't understand why everything makes me so *tired*."

The hallway was cold. I crossed my arms over my chest, then uncrossed them, trying to signal I was totally okay with being naked for no reason. "An action movie? That's so not your thing."

Jeremy leaned against the wall. After a minute, in a new voice, he said, "I keep thinking, if I died—"

"But you didn't die."

"—I wouldn't leave anything behind I've done. Everything I've done would—"

"You'd leave me."

"You're not *getting* it. I don't mean there's nothing I'd regret leaving, I mean there's nothing I've done that would last. I've taught some rich kids math—"

"You want to change *jobs*?" He couldn't leave his job now. He couldn't even stay away from it much longer—only three more weeks—without losing his health insurance benefits. W-K was going to try to lighten his schedule by making two of his classes "advising periods" and then not assigning him any advisees.

"I think we should have a baby."

"Oh, God." The sound of a Spanish-language radio station seeped thinly through the wall.

"I want to know I've loved someone with everything I've got."

"Is that a country song?" I asked, but he didn't smile. "I don't think this is really the time—"

"When is it going to be the time, Claire?"

"Don't shout at me!" I took a deep breath. "Six months. I can get the business on track. You can get better."

"You're just going to have some other reason in six months."

"Are we not dealing with enough?" I saw his mouth quirk at the formality of *are we not*. "You've been really sick. You're exhausted, I'm exhausted, my business is a total mess."

"Your *business*."

"We can wait six months. We'll be parents the rest of our lives."

"Do you even want kids?"

"Yes. *Yes.*" The insistence in my voice sounded forced, but I didn't know what else to say.

After a minute, he reached out, tracing the line of my jaw with his fingers, watching my face.

"You're naked," he said.

He kissed me, then dropped his mouth to my nipple. Usually, he could make me come just like this, but the sensation was far away, wobbly and faint. I pulled him down with me to the floor feeling like I was acting, and doing it badly. Did he really want me? Or did he just want the release of sex?

He groaned when I took him into my mouth. I felt a *tick* of satisfaction before I wondered if he could be imagining Gita. I moved, then stopped, then moved again with what I knew would be frustrating slowness, catching his hand when he tried to pull me up, holding his wrist down against the floor. I sat up to whisper in his ear—*Is that what you want? I'm not sure I should let you have it*—and then stopped before the words could come out. If he wished I were someone else, how pathetic to act all sexy. His eyes were still closed. What if he was basically masturbating into me, like that guy with the lingerie-clothed pillow? It seemed unbelievable suddenly, the inaccessibility of whatever was playing on the inside of his skull. I imagined pushing my thumbs down into the ridge between his brows, through the skin, breaking apart the halves of his brain like a walnut. And still, I'd know nothing. He could be with anyone inside there, he could be remembering anything, he could be anywhere.

"Be right back," I said: my diaphragm.

"Don't put it in."

"We just said—"

"We won't try to get pregnant, and we won't try to not get pregnant. It's a compromise."

"How is not trying to not get pregnant not trying to get pregnant?" I asked.

"Six months from now, it's going to feel the same."

"You want to leave it up to fate." Suddenly the hardness in my lungs broke, and I laughed. "Okay." I didn't have to force the cheer in my voice: hating him was its own kind of joy. He was only about an inch from being inside me. It felt like almost nothing to slide down, onto him.

"Wait," he said. "Are you sure?"

I kept moving. He moved with me for a minute, then said, "Claire?"

I shook my head.

"Wait, stop, we should—" There was a panicked edge to his voice. He put his hands on my hips and I let him pull me up. Right at the top, his grip loosened and I plunged back down.

"*No*," he said, and came.

He put his hand over his eyes. I got up and floated to my studio, leaving him behind on the floor. I fetched a long sweater that reached halfway down my thighs and drank some espresso from that morning. It was cold and thick as motor oil. I found my chisels and, after some hunting and pecking, my second-favorite pair of safety goggles. Somewhere deep inside me, Jeremy's sperm were swimming for their lives. It stopped me in my tracks, the idea of tiny creatures whose only desire in the world was for something of mine.

16

*e*veryone has that one thing that freaks them out dispropor-tionately. Jeremy couldn't think about the ligaments under his tongue. My father, anything having to do with eyes; he couldn't even watch someone putting in contact lenses. For me, it was constricting clothes: as a child, I once hyperventilated and blacked out because I couldn't pull off a pair of rubber boots, and then it happened again when I was a teenager rushing to change costumes during *Oklahoma!*, getting stuck with my arms above my head.

Nicole: needles. Once when we were kids she ran out of the doctor's office and an orderly had to haul her back in and hold her wrapped in his arms while she screamed and strained and the pissed-off nurse jabbed in the vaccinations. She took Xanax now when she absolutely had to see doctors, but still dreaded them.

The first part of her prenatal appointment was just an ultrasound. The tech spread gel on her stomach and Nicole jumped a little: "Oh, cold." In clothes, she didn't look pregnant yet. But here, unmistakably, her stomach was round, veined in blue like the Carrara marble sample I'd done for Diane Winter.

"Oh my God," Nicole said. Her eyes filled with tears.

On the screen were black ribbons and a pale flutter, the baby's heart. I'd been feeling like I was part of Nicole's pregnancy, but looking at her face, stricken with love, I felt how profoundly outside I was. If it were mine, could I love this dark spot, this blur of white?

When the doctor came in, balding and stooped, I had a moment of surprise at not recognizing him—but of course I didn't recognize him, this wasn't the ICU. He introduced himself quickly, over his shoulder, as he washed his hands at the sink. A nurse had followed him in and began to lay out instruments on a tray. Just in time, I put my hand up to shield Nicole's eyes: a long paper package held a needle almost the length of my forearm.

Head averted, Nicole said, "You use really good anesthetic, right?"

"We numb the skin, but you're going to feel it after that," said the nurse.

"And the anesthetic—"

"A little pinch."

Nicole winced. Without looking, she reached for me and I took her hand, which was shaking. She tried to breathe deeply.

"Didn't you take your pill?"

She gave me a look.

"What?"

"God, Claire. *Pregnant.*"

"Oh, wow."

She had her head averted, but she must have felt the needle near her skin because she sat up. "No no no no no. Never mind, I don't want it."

"Close your eyes, honey," said the nurse.

Nicole's head whipped towards me, her pupils huge. "I can't do this, I can't. I don't need the test."

"You can. You can. Look at me."

"Don't do anything," she said to the doctor.

"I'm going to give you a quiz, okay? I'll say . . ." I cast around. "I'll say part of a cheer and you tell me what's next. Um. Okay. 'Your mama, your daddy.'"

"Your M-A, M-A, your D-A-D-D-Y."

"Lie back again. Come on, lie back. Okay. 'I turn around, I touch the ground.'"

"Then I wiggle it, just a little bit."

"Ugh, I always hated that one. I'm going to tell them to go ahead now." I flicked my gaze quickly towards the doctor. "'Wildcats are smooth—' No, wait. 'Wildcats are ready, Wildcats are smooth—'"

"Wildcats are gonna—" She gave a huge, rattling gasp as the anesthesia went in.

"That wasn't so bad, was it?" said the doctor.

Nicole laughed roughly, almost a hiccup.

"Now we wait a minute. . . ."

"Guess what the girls' teams were called?" I said to the nurse. "Wildkittens." It had been a gratifying source of outrage when I took my first women's studies class in college.

"Which one of you was a cheerleader?" she asked.

She had to be joking—but then I realized she wasn't. "Her."

"Okay?" the doctor said to me.

"Um, give me a second. I have to think of another." I tried to summon words, dragging the past up like an anchor. The cheerleaders resented the rule that they had to go to girls' events, not just boys', and so at our basketball games they chanted without leaving the bench, French-braiding each other's hair or trying to thumb-rub away a spot from a saddle shoe. "Hey hey, hey hey, are you ready?"

Nicole smiled, then muffled a gasp when the second needle went in. On the screen, I could see it descending, thin and white. "Fuck!" Nicole muttered, "Fuck fuck *fuck* fuck *fuck*."

A long, trembling moment, and then the bright line on the screen grew shorter and shorter and disappeared. Nicole and I both breathed out hard. She asked, "Can you tell if it's a boy or a girl?"

The doctor handed the syringe to a nurse and peeled off his gloves before taking the ultrasound bulb from her. "We'll know for sure when we get your test results, but, if I had to guess . . ." Gray streamers, grainier than in Jeremy's CT scans, furled and unfurled on the screen. "I'm not seeing a penis."

"A girl," said Nicole. She covered her eyes with her hand.

When the doctor and nurse had gone, I asked, "Isn't that what you want? A girl?"

She said, "If it's a girl, that makes me my mom."

I'd just assumed that women wanted girls. "But—I mean, your relationship with your dad was more messed up than with your mom—"

She'd worn her Meetings Suit to the appointment for some reason; she pulled on her pantyhose, jamming her feet into her pumps. "They're *my* parents. I think I get to say what 'more messed-up' is."

She couldn't really believe that: Costa had retreated from his kids' lives after the divorces; Nicole had had to do an Internet search to find him working at a Key West church. "Wait, are you—why are you mad at *me*?"

Her shoulders sank. "No, you're right. It's not you."

I wanted to tell her that Jeremy and I were kind-of-trying, but I felt strangely shy, like I'd grabbed something she found first. It wouldn't seem quite fair if I got to be married *and* have a baby. She'd always wanted those things and I'd always kind of disparaged them.

"The doctor could be wrong. He said you can't know for sure until the test's back."

"Well then I'm having a boy without a penis, so *that's* good news." She'd finished dressing but didn't move to leave the room, whose lights were still out, the ultrasound screen illuminating her face.

"Your boobs are huge, by the way."

She said, "Jealous much?" as she always did.

And as always I said, "More than a mouthful is just waste."

She sat down heavily on the ultrasound tech's stool. "I think I was so focused on could I even get pregnant. I didn't realize—I mean, I knew this, but—I'm going to be really alone in this."

"You have me."

"You've got so much going on. . . ." she said in a voice that wanted to be contradicted.

I shook my head. "I mean, yes, but I'm totally here for you."

★ ★ ★

From a distance, the "marble" appeared simple, a creamy white, with thick blue-gray streaks. I was glad not to be doing the Rosso Francia: being surrounded by all that veiny pink would have felt like working inside a piece of raw meat. I filled in small patches, perhaps six inches square, putting down white eggshell base and then, while it was still wet, using a thin hogs-hair brush for the mixture of Payne's gray, ivory black, and titanium white, six parts scumble to four parts white spirit. Jeremy was having his central line removed; Gita had volunteered to take him and from inside my impervious bubble I'd been all, *Sure, great*. The bubble had deflated slowly over the days since then, but I stuck with my answer because I wasn't *a jealous wife*.

Suddenly, I couldn't believe my stupidity. I imagined them leaning their shoulders together, their hands too close, and now their hands touching. I imagined them kiss. Here and there, I dug a little flaw into the marble, a smudge of ochre and an even tinier dab of umber near the intersections of lines. The monotony of white and gray tired my eyes; I had to restrain myself from speckling the whole wall with flaws. I tried to imagine Jeremy and Gita fucking. It should have been painful, but finally giving in to the thought felt weirdly comfortable, a place to rest. Then I forced myself to be honest. I didn't really think either of them would cross that line. What seemed more likely was silent yearning, and wouldn't that eventually gutter out? Maybe someday Jeremy and I would even joke about it.

"How's it going?" Diane said behind me.

I jumped, spilling paint thinner. "I didn't hear you." I reached for the cotton diaper to wipe off my hand.

"May I?" she asked merrily.

Diane came and checked my progress at least once an hour. At first I'd thought she was micromanaging, but then I realized she was just aimless, wandering around her mansionette in immaculate yoga clothes until some idea seized her. She leaned her shoulder close to mine. What did she think she was going to discover?

She said, "Nice. Nice work," as she had every time she'd looked. She balanced briefly on one foot, clasping the other behind her with both hands; then she went away.

At home, I called out "Jeremy?" No answer. Late afternoon, that time of day when the light becomes watered-down and unsteady. They were late again. The sadness I'd held so tightly in check the last few weeks stirred inside my chest, delicate, expanding. I walked down the hall without turning on lights. Anything I imagined doing—finding something to eat in the kitchen, putting in some work on the Windsor chairs—seemed like it would do violence to this strange, fragile mood. His appointment had been hours ago.

I found myself trailing my hand on the wall, shoulder-height. It was something I hadn't done in so long, since the very early Naked Family era, that I'd in fact forgotten I used to do it. The rule was I couldn't raise or lower my hand, and I couldn't break contact, so when I came to the bathroom doorway I had to go through it, straining over the tub to keep my fingertips touching the wall. Down the long stretch of hallway, a short round of Jeremy's study, tiny bit of hall, my closed workroom door, and then the bedroom. In the dimness, I didn't realize at first that the lump in the bed was Jeremy, asleep.

Only in the force of my relief did I know I'd been scared. I crawled into bed beside him, putting my arms around his waist. I wouldn't pile dishes in the sink; I'd make sure we never ran out of food or toilet paper; I'd fold the clothes instead of leaving them in the basket. "Jeremy," I said. "Jeremy."

Groggily, he said, "Gee."

Gee?

"Look," he said, fumbling with his shirt. Where his central line had been was a layer of gauze over ragged-looking black stitches. He tried to move my hand there but I jerked back, too used to needing to keep everything sterile.

"It's covered, it's fine," he said. "I'm sorry I freaked out the other night. The baby."

"That's okay." I didn't really mean it, but then I did. "It's normal to freak out."

He pulled my hand towards his chest again; this time I let him. I undressed us. He asked if I was sure and I said yes. I held my breath for a moment, but he didn't say anything more, even when I guided him inside me, even when he came.

Afterwards, I found myself tracing my fingertips over his dressing. Beneath it, the stitches were small and strange, an unreadable braille.

17

*l*iving in a city, I'd developed the skill of sighting a parking space about to come open. People walked differently—I couldn't define it better than that—when headed back to a car than they did headed somewhere else. It was kind of like the way you could tell whether a junkie was headed out for a fix or had just scored, though I couldn't have defined how I knew that, either. A difference in the tilt of the chin, maybe. A difference in where they centered their body weight.

At Dolores Park, Jeremy opened his door, and I looked away to keep myself from helping him climb out. He hated when I did things for him that he thought he should do for himself, but on the other hand if he actually couldn't do something, he also hated having to ask for help rather than my just matter-of-factly stepping in.

It was his first time outside without crutches, his first time using a prosthesis. Two of them had come in the mail a few days ago and he'd held them in his hands, studying them. One—the one he had inside his sneaker now—was about the size and shape of a rubber doorstop wedge. The second one looked like the front half of a ballet slipper. There were holes for his real toes, plus two molded toes. They looked remarkably like the ones he'd lost: thick ivory-colored nails, a few tufts of hair, even the way his first toe overlapped the second. I'd reached out, wanting a better look, but he'd shoved the prostheses back in the box and then shoved the whole thing under the bed.

He went downhill with agonizing slowness, me hovering behind him. His doctor had told him he didn't need to wear a surgical mask in public but he did anyway, to be extra safe. How slow he seemed, how stooped. And how eager, looking all around.

Though it hadn't rained in days, the ground was marshy. We finally found a dry patch on the hill at the west side of the park. I spread our blanket out under a tree. Jeremy lowered himself gradually, as if he might crack. Quickly I bent forward, kissing his cheek. "What should I get you from Tartine?"

Rubbing his skin beneath the mask's elastic strap, he said, "I don't care. You choose." He worked out his phone from his pocket, glancing at the screen. He tapped a quick response, then turned it over.

I'd arranged with Hal to meet here to hand off Fort, and as I crossed the park, I looked for them without luck. I could barely remember the last time I'd been outside for any but the most utilitarian reason: I might as well have been under house arrest myself. I'd cancelled my last three dinner nights with Nicole. The third time, she'd said, *You have to take care of yourself too, you know*. Which seemed a little like what she actually wanted was for me to take care of her.

At Tartine, I stood in line for almost thirty minutes behind two girls in maxi dresses discussing the probable calorie count of every baked good behind the glass. How bad would they let themselves be? One of them suggested splitting a morning bun and a chocolate croissant, and then they giggled the way school friends used to giggle when I showed them *Playgirl*. I hated them. Then the feeling collapsed, and I just felt sad and mean and old. When I finally reached the front of the line, I bought way too much, everything Jeremy might possibly want, putting it on our already-strained Visa because why did it even matter.

He'd fallen asleep by the time I returned, phone next to his open hand. He hadn't been a great sleeper before, but now he could drop straight and fast, like a heavy stone down into a pond. All over Dolores Park, I could see people sleeping, singly and in pairs, sprawled in the sun. Jeremy—curled tightly, his pale scalp shining through his short hair—seemed almost unbearably vulnerable. I scooped up his phone, jamming it in my back pocket, then wrapped the corners of the blanket clumsily around him.

I tried to relax, but my joints buzzed and juddered. I looked around for Fortinbras again and this time saw him across the park. He stood frozen, knees locked, his body tilted a little to one side, and then he exploded into motion. He was so big and so solemn-looking with his huge jowly head and broad shoulders that there was something deeply funny about him playing. He was chasing a tennis ball, not gracefully: he skidded past, then turned and snapped at it, missing. His tongue hung out, his ears flapped. There was Hal grinning at him, hands on knees, wearing shorts with ragged hems and a gray T-shirt so old the cotton looked silky.

I took off towards him. "Fort!" I called, and they both turned. For a moment, Fort didn't seem to know me, and then he tucked his head and barreled forward. I knelt, arms wide, and Fort crashed into me straight on; I let him knock me over, heavy paws on my shoulders. Hitting the ground, I felt clear, wild joy, a high note that could break crystal.

Fort nosed and snuffled at my neck, which tickled, and I yelped, one arm around him, laughing and trying to push his mouth away from my face with my other elbow. I ran my hand down his back.

Something was wrong, a lump.

I bolted up, heart yanked by alarm, before I could fully register that the *something wrong* was just matted, stiff fur. Not a growth.

"Did he roll in something?" I called to Hal.

"What?"

"His fur, it's almost spiked."

"I wanted to ask you. You said to put it in, but am I supposed to wash it out later?" I must have looked totally blank. He said, "The egg."

"Egg—Oh my God." I started laughing.

"You said give him an egg in the morning for his coat."

"That's for—it's not—" I whooped, unable to finish the sentence. I'd been holding myself in so tightly. I collapsed onto all fours, then down onto my elbows. Every time I recovered enough to try, laughter felled me again.

And then all at once I was drained, empty, aware that I was on my knees, my ass pointed up at Hal. I didn't want to be reminded of sex, but of course I was. As a lover, Hal had been generous and a little goofy, contradicting two of my general beliefs about beautiful men. I sat back on my heels, catching my breath.

Hal was smiling, but nicely. "I take it I fucked up?"

"I scramble the egg. He eats it."

"That would explain his total bafflement. *Polite* bafflement, though."

A final giggle escaped me. "Thanks so much for taking care of him this week."

"You're not usually a 'pretty please' kind of person."

"I didn't text you that. Wait—did I?"

Hal held up one finger for just a second, then dug in his pocket for his cell.

I said, "No, no; I believe you."

I knew Hal still had feelings for me. Their longevity came from my having dumped him during college out of the blue. Of course, it hadn't felt out of the blue to me: I'd been more and more obsessed with the idea he'd get tired of me. Because no one else had ever broken up with him, he thought that I saw through him in a way other women couldn't, and I became the Great Loss. But I suspected that if I'd ever agreed to try again, his feelings would have blown away, like dust blown off a photograph with one hard breath.

I lay down again, my leg over Fort's withers and my cheek against his head. "I've missed him so much."

Hal lay down, too, on Fort's other side. "He's a good dog." He reached to pull one of Fort's ears. Fort grunted in satisfaction and dropped his big head on his paws. Hal's gaze held mine. The thought of Jeremy—passed out on the ground, weak and skinny—repulsed me. "I should get back. Thanks so much for helping with him."

"Should I come see your husband?" Hal always called Jeremy *your husband*. Somehow he managed to make the words sound like they had quotation marks around them.

I said no, Jeremy was sleeping, and thanks again, and I took Fort and walked towards our blanket. I'd thought having Fort back would make my throat less scratchy with loneliness. We got settled on the grass. I wouldn't tell Jeremy about the egg: he disliked Hal too much to find it funny.

I picked up the bag from Tartine and ate the chocolate cookies I'd bought. I ate the biscotti, the croissant, chocolate pudding, an open-faced sandwich of asparagus and Gruyère gone cold and oily. I drank the rest of the cooling coffee. When I stuck my hand in the bag and found just crumbs—only then did I even realize how I'd been eating—I licked my fingers and stuck them in again and again, trying to get the last bits from the corners, and then I ripped the bag and licked the creases, head so light from caffeine and sugar and butter that it felt like it might pop off. I squeezed my eyes closed. Prickly nausea rose in my throat, then subsided.

The first of the streetlamps came on and were immediately swarmed by a bevy of gnats. There was something hard beneath my ass. I'd forgotten I had Jeremy's phone in my pocket. I pulled it out, a heavy ingot—he refused to get a smart phone. Nearby, a Frisbee wobbled in the air, and a girl leapt to catch it, her shirt rising to show a band of stomach. She came down hard, hopping on one foot, almost falling, touching the ground with her hand, then rocking back and catching herself. "Whoo!" she said, raising her arms: laughing breathlessly, suddenly lovely. All at once, I knew.

I almost didn't need to look, but of course I needed to look. I thumbed in his code, everything in me suspended, a wave trembling at the top of its swell. I pressed the arrows on his keyboard that took me to the cheery little icon for messages. And there they were, a blizzard: text after text after text after text after text.

Intern is on the phone to
Her boyfriend again
I want to make her get off but also
I
From: aGita
Sent: Mon, Feb 9
11:17 AM

Don't want to have to
Deal with her ether why do
I keep accepting interns?
From: aGita
Sent: Mon, Feb 9
11:17 AM

I mean either
From: aGita
Sent: Mon, Feb 9
11:18 AM

Did you mean "either"?
To: aGita
Sent: Mon, Feb 9
11:18 AM

Jinx buy me a Coke
From: aGita
Sent: Mon, Feb 9
11:18 AM

Luckily you hate Coke, so
That's fifty cents I
Save. (Evil cackle)
To: aGita
Sent: Mon, Feb 9
11:18 AM

There must have been fifty messages just from the day before. Full sentences, no abbreviations or acronyms, broken into haiku on Jeremy's tiny dumbphone screen. Jeremy wrote about how he could still feel the toes that weren't there; he wrote that he'd sent jeans through the wash with a twenty-dollar bill in the pocket; he said, "Remember that time we got lost junior year in Oakland and you were so sure you knew where you were? And then you did know."

I was shivering in the cold; blue shadows stretched across the grass. I'd been the person he could count on to care if his bus sat in traffic for an hour, or if he tracked down online some dead stock of the discontinued Japanese pen he liked for grading. Maybe parents care in that way when you're really young, before about age nine when they can let go and return gratefully to their own lives. It struck me that marriage formed itself, not around the big decisions, but instead around the grit of daily life. He and Gita had become the repositories for each other's days, the person for whom no detail could be boring. And I'd prattled on about how I didn't feel like dealing with billing clients, and Rainbow was stocking again the olives we liked, and my fingers had started kind of flaking, I hoped not a reaction to something in the workroom like that new Russian fish glue I'd ordered.

Occasionally, the tone of Jeremy and Gita's texts conveyed an urgency that I didn't know whether to interpret as passion or only the brevity of the form. From that morning:

Just got to work I
Cannot focus at all
From: aGita
Sent: Tue, Feb 10
9:12 AM

Me too. Not the work
Part.
To: aGita
Sent: Tue, Feb 10
9:13 AM

At all at all
From: aGita
Sent: Tue, Feb 10
9:13 AM

Me too. At all at all.
To: aGita
Sent: Tue, Feb 10
9:13 AM

I scrolled up to the final texts, which were from that afternoon. Three-fifty: I'd been *with* him. His message seemed uncharacteristically sloppy, rushed:

I just miss you so
much all the time
To: aGita
Sent: Tue, Feb 10
3:50 PM

When can i see you soon
To: aGita
Sent: Tue, Feb 10
3:50 PM

I'm yours
From: aGita
Sent: Tue, Feb 10
4:13 PM

All noise around me flattened. I didn't think *I can't believe it* or *I can't fucking believe it* or *I can't fucking believe this fucking shit, can you fucking believe this fucking shit? No me neither.* Not even *No* or *Yes.* My mind felt blank as sheet metal.

18

*Y*ears ago, back when I depended on a mix of bartending and restoration jobs, I worked a wedding at the Harrison Mansion. Burgundy damask muffled the rooms; ornate gilt frames that looked like they belonged in museums held flat, amateurish portraits that looked like they belonged in someone's attic. We set up under the guidance of a wedding planner and her *two* assistants. An extraordinary amount of work had gone towards making sure the wedding was just like every other wedding: string quartet playing Mozart, bride clutching a bouquet the size of a small chandelier.

During the reception, a skinny British man leaned on the bar and asked what he should drink.

I shrugged. "We don't share a body."

His brows jerked up in surprise. For some reason regret zagged through me, needle-fine and electric. To cover, I thumped a rocks glass on the bar and poured a Scotch.

Still watching me, he picked up the glass and tipped it forward, a tiny toast. He had messy dark hair and brows that met over his nose.

A woman joined him. Her violet silk dress was low-backed, dipping to just below the waist, but I noticed he didn't put his hand there. She flashed the little printed menu card with its choice of prime rib or salmon. "How fishy is the fish?" she asked me.

The British man's mouth twisted; our eyes met for a second and I went ahead and let myself smile at him.

"Would you like me to ask the chef?" I knew that of course she would like me to ask the chef. Normally, I would have left the room for a moment, then come back to guide her in whatever I thought was probably the wrong direction. But the question would amuse Sam, so I went into the kitchen. He suggested I tell her, "No fishier than your cunt."

"Definitely to be avoided," I reported back.

After the meal, the British guy came over to the bar again. "Before I ask you what to drink, I first need you to tell me whether I'm thirsty."

I laughed, and the corner of his mouth tugged upward into a smile. His accent wasn't British after all. I'd been thrown off by his appearance—something about the long, knobbly nose and the untidy hair.

"What did you think of the Scotch?" I was pretty sure he hadn't liked it and pretty sure he wouldn't admit it.

"Good."

"Try this, then. It's one of my favorites." I poured him an even smokier Scotch he'd hate even more. He stayed, sipping it. He didn't slouch, but he also wasn't one of those men who stand frighteningly erect, like they're trying to touch their shoulder

blades together behind their backs. Though I never started conversations when I was tending bar, I found myself looking for
something to say. "Are you from out of town?"

He shook his head. "I went to high school with the bride. At
Wilkerson-Kettlewell?"

I shook my head. Closing one eye, he made his finger into
a gun and pointed east. He let his thumb fall, miming a shot.
"About six blocks."

"Private, then?"

"Fifty people in our graduating class."

"I had six hundred."

"Let me guess." He lifted his drink, squinting at me through
it like a magnifying glass. "New York. You went someplace like
Stuyvesant. You got in for math but you hung out in the art
room."

"No to New York, no to Stuyvesant. I wish. A world of no to
math. Art room's only half a no." I leaned back, holding on to
the edge of the bar. "Okay, you now. Cross-country?"

Direct hit: the not-British guy raised his brows in surprise.

"Your best subject was English, and you used to hide novels in
your other textbooks to read during classes. During free period,
you'd sneak off campus with your friends to, like, a coffee shop,
but you were a good student and so the teachers looked the other
way. Your best friend was a girl, and you always hoped you'd get
together, but you didn't except for one Thanksgiving break in college." He seemed a little stunned. I'd always been good at stories.
"You were an only child, after a bunch of miscarriages, and your
mother doted on you. In the summer, you went to genius camp."

His expression was so strange that I knew I'd nailed it.

"That was . . . weirdly complete. I almost believe it, even though it's totally wrong. I never even snuck off campus."

I laughed, disappointed. "But the cross-country part?"

"I did run cross-country," he conceded. "And I did genius camp, except it wasn't really for geniuses, just geeky kids."

"I was trying to be nice."

"Ah." He took a step away, studying me. "I'll remember what that looks like."

He and I both wore tuxes, and he was still wearing his several hours later, after the reception ended. Maybe one in the morning. High overhead, clouds skidded across the full moon. As I lugged boxes of glasses out to Sam's van, someone stood up from the curb. "Hey," he said.

"Jerry."

"Jeremy." He made a motion to take the glasses from me.

"I've got it." With my knee, I bumped the boxes up so I could get a better grip. "What happened to your date?"

"She went home. Things aren't so good with us right now. Hence the—" He mimed tipping a glass to his mouth.

I nodded, filing this explanation under *unlikely*. In my experience, one class of heavy drinkers always tells you how unusual it is that you've seen them drinking heavily. The first time I'd misjudge Jeremy. No, second: the British thing.

"So," I said.

"So."

I'd always loved the moment when nothing had happened yet but you knew it would. I still held the box of glasses. A cool breeze rounded the corner, lifting the edge of my untucked shirt.

★   ★   ★

In the morning, I reached out my foot from where we lay on my mattress, touching Jeremy's tux on the floor with my toe. "Is this rented?"

"What do you think?" he asked.

"I know basically nothing about you."

"You know I went to genius camp." He rolled towards me, then winced: "I drank too much. I'm not usually much of a drinker."

"You mentioned that." I hoped he wasn't too hungover to begin making his way home. For workspace then, I rented the back room of my friend Meara's store. I loved Sundays when it was closed and I got to be alone. I brought bread and cheese and a thermos of coffee and listened to PJ Harvey turned all the way up and left twelve or fourteen hours later, stepping out into the night street dizzy and buoyant, ears ringing, whole body ringing.

"The tux is rented." He propped himself on one elbow. "I'm a high school teacher. I live"—he did the gun thing again, pointing, squeezing off a shot with his thumb—"in the Mission. Folsom and Twentieth."

"The Mission's that-a-way." I turned his pointing hand from the window towards the door. In the sheer light of morning it felt weirdly intimate to touch him. "What do you teach?"

"Math. Calc, pre-calc. This semester, some geometry." He made a face, as though I'd know why teaching geometry sucked. "And then we have to coach, so I coach cross-country in fall, then indoor track, then outdoor. What about *your* tux?"

"I own it. Lots of catering." I rolled off the mattress, kicking away the quilt from my ankles. I lived in the tiny, Dogpatch attic apartment then, with blue walls and a view of the cranes down at the waterfront. I pulled on some old jeans from the floor, a black cotton camisole. I liked that Jeremy didn't move to cover himself back up.

I said, "So, I have work to do."

"Bartending? At . . ." he rolled over, squinting at his watch, "nine-thirty in the morning?"

"Not bartending, other stuff."

"It's Sunday. Let me take you to breakfast. You can tell me about the other stuff."

When I hesitated, he opened his mouth. I thought he was about to repeat the offer to buy breakfast. It would have pissed me off, the idea that fifteen dollars could make me do something I didn't want to do. He might have said, "Come on, I'll treat," and I would have sent him home.

But he said, "Or I won't even make you talk to me, if you don't want." And smoothly as a bus changing lanes, I veered from that other life I might have had, into this one.

19

Some places I cried: at Rainbow Grocery, measuring out bulgur wheat from the bulk bins. In the beautiful, gilded 1920s movie theater on Van Ness, where I'd gone to distract myself with a ludicrous shit-gets-blown-up movie I couldn't even follow. I walked Fort on Twenty-Fourth Street with tears slipping out under my sunglasses. A slight Asian man stacking clementines glanced at me and then quickly, almost shyly, away. So my husband was infatuated with someone else, someone from a simpler time in his life. If anyone in the world could put that in perspective, shouldn't it be me?

Apparently not. I cried in my truck, driving, and in my truck, pulled to the shoulder because I was crying too hard to see. I couldn't sleep, which made me feel that much worse, which made me sleep that much more horribly. On the phone with a client I gasped, "Sorry, I've got to—" and hung up and doubled over, mouth stretched wide and soundless—even as another part of me, so bored, was going, *This again*?

I managed not to cry when I said Jeremy's name at Walgreens to get his prescriptions. Outside, the guy with one side of his skull collapsed like a rotten mango came up to me smiling. I always gave him money but today I found myself backing away. He shook his cup with one hand and pointed to his skull with the other, bellowing *My heh*, *my heh*, and I spun and tripped on the uneven sidewalk and almost fell.

When I'd shown Jeremy the texts, he'd gotten very quiet. "We were trying to stop," he finally said. "We kept stopping and then we'd . . . we'd miss each other and we'd start again."

I cried when I saw my diaphragm in its preposterous Barbie-pink plastic case. I cried in a corner of my studio, knees to chest and fist crammed into my mouth to muffle the terrible keening noise. And on BART—still in sunglasses, because without sunglasses was not an option—listening to some boys from Cal opine that fat girls gave the best blowjobs because they were used to stuffing their faces: whooping, high-fives. In the studio again, under the worktable, screaming into the heavy padding of Fort's dog bed, until I sneezed from the dander and snot ran down my lip and I was forced to laugh at my own absurdity.

In the meantime, when I could scrape myself together, I worked through the backlog of repair jobs. I took them in order—one fewer decision—crossing each off my list with grim satisfaction.

Jeremy came into my studio and leaned against the worktable. "Time for bed?" He'd gone back to teaching, which was a good thing, but it exhausted him.

"I have some catching up to do." I focused on clamping the chair frame I'd glued.

"Claire, please. Talk to me."

I reached for a block of wood to protect the chair leg from the U-clamp. "I am. Listen, did you see the paperwork from the lab? It looks like they didn't bill Blue Cross first but went straight to us. I can call later, or you can."

"Stop it." He grabbed both of my hands in his. "God! You're being so distant." His hands were trembling. "Please don't shut down."

"I'm not doing *anything*. I just have work to do."

"Nothing's going on with—with Gita. We haven't talked since . . . She's known me basically forever. She gets me. It's not that weird that we'd text."

I pulled my hands out from his. "It's not weird that you tried to stop and couldn't?"

"We have now. Yes, that was—I admitted that. But mostly we . . . You knew we were friends."

"Right. Friends who say 'I'm yours.' Actually, I didn't know, because friends don't *say* that."

"It was a text. People use shorthand. Saying 'I'm yours' is like saying 'I'm available.'"

I adjusted the wing nut on the clamp. "I'm supposed to feel better that Gita let you know she's available."

"I can't talk if you're going to deliberately misunderstand."

With pliers, I gave the wing nut a final hard twist. "Isn't it lucky then that you have someone who understands you perfectly? Go text her what a bitch I am." I thumped down the pliers so hard that they spun across the worktable. I lunged forward but failed to catch them and they fell off the edge, clanging on the floor. "*What?* Go."

20

$\mathcal{N}$icole stopped on the sidewalk in front of a three-story building painted flu green, checking the address against the screen of her phone. At four months, her stomach was the size of a cantaloupe; apparently the baby herself was mango-sized. On the building's front stairs hunched a woman from the management company, underdressed for the foggy summer evening in a linen shift dress, arms crossed. The electricity had gone out in the building, she told us, and other people had already taken all her flashlights, but we should go on up to the apartment anyway.

I hadn't told Nicole about the texts. I wanted to, desperately, so I could ask if I was overreacting or underreacting. But I couldn't stand her knowing. As long as no one saw me acting messy and ridiculous, I wasn't *actually* messy and ridiculous.

The stairwell was dark. The second time I bumped into Nicole, she snapped, "*Careful*," then softened it by adding "—wench."

"Sorry, wench."

"You should be, wench."

Inside, other couples opened the refrigerator—a sigh of sour air—and bent, noses almost touching the carpet, to try to make out its color. We followed a guy into the bedroom, his flashlight illuminating the tentacles of a gold plastic chandelier, and then blazing for a moment as it hit the cheaply mirrored closet door.

"Remember seeing the house for the first time?" I asked.

"The Naked House? When we were eight?"

"*Nine*. You were really mean to me that day."

We'd told this story often, to others and to each other, about how badly we'd gotten along at first. "Well, I was pissed off," she said now, absently. "And I wasn't psyched about sharing a room. Would my bed even fit in here do you think? With the radiator, and all the doors?"

"Excuse me." A man with a pierced septum held out a flashlight. "We're leaving. Do you need this?"

"Thank you so much," Nicole said, giving him what I thought of as her Jockhaller smile.

The woman with him also had a pierced septum. Had they gone to do it together? Or had they already had the same piercing when they met, and had it been part of what drew them together? "What do you do?" the woman asked.

Startled, I said, "I'm a restorer. She's—"

"She asked when we're due, honey." Nicole slipped her arm around my waist. "November."

They congratulated us. The woman glanced around, as if the room might be bugged, then leaned in. "We're not telling people yet, but—" She pointed at her own stomach.

"Oh, *amazing*," said Nicole, with another Jockhaller smile.

The kitchen had been updated to look like Every Kitchen Everywhere—tan quartz countertops, oak cabinets, pewter-colored pulls. Off the kitchen was one last small room with vinyl flooring.

I said, "Wait, I thought this was a two-bedroom."

"I believe this is the second bedroom." Nicole flashed her light off a water heater. "They want twenty-four hundred for this place." She sounded grim. Her current studio apartment cost thirteen hundred dollars a month.

"I guess a crib could—"

Nicole was already storming towards the living room.

The woman in the shift dress had set herself up with rental applications, a flashlight clamped between her chest and arm. "Do you girls have any questions?"

"You can't call a room without a closet or window a 'bedroom,'" said Nicole.

"Well, a bonus room. You could use it for anything you like. I believe the last tenants had an office set up there. Did you see the kitchen has granite counters?"

Nicole flicked her phone's screen with her thumb. "'Two-bedroom in Trendy Hayes Valley.' You're advertising an illegal bedroom." She usually kept her sharpness hidden, the razor blade in the apple. "I'm flagging you on Craigslist."

The woman made a little moue of sympathy, but she'd find plenty of people happy to pay twenty-four hundred to live in Trendy Hayes Valley.

"I have to pee," Nicole announced and stomped down the hallway. She had to pee about every half hour. I followed her into the bathroom.

"Hold this." She thrust the flashlight into my hand.

I pointed it up at the underside of my chin, like telling ghost stories at camp. "Just think; if you take this place—"

"I'm not taking this place. Don't do that flashlight thing, it creeps me out."

"No, wait; if you take it, she'll be able to tell her therapist, 'When I was a kid, my mom made me sleep in the boiler room.'"

"She'll have plenty to tell her therapist without that." Nicole ripped off some toilet paper. "Considering how *sordid* her conception was."

I felt normal. Of course, noticing that I felt normal reminded me things weren't normal. Jeremy was in love with someone else.

I took a shallow breath—my lungs felt like they couldn't do more than that. "You're never going to let me live that down." Weirdly, my voice didn't sound weird.

"I am never going to let you live it down." Standing, she yanked up her stretchy pants. Her mixed-up styles seemed less incoherent these days. Or maybe it was that they matched the incoherence of pregnancy. Pregnant women were like centaurs: human on top, strange below.

Someone knocked on the door, tried the knob. Nicole and I looked at each other and I reached over and rattled our knob, pretending it wouldn't open. "The lock's broken!" I said. "We can't get out!"

"Oh, shit," said the guy on the other side of the door. "Do you want me to get the lady?"

Nicole rolled her eyes at me, trying to swallow a smile.

I called, "Tell her there's a pregnant woman in here about to go into premature labor."

His footsteps pattered towards the kitchen. "God, what are you, fourteen?" whispered Nicole.

I clapped my hands. "Now go into labor! Go into labor!"

"I take it back. You're, like, eleven." She took a couple steps back to better see her stomach in the mirror, pulling her shirt tight, twisting back and forth. "Do you want to come over for a while?"

I kind of did. In Nicole's tiny apartment on Bartlett, everything doubled as something else: kitchen table also her office, couch also her guest room. Nicole slept in the big walk-in closet, which was just wide enough to fit a double bed. If I went over, we'd bake cookies and lie shoulder-to-shoulder in bed and read old issues of *Elle*. But I'd end up telling her about the texts.

"I can't. I have plans." Rapid high-heeled footsteps were coming towards us. "Do you want to leave the door locked and go down the fire escape?"

"Yeah, right. *No.*"

I unlocked the door and opened it in one quick movement. The real-estate woman, who'd been about to knock, had to catch herself from stumbling.

"Sorry," I said. "Total false alarm."

Gita lived on the second floor of an apartment building in the Inner Sunset. The building's left shoulder faced the park but Gita's place was on the right, her front windows looking out on Twelfth Avenue and her side windows onto a narrow alleyway between buildings.

This was the fourth time I'd come to her place. Once I hadn't seen her; once I'd seen just the blue flicker of the TV; once after twenty minutes, as I'd been almost ready to pull myself away, she'd walked up the street with groceries. Gita used cloth grocery bags, remembered to bring them to the store, probably kept them in her purse, which was not actually a purse but a KQED tote bag. She'd fumbled with her keys, let herself in. I'd spent another twenty minutes watching her put away groceries, read something from the mail, take a phone call.

If I watched long enough, surely I'd learn what I needed. I'd see the detail that proved Gita was or wasn't better than me. The thing that said no, Jeremy's not in love with this woman. That said yes, Jeremy's in love with this woman. That told me how to live with someone while he got over someone else.

The window went up in her kitchen. She sat on the sill. For a moment, she put her hands over her face, and I thought, *That's it*. She was pining for Jeremy.

Or she was tired, or had a headache, or couldn't remember what she'd meant to do next. It was crazy to think I could see into Gita by seeing her: crazier to think I could see into *Jeremy* here; craziest of all to think I was going to understand something about my most essential self, outlined against what I was not. Still I couldn't quite bring myself to start the truck, even after she stood, and brushed something off the sill, and closed the window.

Our landlord was on the phone when he answered the door; he pointed at a chair, apparently an invitation to sit, though the seat held a precarious tower of paperwork. More paper and folders covered the floor and piled in snowdrifts against the walls. Mr. Makarov was a CPA. It was hard for me to imagine someone who saw this office wanting to drop more papers into its maw.

Makarov spoke in Russian on the phone. He had a sad, turtle face: weak chin, strong jowls, umber under-eye pouches so heavy that the lower lid pulled down slightly from the eyeball. The call seemed to be social, or at least he was laughing a lot and thumping the desk. By his elbow were stacked little plastic containers of half-and-half; every minute or so, he'd lift one, peel up the foil, and toss back the cream like a shot of whiskey.

Jeremy thought it was important to bring the rent in person, and I'd agreed to do it even though I was sure nothing we did could make Makarov stop hating us. He resented the changes in the Mission, the hipsters and artists and gentrification, even as he wanted Jeremy gone so he could take advantage of those very things.

Finally, he hung up and turned, affecting surprise, as though he'd forgotten my presence. "Mrs. Goldsmith! To what do I owe this honor?"

I held out the rent check. He took it, reaching for another half-and-half, which he drank in two or three contemplative sips. I could see a thick brown plug of wax in his ear. It looked like a fingernail could pop it free with satisfying ease.

"I haven't seen Mr. Goldsmith—"

"He's been in the hospital, he was very sick—"

Our landlord sat up, looking me full in the face. Maybe Jeremy had been right: we just needed to humanize ourselves to Makarov.

He said, "You're not on the lease, Mrs. Goldsmith."

I burst out laughing.

For weeks, I'd been angry at everyone—the slow driver in the left lane, the cashier who didn't know how to ring up a credit-card transaction, the men working on the roof next door, filling the air with the thick, charred smell of tar. I got angry at the newspaper for not refolding neatly and the parking meter for jamming and Web pages for loading too slowly.

Still laughing, I said, "Thanks for the bulletin." As I crossed the room, my foot hit one of the stacks, scattering paper across the floor. It was an accident—*on accident*, Kaylyn would have said—but I didn't stop to fix it.

I walked home strangely euphoric. *You're not on the lease, Mrs. Goldsmith.* He'd be glad if Jeremy died. What a fucking *motherfucker*! I began to laugh again. A woman in front of me, hauling two toddlers by the hands, turned, and the startlement on her face actually made me whoop. She yanked the kids up the street and I had to lean over, hands on my knees, until I could breathe again.

At 2 AM, I was in the bathroom with the shower running. I stood huddled in the corner by the door, hugging myself like that might keep me intact. Of course Jeremy couldn't love me. I was all rags and tatters: not funny, or kind, or interesting, or smart, or cool, all the things I let myself believe by daylight.

When we'd gotten involved, Jeremy had broken up with his girlfriend—the woman at the wedding who'd wanted to know about the fishiness of the fish, the one in the low-backed lilac dress. I asked him a few times how the breakup was going.

Actually, I'd say, "How's Fishcunt?"

He winced and shook his head, laughing. "Come on; *Ashley.*"

Initially Ashley hadn't mattered to me. Jeremy was a guy I'd slept with after a job because I was wired and he seemed really into me and I liked his crooked, not-quite-handsome features and why not?

Then I was so swept up by how quickly and fully we were together, marveling at how much I liked this man who didn't even seem like my type—how much we laughed, how seamlessly we *got* each other—that it seemed only natural his girlfriend of nearly two years, a girlfriend who'd begun to push for marriage, would disappear in the faintest puff of smoke. I knew they talked on the phone; I knew they met at Starbucks for a fraught, unhappy conversation; I knew he went to her birthday party during the period they were trying to stay friends.

The few questions I asked Jeremy about Ashley hadn't come from jealousy but from the desire to revel in the singularity of our connection. Ashley worked at Yahoo in some job with a title that sounded totally make-believe. Ashley was in a book club that *didn't bother discussing books.* Now it occurred to me that breaking up with Ashley because of my awesomeness could also be interpreted as putting a new relationship in place before leaving an old one. Marriage had been on the table between them, and he'd just pushed away.

And God, did I have to make everything a metaphor? It wasn't a table, or a meal; it was probably a fair amount of pain that I'd barely given a second thought.

A knock, and then the bathroom knob rattled. I swallowed and called, "I'm just taking a shower."

He sighed. "I can hear you, you know, Claire."

"I don't—"

"You always turn on the shower when you cry, and it's never worked."

I wanted to open the door and fall into his arms. I held my breath until the impulse passed. When I could talk again, I said, "That's been my trick since I was, like, nine."

"It's not a very good one," he said gently. "You might think about switching."

"Apparently." I leaned my forehead against the door. "What's so great about her?"

"But you already know what she's like."

I felt as drained as if I'd just run for an hour. Jeremy sounded exhausted, too.

"I mean why you—why you feel—"

A pause. "You really want to know?"

Panic flashed in my chest. I put my hands over my mouth so I wouldn't say *No.*

Through the door, he said, "She likes me the way I am."

"How Mr. Rogers of her."

"And it's a relief to talk to someone who gives a shit."

"What does that mean? She's enthusiastic?"

"I mean she actually *cares* what it's like to almost die." From the force of the words, I could tell he'd gone a long time not saying them.

For a moment, I couldn't speak. "I can't believe you just said that to me."

"You're always all, 'It's fine, it's fine.'"

"And half the time when I ask you don't want to talk about it."

"Because I get the sense you want me to—like if I'm anything other than totally stoic, it's whining."

In the steam, the bathroom walls began to swim. "I was at the hospital every day." For once I didn't mind that my voice shook; my sense of outrage was too sure.

He sighed. "Yeah, you're right."

"When you were sick, that was my whole life."

"No, you're right, I *said* you're right. I shouldn't have said it."

I reached across the small room to turn off the shower then lay down by the door, the tiles cold under my cheek. After a moment, I heard him lie down, too.

"We're staying apart. I haven't talked to her."

"Okay."

"I *swear*."

The problem wasn't if he saw her; it was if he wished he could.

"Maybe we need to talk to someone," Jeremy said. "A—you know. A therapist."

"You want to do family *counseling*?"

"Couples—"

"Costa made us do family counseling." And he was also our family counselor. "It's a fucking nightmare."

"*Costa's* a fucking nightmare! We have to do *something*."

"You know what we did once? For a week, we each wore a badge that said I.A.L.A.C., for 'I Am Lovable and Capable.' Out of, like, construction paper. And if someone did something that made you feel bad, you showed them by ripping off a corner of your badge."

After a moment, I saw the tips of his fingers reach through the crack under the door. "You know, of all the messed-up things about your family?" he said. "That might be the very most messed up."

I touched his fingertips with mine. I'd never bothered to tell the I.A.L.A.C. story—it wasn't flashy like the porn subscriptions. But he was right. The thought of how earnestly I'd safety-pinned the paper badge to my shirt made me feel wild with regret and longing, I wasn't even sure for what.

"I can guarantee that you won't have to wear a badge," he said.

Don't cry, don't cry, don't cry.

"Claire, just—We can't go on this way."

I opened my mouth. *Okay*, I'd say. *I'll do it, I'll try.* Deep breath. *I mean, for real I'll try.*

He sighed. "So if you won't do therapy, what do you think we should do?"

I let out the breath. "How about you untext Gita five thousand times?"

"It's not about Gita! I won't keep rehashing that with you. It doesn't go anywhere."

"That would have been some super-useful couples therapy then."

A thud; I jumped. Jeremy had hit the door. "You always have to *win*," he said. "You know what? Fuck you."

"*Really?* 'Fuck you' is the most original response you can come up with?"

"Fuck you," he said again. "Fuck you. That is exactly why fuck you."

21

i expected the building where Gita worked to look beachy—maybe made of weathered gray cedar, perched on a cliff—but it turned out to be an old army barrack, squat and cement, with a yellow and blue vinyl banner, *Center for Marine Education*. No frivolity here; they hadn't even bothered to come up with a name that could work as an acronym. A gray afternoon, March, the damp light crouching low to the ground. When I stepped out into the parking lot, I shivered despite my thermal undershirt and wool socks.

Inside, the first floor looked more like what I'd pictured: big concrete tanks holding fish and rocks, the burble of tubing, wobbly sparkles reflecting off the water onto the walls. I found myself next to a model otter, its skin pulled back over the stomach to show its organs and a tiny, perfectly formed otter fetus. The wall plaque said it was a real otter that had died of algae poisoning and been preserved, pumped full of some kind of plastic.

The kid behind the front desk called out, "Oh, hey! Mrs. Goldsmith!"

He looked vaguely familiar—curly hair, volcanic pimples—but I couldn't get any purchase on the memory. "Um . . ."

"Judah!" He patted his chest.

I started to shake my head, then realized Judah had been one of the students who'd come to visit Jeremy in the hospital. "Oh, *Judah*! How are you?"

"Good, good!"

"Good!"

We nodded at each other a few times. I said, "So, Gita Jayaramen—?"

He pointed me across the lobby, towards a velvet curtain. When I pushed it aside, I found myself in a dark room, huge fish swimming slowly past in purple-lit water. At first, I didn't see anyone but a couple of kids pressing their foreheads against the glass, but at a sound overhead, I made out a group of people on a walkway above the tank. I called up to ask if they knew where Gita was. One of them stepped to the railing.

"Claire?" she said, sounding shocked.

The metal staircase clanged as she descended. She appeared through what I'd taken for a wall but was actually another curtain. When she came close, I felt the cold from her wet suit. Her hair streamed down her back, and her clumped lashes emphasized the darkness of her eyes. In the tight suit, she looked almost glamorous.

She started talking very fast with a lot of gesturing. She'd had to unclog a filter, she said, and she described what she'd done and

why she'd done it even though anyone could have . . . But if you
didn't deal with it right away . . . Once, in Boston . . . She caught
herself, actually jerking a tiny bit. "I'm sorry. I didn't expect—"

"You told me I should stop by sometime."

She nodded a few times and then seemed to realize she was
still nodding and stopped. "I could show you around?" she said.

I followed her out into the central hall, blinking as I adjusted
to the light. Gita went to her office to change into real clothes.
A group of kids in red T-shirts clustered around a shallow touch
pool—little kids, maybe three or four.

Jeremy and I were still having unprotected sex. I'd hoped for
my period and then felt a pinprick of regret yesterday when it
came. What might our child look like? I searched the kids' faces,
but none had a big nose or sharp chin. A volunteer helped a girl
with severe bangs hold a red starfish on her hand. The girl pet-
ted it, like a cat. We could make an actual *person* out of practically thin air. All at once, for the first time, I wanted to know
that person with an urgency that wasn't only about Jeremy.

"Ready?" Gita said, emerging. She looked nervous.

I wanted to keep standing there, watching the weird little girl
with her starfish, but I followed Gita out the rear door, down
the green cement stairs. We crossed a parking lot and climbed
a small dune and suddenly the damp salt smell scratched at
the back of my throat. Most of the time I forgot that we lived
twenty minutes from an ocean.

Gita turned sideways to skitter down the steep dune. The
wind pulled at my hair, whipping it into my face.

She said, "I'm glad you came, I've been feeling really bad
about . . . Jeremy said you . . . the texting . . . it was just like
a conversation."

I wanted to smash my hand into her mouth, to shut her up. Why had I come? "I know that," I said loudly, my voice tight.

"I really like having you as a friend. I can see how it might seem—Oh! Oh!"

I followed her finger, which pointed to the gray waves. "What am I looking for?"

"A seal. You're really lucky; we don't get a lot here. It's . . . there, it surfaced again." She reached up, taking my chin in her fingers, turning it to the right, her touch so unexpected and cold that I didn't think to flinch from it.

"No," I said. "I don't—oh, wait." A sleek black rock had appeared in a spot I didn't think there'd been a rock a moment before. As I watched, a second head joined it. "Is that her baby?"

"Mmmm, not sure. Looks like another adult to me, a mate."

The salty wind made my eyes water. I'd felt sure that seeing Gita would tell me what I wanted to know. I hadn't bothered thinking out what to say, and now I felt at a loss. Gita walked with me to the water's edge, squatted down, and began to point out crabs, a sea urchin, an anemone with peach-colored tentacles, velvet-soft. Her hands windmilled around as she talked about starfish, her face animated with excitement though she must have said the same things a thousand times. Here was someone unembarrassed by enthusiasm. Someone who would risk looking foolish, who didn't even recognize it as a risk.

"This fact, I think you'll love it: starfish compete with fishers for oysters. So oystermen used to catch starfish and hack them up and then dump them back in the water, as trash. Except starfish regenerate lost limbs." She was looking at me expectantly. When I didn't say anything, she explained, "So . . . they were creating more and *more* starfish."

"I was an oyster in our school play. In fourth grade. It was called *O Maryland!*" For the role, I'd worn a too-big gray leotard stuffed with newspaper, braying out the lines, *I'm an oyster, not a clam / You can cook me in a pan / Fry me up or eat me raw / Shellfish are delish, by gaw!* To us, the prestigious parts weren't the ones with the most lines—the Oyster, the Wye Oak Tree, Barbara Fritchie stoutly shouting, *Shoot, if you must, this old gray head*— but roles like Nicole's. She'd gotten to wear a correctly-sized leotard and do round-offs in front of a brown square of kraft paper labeled "Dr. Doughnut Factory" while the rest of us sang, *Ain't it sweet, a breakfast that can't be beat . . .*

Looking concerned, Gita asked, "Are you okay?"

"What? Yeah. I'm fine." Suddenly I knew exactly what I had come to say. I made myself laugh; it came out sounding winded, like I'd sprinted. "The hormones are kind of kicking my ass."

"Hormones."

"I'm pregnant."

She stood, her foot coming down wrong so she had to catch herself. The purity of the pain on her face shocked me. Here it was at last, naked between us. We weren't friends. Or no, weirdly, we were—at that moment, maybe we were more aligned than ever.

When I got home, Jeremy was sitting on the back stairs, looking at our concrete yard, his bad foot stretched out in front of him. He didn't turn when I came through the kitchen door. He said, "Gita called." He hunched further into his sweatshirt. "It's really over. Whatever it even was."

My cheeks went hollow. I put my hand out for the doorframe. Was he calling our marriage "whatever it even was"?

Gita. He must have meant Gita.

"We've known each other a long time. We probably both wondered about—I mean, we have a history, it's natural—but I swear, nothing happened. I love *you*." He closed his eyes and blew out. "She seems to think you're pregnant."

"What did you say?"

"I said, 'Thank you.' I mean, she'd just congratulated me. You're not, are you?"

I shook my head. A shallow wind blew back the tree leaves so that they showed their pale undersides, like Fort flattening his ears against his head.

I nudged his hip with my foot so he'd scooch over to make room. Wedging myself onto the step beside him, I asked, "You okay?"

"Yeah," he said. Then, "Not entirely."

He was going through the pain of a breakup. I pitied him and hated myself for it. The two should have cancelled each other out. But instead they felt like parallel lines that could stretch forever and never touch.

He went on, "It's been so weird, everything going back to normal—I mean, aside from the toes. But otherwise, I can live like nothing ever happened."

"Unless you're hit by a bus tomorrow."

He laughed. "Yes; the bus, the bus."

Without looking over, he reached to interlace his fingers with mine, holding on really tight. I felt as sad as I ever had in my life.

22

*J*eremy came to the door of my workroom. He had an evening staff meeting at W-K he'd forgotten about. "I feel like I have to go. They're being so generous. The advising periods and all."

"Okay."

"I mean, I should do whatever I can."

"No, it's fine, I get it. You should go."

"I think people are getting a drink afterwards. I just want to show I'm still part of the team."

"Whatever you think is best." In truth, I was glad he had a meeting. It had been a week since I'd seen Gita at the marine center, and another two weeks before that since I'd spied on her apartment. The urge to go back, the sense that by seeing her I might understand something I needed to know about myself, had begun to gather in me like a storm front.

"It might go kind of late."

"It's *fine*."

I parked across the street. Gita could have recognized my truck, of course, but I felt much less naked slouched down in the driver's seat than if I'd just stood on the sidewalk. Twenty minutes, I told myself. After twenty minutes, I was going home, whether or not I'd learned the Single Magic Truth about myself that I imagined Gita could show me.

Dusk began to gather, a drawstring slowly pulling closed. Gita's lights went on—right window, long pause, left window—but she was too far back to see. Twenty minutes had passed, then more. This was absurd. I put the key in the ignition and watched myself not turn it.

Ten more minutes, I told myself sternly, and at this reprieve I sagged with relief.

After ten minutes, I told myself, *ten more, and then that's really it*. In the window of the pho restaurant nearest me, a neatly hand-lettered sign read WE ARE CLOSE TODAY. A man turned the corner from Lincoln, pinching the throat of his jacket. I watched his approach, a messenger bag slung across his body. He passed under a streetlight. A buzz raced up the back of my neck.

He wore the gray corduroy jacket I'd given him. I slid down in the seat, heart thumping. Across the street, Jeremy had his forearm braced on the wall above the intercom and his face close to it, as if he was talking to a girl at a party. After a moment, he jumped to open the gate and slipped inside.

My pulse galloped. From this angle, I was too close to the building to see more than a foot or two through the windows. I slid across the seat and out the passenger-side door to the sidewalk. "*Excuse* me," said someone I'd just jostled. I startled, looking around, half expecting everyone else to have frozen to stare at Gita's window, but of course they laughed on their cell phones, or walked with fists jammed into their front pockets. A man passed me with a baby carrier strapped to his chest, the baby inside wriggling like a pinned beetle.

Another step back, but all I could see was the empty living room. And then Gita came into view, walking towards the window, head turned to talk over her shoulder. Jeremy entered the frame, his hand resting on the strap of his bag: a posture so utterly familiar that when Gita pulled the curtains closed, it shocked me to realize I wasn't inside.

Any moment, he could come out the front door, carrying the movie he'd stopped by to borrow. Gita was sponsoring CME internships for W-K students; he could be stopping by to go over paperwork. I needed to pee but didn't dare take my eyes off the door. A man emerged from Gita's building and my heart surged in my chest, but he was heavier than Jeremy. I shook my hands, trying to fling something off, then bent double to steady my breath. An older woman in periwinkle linen looked at me curiously and I straightened up to shout "*What?*" Truck door hanging open like a dislocated shoulder, the interior light weakly illuminating the pavement.

The neighborhood began to shift and settle, grumbling its way into night. There was an explanation. I crossed my legs, pressing them tight together. I willed so hard for him to come through the door that it seemed to shimmer.

My phone buzzed in my pocket: new text from Jeremy. My fingers were shaking; it took two tries to hit the code that unlocked my phone, and I almost dropped it.

Getting a drink with some people.

A great, heavy cold descended through me. I crossed the street, dragged a trash can below the lowest rung of the fire escape. With each step, the ladder creaked and swayed. Luckily Gita lived on the second floor.

The window was a couple inches open. Sliding my fingers under the sash, I pushed it up as silently as I could. Halfway, it stopped. Smushing my face against the glass, I jammed my arm up inside, twisting my hand to find the obstruction, a dowel. After a few tries, I yanked it out and pushed the window the rest of the way. The opening was only about a foot wide. I decided to go headfirst. My hips got stuck long enough to alarm me—it seemed brilliant to just materialize inside the apartment, but not to materialize *halfway* into the apartment, like Winnie the Pooh. Then I twisted and slid through.

From the other room, a rustle—sheets being thrown back— and Jeremy's voice asking, "What was that?"

Footsteps came towards me.

I was in Gita's apartment. I felt winded with fear—not of being discovered, but of discovering them. As long as nothing was acknowledged, it might still be reversible.

"Oh my God," Jeremy said. "Oh fuck. Oh my God."

I was the one who got him to wear boxers; he used to wear the same brand of dingy white cotton briefs his mother had bought him in first grade.

"Tell me," I said.

We stared at each other. I was dimly aware of Gita behind him, but I couldn't have broken our gaze even if I'd wanted to. From Gita, a soft click, intake of breath; she was about to say something. Without looking over I said, "Don't!" To Jeremy: "Tell me."

In a small, miserable voice he said, "I was here."

"Um, I *know* you were here? Obviously? I don't go climbing into random apartments in case one happens to—"

"Don't do that! Jesus, Claire."

"Just tell me where you were."

"Claire—"

"Stop saying my name, I'm not *five*. Tell me where you were."
He let out a long breath.

"Just say it."

"In the bedroom."

"Were you—" But then I couldn't bring myself to say having sex. *Making a baby without making a baby.* "Hmm, let me guess." I wanted my voice to come out casually but it shook.

"I'm so—" Gita said.

"You! You are the most boring person I've ever met. You're like, you're *nothing*."

Jeremy took a step towards her. "Come on. You don't need to—"

"Don't tell me what I 'need to'! God!" I grabbed a wineglass from the table and threw it against the wall; it bounced then shattered, musically, on the floor. I picked up the other glass. Pride swelled in the back of my throat—here I was, not holding it together for once—but as soon as I thought it, conviction deserted me. I covered my face, swaying in place.

When I dropped my hands, Jeremy and Gita stood together across the room, too close, her hand over her mouth. Jeremy started to lift his arm, as if to put it around her, then jerked and stopped himself. My groin felt like it was on fire, but I would rather have died of a burst bladder than ask to use her bathroom.

He said, "I was planning . . . I didn't want to hurt you."

"That was a very excellent strategy."

"Yeah, apparently."

My heart dented.

"Do you—" Gita said. "Do you want some tea?"

I glanced at Jeremy. I wanted to say, *And we always thought she didn't have a sense of humor*, but I couldn't wait another second. "Bathroom!"

Gita was saying, "What?" as Jeremy pointed and I pushed past them, shoving open the door with my forearm, kicking it closed. I ripped at my fly's buttons and at this signal my body let go. Urine splashed my wrist and jeans while I struggled to get them down. I flung up the toilet lid with a crash and peed and peed, the stream tapering then surging, as if beginning all over again.

For a long time afterward, I stayed with my head on my knees, wet clothes yoking my ankles. The bathroom began to feel very hot, the edge of my vision starting to buzz. I stood, trying to drag up my pants, and almost fell over. Sweat prickled at my hairline. I lunged forward to lean on the sink, running some cold water on a washcloth, pressing it behind my neck. My vision cleared, the heat receding. Beads of cold water ran down my back.

They sprang up from the kitchen table when they saw me. Jeremy had gotten dressed and Gita had pulled on some burgundy sweatpants. "Are you okay?" Jeremy said.

"I'll do it," I said in what felt like a calm voice. "Couples therapy. I'll do it."

Jeremy looked very tired. "Claire—"

"We're *married*."

"Claire—"

"And I know you've been through so much, and that I wasn't

always there in the way I wanted to be, and that it must have seemed easier to throw yourself into something new—"

"Claire, that's—"

"What we have is, people don't just find that and then throw it away. It's—"

Jeremy raked his hair back from his forehead with both hands. "Claire, my God! You asked if we're sleeping together and I said yes."

"Well, you didn't actually say yes; you inclined your head regally to imply it."

"You can't let the littlest thing go. The littlest thing."

"Is this 'the littlest thing'? Fucking someone? Fucking someone who—please don't tell me those sweatpants say 'Harvard' across the ass."

"You see? Why can't you be real for one second?"

"I just said I'd do couples therapy."

"Claire, no! Stop. Right now is exactly why this isn't working. It isn't going to work."

The overhead bulb trembled. "That can't—That can't—" I looked over at Gita; her expression was twisted with pity. "Shut up!" I told her, and suddenly saw how I must look in the fluorescent light of the kitchen, flushed and loud, wearing piss-soaked jeans, clutching my hair and breathing too fast.

Jeremy said, "I was telling the truth before. Nothing physical happened until . . . Well, mostly nothing."

I stood up very straight. I pulled my shirt down, smoothed my hair with my hands. I licked my thumb, stepped forward to press it quick and hard against his forehead.

He jerked back. "What was that?"

I said, "That was your gold star."

part three
the naked family

23

*t*uesday night was Caring for Your Newborn. Thursday we had Labor. There was also a two-Saturdays Lactation class, but I'd begged out of that one. Tuesdays, a laundry basket was passed around so that each couple could pluck out one of the dolls, which seemed to be stuffed with wet sand. I tilted ours, its heavy head hanging back and then flopping forward with a disturbing thud.

"Resuscitation. This is not the same for a little one." Joelle was a ruthlessly cheerful RN in her forties. I'd thought at first that she wore the same silky cheetah-print shirt every class but then began noticing subtle variations—a puffed sleeve, a covered placket—that indicated she had a wardrobe of silky cheetah-print shirts. I spent class mostly waiting for moments of high emotion, when her carefully repressed Tennessee accent emerged.

Otherwise, I looked at the other couples and tried to imagine their stories. Five straight couples, one lesbian couple. One gay man and his straight woman best friend. We couldn't tell if Gary had fathered Andrea's child or if he was just being supportive, like me with Nicole. Normally I would have admired their privacy, but it had a smirking smugness: they'd think having any curiosity about them was unimaginative and heteronormative. I decided now that Gary was the biological father, but they wouldn't have wanted to have a doctor do the insemination because, you know, *the medical establishment*, and when Andrea had said, "We could . . ." Gary hadn't bothered to hide that the idea of sex with her repelled him. Alone in the bathroom some weeks later—naked from the waist down, her legs up the wall, having basted her cervix with sperm—Andrea cried a little with loneliness, but told herself she was moved by the significance of the occasion. A few years from now, they were going to have a massive falling-out and Gary was going to get very self-righteous about his custody rights, even though he hadn't been all that involved, and the legal stuff would be a total nightmare. I began feeling bad for Andrea.

Nicole pushed herself up from her chair. It still surprised me that all the normal rules of pregnancy applied to her: her face had filled out; she walked with that cowboy swagger, like someone just off a horse. She was at thirty-six weeks.

Jeremy had been gone four months.

Joelle said, "Don't be shy, ya'—*you all*. Come in close."

The room was windowless, fluorescents buzzing overhead like gnats. Joelle briskly sanitized the doll's face, then pretended to find it unconscious and gasped loudly, as though her performance needed to reach the back row of a theater. Stricken, she shook the doll's shoulder, shouting into its face, *Bye-bee, bye-bee, are you oh-kai?* I didn't look at Nicole, and I could feel her not look at me so we wouldn't laugh and have to fake coughing fits and run from the room like in ninth-grade health class when someone used the phrase "girl parts."

Caring for Your Newborn started in late afternoon, still light out, and so it always felt strange afterwards to emerge to early evening, air the soft blue of carbon paper, telephone wires stitching the sky. Nicole was going to have the baby at the same hospital where Jeremy'd been, but luckily her classes were in a weird office building a few blocks down Van Ness.

I waited on the stairs for Nicole, who was peeing for about the eighth time. Little kids played across the street. One had a toy gun; the others were probably not allowed them, which meant they'd turned anything they could find into guns: plastic bottle, stick. "I killed you to death!" shouted a boy who looked about six. He wore a Smiths T-shirt and wielded a twisted-up newspaper.

When Nicole emerged we walked down to Hayes Valley. Blue Bottle was the only coffee shop I could tolerate these days. Ritual was full of lovely, ironic girls in too-short bangs and Gunne Sax dresses. Four Barrel was full of people too cool for Ritual, girls so luminous that even their mullets and Iron Maiden T-shirts and slightly-infected lip piercings didn't dent their loveliness. I felt Jeremy's absence as something narrow and sharp lodged in my chest. As long as I didn't breathe in too deeply, I almost didn't feel it, but certain things made it wobble dangerously. For example, girls in Gunne Sax. If Jeremy had fallen in love with someone like that, someone younger, serene in her own beauty, at least I'd understand it. Then I'd think,

That's exactly the kind of thought Jeremy would see as shallow and beside the point. Except he'd think the fact I'd have such a shallow and beside-the-point thought was exactly the point.

Blue Bottle consisted of a counter across the mouth of what had been a garage, in a narrow alleyway. I ordered a Gibraltar, not on the menu—you had to know about it to order one. In my head, Jeremy sneered at this pretension, and I had to remind myself I wasn't showing off: I actually thought the Gibraltar was the perfect drink. Since Jeremy had gone, my whole personality felt unstable. I was supposed to be wanted, not the obstacle to what was wanted.

There was only one table at the café—everyone else sat on the sidewalk, or stood in little clusters in the alley, moving out of the way for the occasional car. When Nicole and I turned with our coffees, the guy at the table—a bike messenger with muscled calves and a shaved head—glanced over idly before seeing Nicole's belly and jumping up from his seat. He looked like the guys I dated before Jeremy. On his shins and forearms were tattooed austere and oddly beautiful line drawings of the bones below. Nicole thanked him, putting her cup down very carefully, then backed into the chair and lowered herself slow as a winch. The bike messenger moved a few feet away and leaned against the wall. I remembered Jeremy lifting his bike from the street, his leg bleeding.

Nicole jerked upright: "Oh! She's kicking!"

She grabbed my hand, moving it under her shirt and onto her stomach, which roiled and leapt. Something about it made me feel motion sick: maybe that the kicks seemed so random and unpredictable, or maybe that I couldn't tell what part was writhing under my hand. I held on just long enough to demonstrate my appreciation for the miracle of life, then took my hand away. "Wow." The word came out anemically, and I was glad Jeremy watched only from inside my head. Every thought led back to him. I could make any stick or bottle into a gun and turn it on myself.

"What if it's really, really painful and I can't handle it?"

"You'll handle it," I said automatically.

"I don't want drugs. I want it totally natural. Don't let me ask for drugs."

"Okay, I won't." We had this conversation at least twice a week. Before she could add, *Not even if I really, really beg*, I said, "Not even if you beg."

She nodded, relieved. "You promise you'll keep your phone charged? And near you?"

She still had five weeks to go, but I said, "I'll charge it anytime it's even just down to two bars. *Nicole.* I'll be there."

She smiled ruefully, then said, "Oh! That was another!" putting her hand on her belly. The baby kicked so hard that Nicole's arm jerked. Sharp and precise and sudden, I had a memory of Jeremy standing next to Gita in her living room, the moment he'd almost put his arm around her then stopped himself.

More and more, every moment seemed clogged by memory in this way. I'd be at Rainbow, plonking green apples into a bag, and out of the very corner of my eye my earlier self would be there, too, picking out a wooden cutting board for Jeremy for the first night of Hanukkah. Maybe when old people said they felt ready to die, it was because every moment was so thickened with associations that they could barely move.

Nicole stirred sugar into her decaf latte, spoon clicking against the cup. "Have you thought about what you guys'll do about your place?"

"I don't know." Tiredly, I scrubbed my face with my hands. I felt like I had sand inside my eyelids. "I guess, eventually . . . I don't know. He's coming over in a couple days so we can talk."

To my surprise, Jeremy hadn't moved in with Gita but with his friend Steph and her three boys, sleeping on the pullout couch. He hadn't told his parents we'd separated, which seemed like a mark in my column. He said, *I need some space to figure out what I even want.* Clearly he was wrapped up with Gita in some romantic way—I mean, they'd *fucked*, so: obviously—but I had no depth perception. Was I looking at something big, or just something extremely close? If I was good enough, Jeremy might return. I finished jobs on time, I didn't yell at an oblivious driver, I sat at the kitchen table every morning and dutifully read the front page before the arts section. The sense that my virtue registered on some great, cosmic whiteboard made me feel less helpless.

And then three in the morning might find me bursting out of our house with a groggy but game Fort, race-walking the streets until night began to leach from the sky and we stumbled home to collapse for a couple hours on the couch. I avoided the bedroom Jeremy and I had shared. Aside from Fort, I didn't want to be around anyone but Nicole. Even with her, I made sure to keep my dark hemisphere turned away.

She twisted her cup on its saucer to the right, then left, like working a combination lock. "You could get a roommate."

"I'm too old to live with a stranger. Even in college it didn't work for me."

"Right, Rat Girl." My frosh roommate at Santa Cruz had carried her pet rat around campus inside her bra and let him run free around our room. "Anyway, I wasn't thinking about a stranger."

"Who then?" I asked. "*Oh*. No way."

"Why?"

"Just because there's no way."

"I've been thinking about this." She jabbed out one finger. "You have a huge place—"

"Not *huge*."

"—which you can't afford, even if your landlord doesn't figure out Jeremy is gone." A second finger: "I can't do two flights of stairs with a baby and a stroller and groceries." Third finger. "Schlepping my laundry to Gymfinity is kicking my ass."

I couldn't admit that I thought Jeremy might come back. *Really?* Nicole might say, and the doubt would scare away the possibility of his return. "My house isn't exactly a healthy place for a baby. It's full of, like, paint thinner."

"So you'll get a lock for your studio."

"Nicole, no. I just—I have all my stuff. No."

"Why does everything have to be exactly the way you want it?"

"Right. Because this is *exactly* what I wanted."

Nicole glared at me and heaved herself up. She stomped down the alley, past the store selling fetish-wear corsets and the greasy pavement of the engine repair place, towards the little park wedged between Octavia and Laguna. I stayed at the table, waiting for her to work it out and come back.

Over the months we'd lived apart, Jeremy and I had maintained contact. I texted about bills, or to tell him his alumni magazine had come and what should I do with it? He stopped by the house to pick stuff up—clothes he'd forgotten because they were in the wash; some books. If he'd really wanted to avoid me, he could have bought new copies, right? Another mark in the ongoing tally. And then we crossed paths occasionally by accident. San Francisco wasn't small, but Jeremy hadn't yet figured out a new set of resources: he still got his shirts dry-cleaned on Twenty-Fourth Street, still shopped at Rainbow, still rented DVDs at Lost Weekend. In fact, he still used our shared membership and once, missing him, I took out the Turkish movie he'd just returned. Watching it, I was so distracted by imagining what he might have thought—and had he watched it with Gita?—that I switched it off midway. I ejected the disc from my computer and walked with it to my workroom and dragged the tip of a skew chisel across the back, etching a long, deep scratch. Jeremy's credit card was the one linked to the account.

I would never have guessed the power of a lie to make the whole world seem unreal. I didn't trust my feelings about anything—but then I didn't trust even *that* feeling. Hadn't I known all my life that people cheated? That you couldn't be surprised by it, or even blame them really? If infidelity was so understandable, how could it so unmoor me?

When it became clear Nicole wasn't coming back, I got a paper cup for the rest of her cold latte. She was at the edge of the little park, watching a father and daughter scramble around on the rope jungle gym.

I touched her shoulder. "Are you oh-kai, bye-bee?"

She took the cup without looking at me.

"It's just—living together seems so hippie and utopian," I said. "Like something our parents would be into."

"It's so different I don't even know where to begin."

"Plus people get *shot* in my neighborhood."

Still watching the girl climbing with her dad, she said, "Don't pretend you're not into that."

"People getting shot?"

"You love how edgy you are. You're like a tourist of sketch."

The pointed thing in my chest shifted, a sharp jab. I didn't mind the words themselves; hearing even an unflattering truth made me feel known. It was that only she and Jeremy knew me well enough to see through my postures.

"How many of your neighbors have you ever even talked to?" she asked. "I mean, talked to enough to actually know anything about them."

"Fine. If you want *honesty*, don't pretend you're not glad Jeremy left."

"What? I like Jeremy."

I raised my brows at her. Liking him wasn't the point. She didn't want to be the only one who couldn't make a relationship work.

She dropped her gaze from mine. "Just say you'll think about it."

24

*O*n the day we'd agreed to meet, Jeremy showed up exactly on time, carrying two cardboard boxes that had once held Girl Scout cookies. He took off his jacket—the gray corduroy one I'd given him—and slung it, unthinkingly, over the back of his chair at the table, as he'd done thousands of times. Part of me went, *Wait, boxes? Wait, boxes? Boxes?*, the familiarity and unfamiliarity of him there too overstimulating.

In the months Jeremy had been gone, he'd gained weight. He'd always been very thin and so the extra pounds hardly made him stocky, but he seemed more solid than ever before. He'd grown a beard, which had come in patched with gray. In the past, I would have mocked it a little. *Wow, you've got quite the Amish thing going.* The words sounded so clearly in my head it felt like hearing an echo.

He would have laughed and replied, *Wow, you've got quite some manners going.*

"Hey, you." I was determined to demonstrate how very excellently I was holding up, and maybe how wrong he'd been to leave such an excellently-holding-up person. I kissed him quickly on the cheek, which seemed friendly and detached, all *I'm so okay with things I can kiss your cheek and it's no big deal.* The kiss had been part of the plan, but I hadn't planned on my heart racing.

I could see the kiss took him aback. "Listen, Claire; I want to say—"

"Want some tea?"

He glanced up sharply and I realized he thought I might be making fun of Gita. I kept my face mild. I'd thought I'd want to hear about her, but now I found myself terrified by the prospect.

"Um, yeah, I guess. Sure."

The instinct to reach out and touch his face was so strong that I balled my fists in my pockets. His beard made me think of days he hadn't shaved, the way his stubble rasped my thighs when he went down on me. In the past I'd touched every part of him, this half-stranger who was still my husband. If I commented on the beard, in actuality he'd probably shake his head, looking away from me. *Why are you always so bitter?*

Fort had heard Jeremy's voice; he came skidding in from where he'd been sleeping on the couch. Jeremy knelt, grinning broadly, saying, "Oof" happily as Fort crashed into him. He laughed and pulled Fort's ears. "Whoa, big guy. You don't know your own size."

"So, um, boxes," I said.

Jeremy looked up, warily. "I thought you—I mean, I said—"

Somehow—shamefully—I'd heard whatever he'd said about *needing to talk about next steps* as ambiguous. "I was stating a fact. You brought boxes. You're moving in with—?"

"Yeah. I'm sorry."

My stomach felt painfully hollow. With some idea that it would make me seem admirable and quiet, I'd dug out a skirt and ballet flats from a temp job I'd once had. I'd stayed up most of the night to clean, trying to construct a stage set for the play called *My Life's Not Pathetic, In Fact It's Bitchin'*. I felt tissue-thin from lack of sleep.

But for all the ways my childhood had ill prepared me for adulthood, at least I was good at pretending to be fine. "Obviously, I knew it was coming eventually. Let's just do this."

"We don't have to."

"I don't want to drag it out. Take the things you want and, I don't know. I guess if it's not equal, you should keep more of the savings."

He gently pushed Fort's muzzle aside. "Okay, boy. Enough for now."

I looked around the kitchen, trying to seem like I had a plan. I opened the nearest cabinet. "I guess we can begin anywhere. What about the stockpot?"

"You can keep it," Jeremy said. "We have one."

To hear him say *we* and not mean us. I paused, letting the wound open in me, slow and voluptuous. Then I lifted the pot. "I think these cost about eighty dollars, and it's three years old, so do you think it's depreciated—what? Like half?"

"Come on, Claire. I'm not going to let you pay me for the stockpot."

"Not pay; how we divide our savings."

"Still."

"Fine. Then we'll make that corner the Goodwill pile." I heaved the pot so that it hit with a crash, skidding across the linoleum. My phone buzzed and I glanced at it: Nicole. "Do you want the knives?"

"I'll take the big one."

I handed it over. "What about the others?"

"You can have them."

"I only ever use the big one."

"Jesus, Claire! Then take the big one. I'll take the little ones." He crossed his arms over his chest. "You're really skinny."

I shrugged. "Not super-hungry."

"You can write a bestseller. *The Infidelity Diet*."

I laughed, then stopped because it hurt. No one else would have made that joke, or known I'd find it funny. "Radio?"

He sighed. "This is going to take forever. Why don't I just tell you which things I want and you can keep the rest?"

"I'm *trying* to be fair." I took a step towards him. How many times had we kissed in this kitchen? How could something that existed stop existing?

"Pot rack?" My voice came out clotted.

He shook his head. I dumped the pot rack into the corner with a crash.

"You're acting like I meant for this to happen." Jeremy walked over to the stockpot, pushing it neatly against the wall with the side of his sneaker. Was he limping more, or had it just become unfamiliar to me again? "I always felt like it was *you* who had one foot off the ground. Like you always thought you could get out if things got bad."

"Like if maybe you almost died?"

"You're not going to let anything I say be right."

Actually he *was* partly right. When we married, I didn't think *yes, the rest of my life, no matter what.* I could see only a few feet in front of me. Love for him filled that space; I'd hoped it would be enough.

I said, "Bath towels? Sheets?"

"Our bed's a double."

Our bed. Deep breath. "So how much do you want for the sheets?"

"I don't want anything for the fucking sheets! Can't we do this and get it over with?"

"I'm trying to be fair," I said again. I wasn't going to accept so much as a soap dish or a roll of paper towels; I couldn't stand to be even that much in his debt. I opened the drawer where we kept brown paper and stamps. "How much do you want for this stuff?"

"A hundred dollars?"

"Come on."

"You're right. One-fifty. That's my final offer, though."

"Don't *jolly* me."

His smile slid off. "You can't see that it's even a little bit humorous that you want me to sell you our old packing tape?"

"You just want to get done as fast as possible!" I hated the way it escaped, shrill and childish. He opened his mouth and I threw my hand up: "No!"

"I was going to ask what you want to do about Fortinbras." "*Do?*"

"We could split the week, maybe," he said. "Or alternate weeks." I must have looked shocked. "He *is* both of ours."

"Jesus." I raised my hands, then dropped them. "Do you have to want the one good thing I still have?"

"Fine," Jeremy said quickly. "You keep Fort."

Hearing his name, Fort lurched up again, tags jangling. He headed for Jeremy but I caught his collar, dropping to my knees to hug him, which he suffered nobly. I'd be better to him; I'd walk him more, and take him to the park. I put my hand behind his neck, pressing my cheek against his hard, round skull. They were going to leave him in Gita's apartment while they were off at work all day? What were the chances her building allowed even small pets, let alone a dog that weighed a hundred and ten pounds? Probably Jeremy had brought it up so that then he'd have the chance to give in and seem generous.

"Don't think you get points for this," I said.

"Points. *God*." His look of weariness would have filleted me if I'd let it. "I'm not the bad guy, Claire. Maybe you need to see things that way, but we just aren't good for each other anymore."

There were a dozen ways I could have argued. The urge felt like an allergy, a pressure in the sinuses. But what would have been the point? I buried my face in Fort's back, which smelled of cedar from the bed I'd made him.

When he'd gone, taking nothing with him, I let Fort out into the backyard and lay down on the kitchen floor. The wood under my cheek was cool, gritty with dirt. The light faded, the day collapsing in on itself. It was my devastation that devastated me. Who *was* this person lying on the floor because her marriage was over? Back in elementary school, we had watched a film about drug dealers who supposedly hung around playgrounds. The guy playing the long-haired, denim-jacketed pusher rasped, *Whaddya want, kid? I got 'ludes, I got dust . . .* I felt something like that now, tricked into dependence on something I hadn't even *wanted* before Jeremy offered it.

Fort whined and scratched at the door screen. *You're not awake and not asleep*, Costa used to say when I "went back." *You're not yourself.*

Night crept in.

My phone buzzed. Nicole, shaky and joyous.

I expected the second we arrived at the ER to be whisked to Labor and Delivery, but they seemed unconcerned about Nicole's state, at least unconcerned enough to spend time getting her insurance information and ask why she hadn't preregistered.

"I'm three weeks early," she said.

"That's barely anything," the woman muttered. She licked her forefinger to begin pulling out paperwork from her desk cubbies.

Labor and Delivery could be the name of an alt-country album, I would have said to Jeremy. I'd known being back here would feel weird, but I hadn't expected the total sense of dislocation. For the first time in months, I felt married. Technically, I *was* married. But now I felt Jeremy right there, right upstairs, waiting for me.

"I'm going to call up to L and D," the woman said. "You can have a seat."

I got Nicole to a chair, but the thought of sitting down made my legs ache.

"They've stopped," Nicole said.

"What have?"

"Contractions."

"We should go, then." Relief flooded me. We'd go home, and by the time she went into actual labor, I'd have had the chance to steel myself against the mindfuck of reentering the hospital, site of my failures. "It was a false alarm."

She looked uncertain.

I saw an orderly with a wheelchair stop at the reception desk. "Let's get out of here."

"You're freaking out," she said, amused. "You're freaking out more than me." And then she gasped, grabbing the sides of her chair seat, rising partway to standing. "*Wow wow wow*," she breathed.

The orderly was beside us with the wheelchair. Why had I just taken Nicole's word for it that it was time to come in? I tried to explain to the orderly that she probably wasn't in labor after all.

"No, I think this is it," Nicole said.

"Here is my motto." The orderly drew himself up, mock-serious, and pointed one finger towards the ceiling like an orator. "'Always listen to the pregnant lady.' Otherwise, pregnant ladies turn into rhinos." He put his hand to his forehead, where a horn would be. It was clear he'd made this joke a lot: he scrunched his face, then dipped to suggest a charge. Straightening, he laughed loudly.

Over the next hour, we heard variations on this theme: an irate pregnant woman would rip you to shreds, and you'd have no one to blame but yourself. It was said in tones of voice that ranged: sympathy, mild joshing, scorn accompanied by a hard glance at me that meant *pull yourself the fuck together, girlfriend*.

Nicole leaned into the wall, head on her arms. "Counterpressure," the nurse checking Nicole's IV line said to me.

I looked at her blankly.

"Counterpressure. You want to do this." She fit one leg behind Nicole's leg to brace herself, and pressed both hands hard into the small of Nicole's back. Nicole groaned.

My forehead was hot and prickly; my vision began to dim, contracting from all sides. "See?" the nurse said, her voice coming from far away, like she was speaking through a metal pipe, and then the pipe filled with gushing water. I felt faraway hands pushing me into a chair.

I breathed raggedly until my vision cleared. I hadn't slept the night before, and I'd barely eaten. I stood when I felt like I could manage it without falling. "Fresh air. I think I just need air and maybe something to eat."

The nurse said, "There's a cafeteria—"

"Basement, I know."

Running down the fire stairs, through the lobby, pushing the heavy revolving door. It felt like being underwater, desperate to get to the surface.

Outside, I took deep gulps of air, lungs burning, face rashy with heat. I started to sit on a low wall by the front steps, but my chest felt too tight. I walked up the sidewalk, trying to calm the jabbering inside me. When I got to the edge of the hospital drive, I turned back, walking to the stairs. I don't know how many loops I made before I began feeling like I could breathe most of the way again. How long had I been out here? Thirty minutes? Five? I headed for the stairs, but the sight of the heavy front doors made me seize up.

"Okay," I said out loud. "Okay." I'd give myself another minute. I walked to the end of the sidewalk, to the stairs.

I hesitated.

The baby was going to be born if I was there or not. People up there knew what to do.

Half-experimentally, I took a step off the curb. It should have felt like jumping out the back door of the school bus. I almost expected alarms. But of course: nothing at all happened. I could just walk away.

25

*f*or almost a week, maybe more than a week, Fort and I barely
left the couch. Magazines and sections of the *Times* littered the
coffee table and spilled over onto the floor. Fur hazed the rug,
blankets, upholstery. I let clients' calls go to voicemail and deleted them without listening. I scratched dead skin from my
scalp until it bled, then forced myself to avoid the spot until a
scab could form. Nothing else was as good as sliding the very
edge of my fingernail under a scab, all the way around, and then
pulling it up, brittle and bumpy, the size of a tick. I pressed a
finger against the sting on my scalp, feeling the drop of blood
and a tight, sour pinch at the back of my throat.

The day I'd deserted my post at the hospital, I'd driven down
Van Ness, the glass storefront of the Bentley dealership glitter-
ing in the late-afternoon light, achingly beautiful. When I got
home, I discovered I wasn't hungry. I brushed my teeth while I

showered, a habit Jeremy had always thought was weird, and for once the thought of Jeremy didn't hollow me out. There was no freedom in the world like not caring.

I slept. When I woke up around 4 AM, I remembered that something wonderful had happened. Then I remembered what it was and sat up with a gasp.

Gray, underwater days. I thought about Nicole until it got too painful; then I switched to Gita and Jeremy until it got too painful; then I thought about Nicole. I remembered her turning handless cartwheels in Matt Sarnie's trashed living room, then lifting her beer bottle to take a dainty sip. How she held in a smile while we clapped, and how this failure at modesty had made me love her more.

At the edge of the coffee table—next to the old, mistaken condolence card *so sorry for your loss*—was a picture of the day we got married, Jeremy wearing his good suit and me in a periwinkle-blue dress from the twenties, heavy with glass beads. Jeremy's arm around my shoulder, both my arms around his waist, grinning like little kids. It had been five months since we met. The myth we spun around ourselves had always been about the randomness of fate: what if his girlfriend hadn't asked about the fish, what if we hadn't shared that ironic glance, what if the next day I hadn't agreed to breakfast? How easy, though, to turn the story of a lucky accident into just an accident.

I googled everyone Jeremy had ever dated. Allegra taught painting at a state college in Maine; the girl who'd been his first kiss at CTY had converted to Mormonism and had five children. Ashley, Fishcunt, still worked at Yahoo as an Interaction Manager. The housemate he'd dated for a short while had published a novel, to little notice, apparently narrated from the perspective of an undocumented migrant fruit picker.

I called up press releases from the Center for Marine Education. I read an old interview with Gita in the *Globe*. I couldn't blame Jeremy for wanting someone great. And when I seemed to find evidence of her ordinariness, that felt awful, too, since then I'd been not even as good as someone ordinary.

On the seventh or eighth or ninth couch day, the doorbell rang. *Jeremy*, I thought, then *Nicole*.

But it was Hal, holding a box. He peered past me, at the murky hallway.

"Wow. This is really depressing."

"I've been busy. And I wasn't expecting anyone."

"Maybe if you checked your phone. Are you going to let me in? This is heavy."

I had checked my phone, obsessively, but I'd deleted anything not from Jeremy or Nicole—which was to say, all the calls I'd actually gotten. I stood aside and Hal pushed past. In the kitchen, he used his foot to shove aside one of the half-filled boxes—pot rack, knives—then put down the box he'd been holding. "Oof. That's his leftover food. And I found some other things around the house, that cloth water bowl thing, and the other leash. And that soft yellow toy is in there."

"The duck?"

"No, elephant."

"Right." I felt worn-out from having to string together so many words in a row. "I have kind of a headache. Jeremy and I . . ."

When I couldn't finish, he nodded. "Bella said."

Hal followed me into the living room, checking out the tiny skyline of empty wine bottles I'd erected against the wall. While

I waited for him to tell me how awesome I was for not bathing, I reached for the aspirin. My headaches had been so constant that I didn't even bother putting the cap back on the bottle after shaking four pills onto my palm. "I should invest in Excedrin."

"You should invest in some *food*. When's the last time you had a meal?"

"I'm really not in the mood for—"

"Because you look fucking awful."

I gaped at him, then laughed. It felt like the most honest thing he'd said to me in years. Laughing made my headache worse, and I cradled my forehead in my hands. After a minute, Hal sat down and put a tentative arm around me.

I sagged against his shoulder, then caught myself and sat upright. "That was weird. Sorry."

"Why do you always do that? Act like we barely know each other?"

"Please don't," I said. "I can't talk anymore about how messed up I am."

"I didn't say you're messed up."

"Okay, well, at Jeremy's girlfriend's apartment, I pissed on the floor."

"On purpose? That's badass."

"It could not have been less badass." Fortinbras, sleeping in the corner, woke and lifted his massive head a few inches and straightened his legs, his whole body trembling with the stretch. "I know you don't like Jeremy much—"

"Jeremy was fine. I just didn't think he—I never totally got you *marrying* him. He seemed like such a normal guy."

"He was so much better than me. And I'm probably going to get evicted, and I haven't done any work in, like . . . And then Nicole had her baby, and I . . ." I pressed my lips together, unable to go on. "She wanted to move here with the baby, and I said no because I can't, I just can't, and everything I touch, *everything* I touch, turns to shit."

Hal took my hands, hauling me to my feet. "I'm taking you to dinner." From a pile on the couch, he dug out Jeremy's gray corduroy jacket, forgotten behind on the day he'd come over with his Girl Scout boxes. I'd been using the coat as a pillow, periodically turning my nose to huff its fumes.

Hal held up the coat. What was I supposed to do next? He stepped closer, taking my arm and threading it into the sleeve.

"You're being so nice," I said.

"You probably won't believe this—I know we don't hang out much. But you mean a lot to me."

"No offense, but that's pretty sad."

I regretted the words immediately. Why was I always so bitter? Hal raised his eyebrows and I felt my shoulders pull up, but then to my relief he shook his head and half-laughed through his nose.

"Quit stalling." He did up the snaps on my coat. "I'm your friend right now whether you want one or not. You're going to have to wait to pick a fight until after you've had something to eat."

26

*N*icole lived in a studio apartment on Bartlett, the street that divided the gentrified and less-gentrified parts of the Mission. One block west was Valencia, all perfectly curated vintage stores and Belgian frites; one block east, Mission Street, with its taquerias and discount furniture emporiums. On Mission, you could buy a life-sized ibex statue with gold horns, or crack. On Valencia, a custom-written letter smaller than a postage stamp and a magnifying glass with which to read it.

I knocked on the door of her apartment and heard running. The door swung open to show Nicole in a baggy maternity dress that reached midthigh, one hand pressed to her abdomen. "It's you," she said flatly.

Since Hal's visit, I'd been calling her twice a day. She let my calls go to voicemail. I held up peonies. "I brought you these."

"She's asleep. I just got her *down*." On cue rose a thin wail. "*Fuck*." She turned and made for the walk-in closet, which she used as her bedroom, leaving me in the open doorway.

The baby's crying swelled, then cut off midhowl. Nicole hadn't indicated I could come in, but she hadn't slammed the door on me, either. I took a step into the room. Normally, she slept surrounded by hanging clothes, but now everything was piled on the couch still on its hangers, slacks and workout clothes jumbled together. The apartment reeked of sulfur and iron: boiled cabbage, blood.

I found an old spaghetti sauce jar for the peonies and stuck them on the table, then approached the closet slowly, as though a sudden move would startle Nicole into remembering to kick me out. She knelt on the bed, a baby tight against her shoulder. She didn't meet my eyes or acknowledge she knew I was there, and for a minute we stayed that way, Nicole jiggling the baby and crooning to her until the lines of the baby's body softened into sleep. In my imagination, housing an extra tiny person in this apartment hadn't seemed like a big deal. But the baby took up much more space than her actual size.

I whispered, "Listen, I am so sorry. More than sorry."

"That you even think you can apologize shows how much you don't get it." Nicole's voice was trembling, but she kept it quiet.

"I know."

"I kept saying, 'My sister's coming back, she'll be here any second.' It hurt so much, and I was screaming and everyone around me was a stranger."

"I'm so, so—"

"Shut up! Just shut up!" She started to cry. She gripped the baby, tears running down her face and over her tightly clamped mouth. "It's not about you." She swayed, burying her face in the baby's shoulder. The baby slept on. Leaving Nicole alone had probably been unforgivable. I knew she was crying because she had to forgive me anyway.

I whispered, "What can I do, if I can't apologize? I'd do cartwheels if I thought that would help."

She wiped her face with a pillowcase. "You can't do cartwheels."

"I would learn."

"I might hold you to that."

She had set up some kind of baby nest—it looked like a padded roasting pan—on top of the bed. She lowered the sleeping baby, who had a little dried-apple face, bunched and mottled. Grumbling, the baby turned towards Nicole, eyes still closed but mouth opening like a bird's. Nicole laughed, drawing her finger down the baby's cheek—her *daughter*. Nicole's face had an expression I'd never seen before, so soft she seemed blurred. I missed her terribly.

"Look." She pulled down the zipper on the baby's sleeper: on her stomach was a big black scab above something like a plastic barrette. Below that, a diaper as tiny as a maxi pad.

The cabbage smell was stronger here. The baby wiggled, making tiny chirps. Her eyes opened—chips of dark gray—and she squinted towards me.

I didn't want to ask her name, reminding Nicole again of all I'd missed. "She's thinking, 'Who's this messy lady in my bed?'"

"Her eyes aren't that good yet," Nicole said. "Do you think—"

My neck and shoulders tightened.

But she was saying "—you could grab the hand sanitizer from over there? I can do it, but it hurts."

"It hurts?"

"I have some stitches. You really want to know?"

"No, you're right; no." Actually, it would have been fine—I'd heard about episiotomies when we did childbirth classes—but my job was to be squeamish about this stuff so Nicole got to be matter-of-fact. The rubbing-alcohol smell of the sanitizer rang a note in my head, *hospital*. I didn't let myself follow the thought.

Nicole gathered the baby in, kissing her head over and over, then hitching up her baggy dress. She pinned the dress's fabric with her chin, one hand behind the baby's head. With the other, she tried to lift her breast and push the baby's lower lip down at the same time.

"Are you going to be one of those people who's always hauling out their nipples in public?"

"Are you going to be one of those people who has a problem with that?" Nicole yanked the cloth clear of the baby's face and tried to scooch herself further up the pillows, then muffled a yelp. The dress had gotten bunched up and twisted around her torso. "Could you do something here, please?"

Awkwardly, I helped Nicole out of the stained and faintly smelly dress. Her body still looked pregnant, her stomach a soft white hillock. She had on some kind of white cheesecloth underpants, a tangle of pubic hair showing through the weave. At my expression, she said, "The nurses gave me a bunch when I left, and I haven't totally stopped bleeding, so." Nicole had always been modest, but now she seemed barely even to notice that she was essentially naked. "Come on," she muttered to the baby. "Everyone at the hospital kept saying how pretty she is. I mean,

I know they probably say that to everyone. But with Alice, they really meant it. I could tell."

Alice had never crossed my mind as a baby name. Somehow, I'd imagined Nicole and I would have the same list.

I sat down at the foot of the bed, then lay down on my back. The baby snuffled softly. I closed my eyes, realizing how tired I was. The bed seemed to sway almost imperceptibly, a raft. Once as a kid, lying on our scratchy white wall-to-wall while Costa counted backwards from a hundred, a whole story had come to me about crossing the Atlantic as a colonist. The smells of salt and fish and sweet-sour vomit, the roughness of my own chapped cheeks, moisture cobwebbing my wool skirts. Another life, so vivid and complete that for a moment it had almost seemed like a memory and not a lie.

When I opened my eyes, the closet had grown dim. "Nicky?" With my foot, I pushed open the door, letting in light.

They'd fallen asleep, too. The sheet covered them to the waists; above that they were naked. Nicole's hand cupped Alice's shoulder blades. Alice's whole hand gripped Nicole's finger. Her open mouth had slipped off the nipple, but a strand of saliva still linked them, fine as a thread.

27

On our walks, Fort and I passed the artisanal ice cream place that had flavors like Secret Breakfast, bourbon with cornflakes. And then a few doors down, Famous Cuts, the pictures in its front window twenty years out of date: scowling models with hair teased into a foam, triangles of magenta blush high on their cheekbones.

The convenience store on our corner blasted classical music, which had the desired effect of shunting away the gangbangers. A new piece began and I was stopped in my tracks before even registering why: this had been the hold music at our insurance company. Our PT office used Vivaldi, and the lab had an instrumental cover of "Here Comes the Sun" on an endless loop, but Moonlight Sonata was the piece I'd listened to most, the phone lying on the worktable switched to speaker because I might be on hold for forty minutes before I reached a person.

Sometimes I waited so long I forgot I was waiting. The music ceased being irritating and began to seem like just a condition of being. Once, after almost an hour, a human voice had interrupted the hold music, startling me so much that I'd accidentally hung up.

The world felt riddled with holes. It wasn't the past that felt insubstantial but the present. Here I was, standing on the sidewalk with Fort. The Moonlight Sonata had ended. Late afternoon, the air gone chilly and purple.

I glanced over my shoulder: one of the guys fixing the former crack house, the one with the mustache running halfway down his neck, waved at me. He wore a collarless button-down and thin leather suspenders, the whole look very Edwardian if you ignored the tattooed sleeves peeking out from his cuffs. "You guys live across the street, right? I'm Mark."

I shook his hand. After a minute he said, "Do you have a name?"

"*Sorry.* Claire. Claire Hood." Trying to sound a little more with it: "How's your cleanup going?"

"It's done. We hauled out two Dumpsters' worth of shit. I mean, some of it *literal* shit. I guess if the water's turned off . . ." The idea of how seedy the house had been made him cheerful. He described their plans for the space, some kind of artists' collective.

"You have to see this." He turned and jogged up the stairs, emerged holding a white plastic bag from Walgreens that he opened to show two-thirds filled with vials. I nodded. Apparently not the reaction he'd wanted because he prompted, "From *crack*."

"No, I know."

"And H." He bounced the bag so the contents shifted to show a needle. "We're thinking maybe of doing some kind of mural with them in the lobby."

"How poignant."

He jerked back, almost imperceptibly. I felt for a moment the ghost of the sexy, mean bartender who didn't care what people thought. Maybe I could be her again, after all.

In the next second she dissolved, leaving me alone. She'd only ever been a story I told. I'd always, always cared what people thought.

A Muppet Girl who taught at Gymfinity and her boyfriend helped with the move. I took what had been Jeremy's study for myself. Alice and Nicole would share the bigger bedroom. We moved Jeremy's Steelcase desk in there, the one I'd found in an alley and spent hours refinishing as a Hanukkah present. A changing pad on top; diapers in the drawers.

I said, "This was my ex-husband's," and the Muppet Girl nodded, polite but distracted, as if an ex-husband was the least remarkable thing in the world.

Nicole's first night at the house, Alice asleep inside, we sat out on the front steps drinking Baileys Irish Cream, a nod to our high school selves. At Two Fingers when people ordered absurd drinks I would make fun of them to their faces. If I was in a particularly bad mood, or if the person seemed like they probably lived in the Marina, I'd say, "I won't serve you that." Half the time, they apologized. Sometimes they got mad, but whatever: they were on the wrong side of the bar for it to matter.

I rattled the ice in my glass. "Do you ever talk to your mom about why she thought it would work, moving her family in with mine?"

Nicole pulled her knees up to her chin. "You think about that time a lot." Without looking down, she patted the air above the step until she found her drink.

"Don't you?"

"Hardly ever. Was this stuff always so nasty? It's like sugared mucus."

"That's actually their advertising slogan. But you know how your taste buds change every seven years? Maybe—"

"Wait, your taste buds change every seven years?"

"All your cells change every seven years."

"It's not like they *mutate*. You don't get a different-shaped arm every seven years." She sipped from her glass. "Whoa. I just sounded exactly like you."

I laughed. I had my back up against Fortinbras, who grumbled in his sleep. The night was clear, and we could see what was—for San Francisco, at least—a lot of stars, a faint dusting across the sky. From a couple streets over, a muffled bass thump approached, then faded.

Nicole said, "If Holly and I talk about it, she usually gives the line about how she thought it would be easier on me and Shawn. But other times, she's more, 'Parents can't make their whole lives be about what's best for their kids.'" Nicole clicked the glass rim a few times against her bottom teeth. "She's always said I'd understand when I had a kid, but I feel the opposite. Like, if it's not your job to protect your kids, what are you doing? I think that's what fucked us up. You and me, I mean."

"So you're mad at her?" Nicole had been the most pissed-off of the three of us back then—she practically walked around in her own weather system of resentment—but in adulthood, I'd been the one who held a grudge. Presumably Shawn did, too, since he refused any contact, but it wasn't like I could discuss it with him.

Nicole said, "More like I could be mad if I wanted to give the energy over to it. I like how you didn't even register that I called you fucked up."

"No, I did."

"Because if you can't trust your mom, you can't really trust anyone, you're totally on your own. But maybe I'm wrong. I mean, it was a different world for her. Up until your dad, she pretty much always did what she was supposed to." She went still, listening to something from inside. "Was that her?"

"I didn't—"

"Just a sec." She jumped to her feet, disappearing inside.

I took another sip of Baileys. The rest of the bottle would probably go into the back of the pantry, in the space my mom and I had cleared of the yeast medication and canned pâté left by old housemates, and which I'd filled again with Jeremy's unwanted clothes and books, and the abandoned pot rack, and our small knives. It felt like there were two stories I could tell about his leaving, both equally plausible. Gita was his soul mate, and nothing I could have done would have stopped him. Or: after almost dying, he'd flailed around, ready to seize onto anything. I could live with either narrative, I thought, if I could just figure out which I needed to live with.

Nicole bumped open the door with her hip. Alice fussed in her arms—a month old now, still in the grub stage.

"Bye-bee, bye-bee?" I said.

"She's oh-kai." Sitting back down, Nicole yanked up her shirt and sports bra with one hand. "I need to buy one of those ones with the snaps," she muttered. "Up, sweetie. Up . . . good." Alice grunted and snuffled. "Little piglet. I can't believe I wanted a boy."

For a while, we sat quietly, watching the street. A woman with a string bag hung over the handlebars of her walker shuffled towards us, hypnotically slow, gathering herself between each step, then stretching forward like an inchworm.

Nicole asked, "Whatever happened to your freshman roommate? Rat Girl."

"Shayna? She was one of those people who went to China or someplace her junior year, and senior year she'd only use chopsticks. You know, 'Forks just don't feel comfortable to me anymore.'"

"I like how you say 'one of those people,' like I would know lots of people like that." She took a last swig of sugared mucus, then reached up under her shirt, pulling her bra down into place. "Asleep already. I have to pee—?"

She meant, would I hold the baby. I'd managed to avoid much holding, instead offering to do things for Nicole so that she didn't have to put Alice down. I couldn't pee for her, though. I shrugged, okay. Nicole shifted the baby into my arms and went inside.

I sat there stiffly, scared that any movement would wake Alice and she'd start screaming. She shifted in my rigid arms and settled. She seemed to be dreaming of nursing: she frowned, mouth working in and out. With one finger, I touched her wrist, shocked by its petal-softness.

Coming up the sidewalk were three teenagers in 49ers jerseys down to their knees, jostling each other and laughing. The one with the long dark ponytail swerved away from the other two. "Boy or girl?"

"Girl." I felt an odd pride, as though I shared some of the responsibility for this baby's existence.

He leaned down. "Hey, Mama," he said softly to Alice. He knew to run his finger down her cheek; in her sleep, she twisted towards him, mouth opening, and he laughed gently. To me, he said, "We thought you was making them babies *up*," then turned and jogged to catch his friends.

28

We met at the Starbucks on Eighteenth at Castro, late on a Friday afternoon in December, a little more than a year since he'd almost died. Hazy jazz, ridiculously over-air-conditioned air, the mermaid holding open her fins like a centerfold. I hadn't wanted to meet at Blue Bottle and risk its being ruined for me, like St. Francis had been ruined, and Dolores Park, and the whole Inner Sunset. Whereas I already had no interest in ever going back to this Starbucks.

"Here." Jeremy handed me a cup. "You've got on the Boots."

I'd worn my ancient steel-toed Red Wings from Dr. Doughnut, hoping to feel as solid as possible. I tilted the cup towards him a little. "Is this—?"

"Yeah. Of course."

Right, of course. That we didn't still share our days didn't mean we would cease to know basic facts about each other. Like: the only thing I'd drink at a Starbucks was an Americano made with half the usual amount of water. Like: the exact way he pulled his satchel off over his head, then smoothed down his ruffled hair, a movement so familiar I couldn't believe it was nearly—almost, about to be—lost to me.

Flipping open the satchel's front flap, he pulled out a manila folder. Apparently you could download divorce papers from the Internet. He smoothed the forms on the table between us. "So I guess—I don't know. I guess we just begin. Do you want to be 'Petitioner' or 'Respondent'?"

"No."

"Right. I guess that makes you 'respondent'." He looked a little thinner and a little paler than when I'd last seen him, the day of the Girl Scout cookie boxes. I almost asked and then thought, *Let go.* I wasn't the one who could monitor those things anymore. I could barely admit the small relief mixed into the realization. It was freezing in Starbucks, any power I might have derived from the boots cancelled by the fact that I was hunched over, arms crossed. I started to reach into my book bag for my jacket, then realized I'd stuffed in the corduroy one, Jeremy's. If I pulled it out I'd have to give it back.

He entered the date of our marriage and separation under "Statistical Facts," peeling our history back to its barest bones. Jeremy had taken half the money from our small joint bank account but we hadn't closed it: the rent checks needed to still appear to come from him. We checked the box next to "no spousal support." Next to "no name change." Next to "no custody arrangements." What would have happened if one of our not-quite-attempts had resulted in a pregnancy? If what he'd needed was change, a clean break from his old life, would he have fallen in love with the prospect of a child?

We had two choices for the dissolution—"irreconcilable differences" or "incurable insanity"—and we looked at each other for a moment and smiled. Jeremy checked the first box.

Today was just for going over details—he'd type them into the forms and then we'd sign in front of a notary next week. Still, it surprised me how quickly we finished. Shouldn't the paperwork have been hundreds of pages long, not two? The language of no-fault divorce was that there'd been an "irremediable breakdown of the marriage."

"You're really sure?"

"Claire, please. I don't have it in me."

If he didn't want remedies, I guessed that meant the same thing as there being none. We filled out a declaration of property, jimmying the numbers until the furniture plus my truck were worth the same amount as his Honda. How did we have so little of value? My parents had owned a house filled with furniture, they had owned two cars, they had a push lawn mower and a riding lawn mower and a washing machine and dryer and stove and two fridges, they had closets of luggage and guest towels and a tool bench in the garage, rakes and a vacuum cleaner and a safe bolted to the floor of the guest-room closet. And that was *before* we'd moved in with the Kapetanakoses.

"What's funny?" Jeremy said.

"Nothing. I was thinking of the lawyers who had to deal with my parents' divorce. There were like eight different bank accounts by then. That must have been some brutal paperwork."

"Lawyers have probably seen it all."

I shrugged, unwilling to concede that my family's unhappiness might have been anything other than completely unique. Maybe it hadn't been, though. Plenty of people tried to find a way to salvage broken things, even things they hadn't taken care of in the first place.

"Life insurance," he said. "I think I get sixty thousand through W-K. Does that mean—I don't know what that means. I guess this is why we're meeting. I'll talk to HR."

"Okeydokey." I read the next line: "Equipment, machinery, livestock."

The corner of his mouth creased.

"Go ahead, say it."

He shook his head.

"You were going to make a joke about your equipment, weren't you? Are you twelve?"

He laughed. Maybe, free of me, he was free to like me again.

"My saws were expensive," I offered.

"I'm not going to try to win custody of your saws."

"That's a good thing. You don't argue with a woman holding the saws."

He smiled. "I don't even know what that means."

"Aha. But it sounded like it meant something, right?"

"It sounded like a T-shirt. 'Don't argue with the woman with saws.' Your stepmom probably sells it at her store."

You could attach another sheet of paper to the divorce forms with more information, but we didn't have any more. He slotted the forms carefully into a folder, slotted the folder into his satchel. "Why do they keep it so cold here?"

"Totally, I know." I took a sip from my cup. "So. What will you do now?"

"*Now* now? Or—?"

"From now on."

"We've talked about having a kid." He watched to make sure I didn't freak out.

I kept my face still, which I'd practiced for approximately my entire life.

"She's almost forty, so . . ."

"I know."

"Yeah, I guess you . . . I mean, of course you would. Know. Anyway, if it's a boy, what do you think of 'Wilkerson'? We'd call him Will."

"*Wilkerson?*" He'd name it after his workplace? No, of course; he and Gita had met there. It was one of those fake-preppy kid names I hated. Also it reduced the kid to just part of its parents' story. Or maybe all kids should have names based on the conditions of their conception: Broken Condom; Trying to Save the Marriage; We Got Drunk and It Seemed Like a Good Idea at the Time. "Do you actually want to know what I think of it?"

"That pretty much answers my question." He pulled his cuffs down over his hands. "What about you? From now on."

I shrugged. "The business. Nicole can get me on her health insurance if we say we're domestic partners." I saw a momentary wobble in Jeremy: he had a strict sense of ethics around this kind of thing. I pointed out, "You took advising periods and no advisees."

"But that's different."

"Just because everything feels different to the person who's *doing* it."

He nodded, okay. "Alice is what—four months?"

"Seventeen weeks. She's great. I mean, she's a baby. It's not like there's a lot of *mean* babies out there."

"Right; those mean babies. I *hate* those."

"They're the worst." I stopped; it felt too strange. "I should get going, probably."

He straightened up. I could see that he'd forgotten for a moment who I was to him now. "Right. Gita's waiting."

His inflection made me say, "You mean here? Like, in the car?"

"I've been—not *sick* sick, just a little run-down."

Still, as always, a cold pinch of fear at the back of my neck. "Did you see Dr. Wu about it?"

"She said it's nothing. To come back if it doesn't let up in another couple days or so."

So not quite nothing.

He said, "Well, I guess this—"

I blurted, "What happened to us?"

He raised his eyebrows.

"No. Really."

He scrubbed at his eyes, looking tired. "I love Gita. Maybe it's not like—" He closed his eyes for a moment. "I miss you. I don't know if you want to know that or not. But I miss you."

Something very messy—grief, fury, I didn't even know—was waiting for me if I let his words in. Instead, I reached into my bag, pulling out his corduroy jacket: "Here. I almost forgot."

"I wondered where I left it."

"That's where you left it." The jacket had been my first present to him. He took it from my hand. I watched him, trying somehow to hold on, slow time. *This.* My husband for a little longer. But he was just putting on a coat. The moment lasted only a moment.

He slung his satchel across his body and I did the same with mine, and we walked towards the door, arms folded over our chests, dark Levi's, both of us the same height, falling automatically into step. He didn't limp now. We stopped at the door. Somewhere beyond it, Gita was waiting for him.

I didn't feel ready to leave and I could tell he didn't, either. How could coolness take so much work, and yet mean nothing? And how could I only be realizing it now? There must be something to say that would keep him here. He raised his hand, goodbye, but I thought, *you want to high-five?*, and in that moment of confusion, he turned. He pushed open the door, letting in a heavy sigh of warmer air, and was gone.

29

*b*efore we moved in together, before I had any sense of the Kapetanakoses as significant to my life, our families went camping together one weekend. We went to the Eastern Shore, and I spent the day crab fishing with Nicole and Shawn on the dock, sprawled on our bellies, dangling chicken necks tied to string into the water. They didn't use sunscreen and so I didn't, either, not wanting to seem prissy. I would learn later that their olive skin didn't sunburn.

That night, I lay in the tent, my back aflame. Nicole and Shawn breathed steadily. I shifted and heat lightening flashed across my shoulders, so sharp I had to muffle a gasp.

Shawn and Nicole had taught me a playground rhyme. Once they realized it bothered me they'd chanted it all afternoon. In my brain now it lurched, like a rusty Ferris wheel, into motion:

Lincoln, Lincoln, I've been thinkin'
What the heck have you been drinkin'?
Looks like water, tastes like wine.
Oh my God: it's turpentine.

I sat up and pitched myself towards the zipper, scrabbling on my hands and knees, the tent flap in my face like a bat that I pushed away, beginning to panic. And then the outside air suddenly cool and wide and throbbing with insects. My dad sat on a picnic bench and my mom perched on the table, her feet next to his thigh. A second later, a photographic slide dropping into place in the tray, I saw the woman was Mrs. Kapetanakos.

"Hey, Claire-Bear," said my dad. "Bad dream?"

"Where's Mom?"

My father pointed his chin towards their tent.

It seemed weird that he and Mrs. K. had stayed up, but they must not have been tired. I stood awkwardly, brushing off my knees. The adults were still looking at me as if I'd missed my cue. "I guess I'll go see her."

My father reached out suddenly to ruffle my hair. The weekend had been filled with bewildering affection—nicknames he hadn't used in years; sudden and engulfing hugs. He said, "I'm sorry you had a bad dream, Bear."

It wouldn't have occurred to me to locate the disquiet as coming from my dad and Holly—I didn't think of adult relationships as shifting things that could heat up or cool off, expand or contract, accelerate or slow—and so I felt like I'd made the moment awkward. I tried smiling, but the smile came out big and showy and then I didn't know how to get rid of it. I shifted my gaze, as if I were thinking of something else, letting the smile fade. I hummed a little tune. When I turned back to Holly and my father, they were looking at each other, Holly's head tilted quizzically.

I cleared my throat, which sounded funny and formal, so I laughed and cleared it again, but they didn't laugh. "Okay. So, good night I guess."

"Good night, honey," said Holly. My dad raised his hand absently.

I crossed the small clearing and awkwardly knelt, unzipping the tent. "Mommy?"

She sat up at once, not asleep at all. "Did you have a bad dream?"

I nodded, not wanting to admit I'd scared myself with a playground rhyme.

My mom had on the same flannel nightgown as always, white with little blue flowers, her blond braid mussed. At home when I couldn't sleep, she got me water and walked me back to bed. But now she lifted the corner of her sleeping bag. "Come on."

I hesitated, still halfway into the tent. "What about Dad?" I couldn't imagine him letting me sleep with them.

"What about him?"

"Will he be mad?"

She reached out, gathering me to her. I gasped a little in pain.

"What?" She lifted the hem of my T-shirt. "Oh my heck. What were you thinking?" She ran the very tips of her fingers over my sunburn, a light, tickly touch that made me shiver. She said, "You used to be my little, little baby. Can you believe once upon a time you were in my tummy?"

Just a couple months later, we'd be living with the Kapetanakoses. We were supposed to think of the four parents equally and they were supposed to feel the same towards the three kids.

Here, just one moment longer: my mother was only mine. She fit her legs behind my legs, she ran her fingers over my back.

"Can you believe you were ever that tiny?" she murmured, but I was sinking into the ground, nearly asleep.

Nicole wakes me. "She has a fever."

"What time is it?"

She turns the alarm clock: not quite seven. Around the edges of the blinds, the light's the dusky lavender of a mimeograph. I want to pull the covers over my head, but instead I sit up. My workroom's also my bedroom now. It's not an ideal arrangement but when Makarov doubled our rent, I moved in here so we could take on another roommate. I press my fingers to my eyes. "Okay okay okay. Are you taking off work?"

"I've got a staff meeting. Can you?"

"I've got the Pac Heights job." More than half my work these days is trompe l'oeil, word-of-mouth referrals grown out of fossilizing Diane Winter's powder room and dining room and eventually two of her guest rooms.

Nicole sits down on the bed, jouncing me. "Shit," she says. "*Shit*." Alice's first year of preschool has been a litany of minor illnesses: colds, an ear infection, pinkeye.

"Can you just give her Tylenol and send her to school?"

Nicole rolls her eyes.

"Did you ask Sherry?" I'm joking, though. Sherry is our third roommate. She works for an Internet company and barely speaks. We can't decide if she's actually autistic or just cripplingly shy.

"Can you just do 'til noon? I will massively owe you."

I'm good on my own with Alice in small increments—a book, a snack. Combing the tangles from her hair. A walk with Fort. Even the walks bump up against my limits, though: I'll realize Alice is half a block behind, squatting, enraptured by a clump of weeds, a shiny foil gum wrapper, iridescent pigeons jostling for access where some drunk has vomited on the sidewalk.

Over these last couple years, Nicole and I have figured out how to act as though there's no damage between us. The patch is pretty good, visible only from certain angles—moments like now, when I might let her down.

"I'll cancel Pac Heights."

"God, thank you," Nicole says.

I say, "Shut up."

Alice, lying on the couch, has what we call her glazed-doughnut look, flushed and glassy.

"How's it going, Bear?" When I brush her bangs back from her face, they're damp with sweat. "Look, Tylenol. Bubblegum or grape?"

She turns her eyes towards me, blinking as she refocuses. "I hate Tylenol."

"No you don't."

"I do!" she shrieks, bursting into tears.

Nicole is in the kitchen, making breakfast before she heads to Gymfinity. Normally, the advantage of being the un-mother is that I can just leave when Alice is in one of these moods. I take a deep breath. "Bear. You ask for Tylenol all the time."

"I!" She takes in a deep, rattling breath: "Do!" Another breath: "Not!"

"Well, yeah, you do."

She puts her hands over her ears and screams, kicking the sofa.

"Well argued," I say.

I stomp into the kitchen, where Sherry startles, as if I'm an intruder. She's at the table hunched over a bowl of what looks like Count Chocula cereal as if someone might steal it if she's not on guard. At the stove, Nicole stands with her weight on one leg, the other foot tapping the floor behind her. Dirk Hertzberg's driver's license is thumbtacked to the bulletin board, next to the envelope where we keep receipts. Dirk's round eyes make him look astonished to find himself pinned here like a pithed frog, watching over us.

"She claims to hate Tylenol."

Nicole shakes her head, trading me the spatula for the medicine bottles, and heads towards the couch. She's making scrambled eggs for us and Fort.

"I still take that," says Sherry, making me jump. Usually she floats around mute as a wraith, the Ghost of Housemates Past.

"Take what?"

"Kids' Tylenol. The grape kind. For cramps."

"Oh. Huh."

"It's *really good*." She says it fiercely, as if I'd argued. She lifts her spoon, hesitates like she might keep talking. I wait, but nothing more comes.

By the time Nicole and Sherry have left for work, the Tylenol has had a chance to kick in and Alice has perked up. We walk to the playground on Nineteenth, passing the purple Victorian. It's no longer a performance art space—and, actually, it's no longer purple but a tasteful charcoal gray, having sold for something like three million dollars. A Google bus glides by us, sleek as a Great White. As we walk, Alice will stop suddenly in the middle of the sidewalk, and Fort—his back as high as her head—will freeze, standing watch. I keep almost tripping over them both.

At the playground, she spins toward me and away, toward me and away.

"Do you feel like an apple?" I ask her when she comes close.

"Claire, Claire, Claire," she singsongs. "Claireclaireclaire-claireclaire. Do something good."

This has been her request lately of Nicole, whose gymnast past lets her rise to the challenge. I try not to let frustration tinge my voice. "That's your mom's thing. Do you want string cheese?"

She shakes her head, closing her eyes as her hair whips to-ward them.

There's a mom there with a similarly-aged child; loneliness wafts off her like body odor. She's talking to her child in a voice pitched for me, and when her child says something, she turns her head to check whether I've appreciated its brilliance. I keep my body angled away, pretending obliviousness.

My phone bubbles: Jeremy. Ironically enough, we communi-cate mostly by text these days. He'll send me a picture of some-thing like a restaurant advertising Donut Burgers. I update him about Ripley, the hairless cat that lives in the bookstore on Valencia. Nothing we say is intimate, except in that we know each other well, but I have the sense that Gita doesn't know we're in touch. Sometimes this idea fills me with satisfaction of the orthopedic-shoe-on-the-other-foot sort. Other times, laugh-ing at something he's written, beginning to thumb a reply, my throat closes with sudden rage. I'll fling the phone down on the worktable and walk away, feeling sullied, thinking *asshole* at us both.

Recently, though, I've been wondering if maybe everyone wants to be complicated, but wants everyone else to be simple. We only get one life, and we spend a lot of it doing repetitive things, and in the meantime all around us, stretching to the horizon, are other lives we could have lived. Who wouldn't wish sometimes for escape?

His text says, *Just saw a guy in Sebastopol oh-so-carefully putting a club lock on his steering wheel.*

Sebastopol is bohemian, rural, full of beekeepers and people who have two-story libraries in their homes. I write back, *I suppose more cars get stolen in rich neighborhoods?*

There's a pause, then the blipping ellipsis that shows he's typing. *Who's this nice girl who's commandeered your phone?* More ellipses. *She's totally mellowing on my harsh.*

I laugh, and then brace myself just a little, waiting out the phantom pain that follows.

There was this night when I was driving back to Jeremy at the hospital, and just at the top of a hill, an old song came on the radio. I turned it all the way up, wanting the music louder than the radio could actually go, wanting to merge with it. I had the truck windows open; dark, fragrant air wrapped around me. The light turned green. I stepped on the gas, flooded with joy.

It makes no sense to be nostalgic for that time. I was scared, exhausted, fragile as old glass. Part of what I miss so fiercely about Jeremy—my trust he wouldn't hurt me—wasn't even true. But knowing these things makes no difference. The truck swooping down Filbert, a block so steep that it seemed like the wheels might lift off the pavement. The currant trees filling the air with their strange smell, at once spicy and musky, like cloves and cat piss but somehow invigorating, not unpleasant. I shouted along with the radio. I can only look at the image for a second; the longing's that bright.

Lonely Mom has given up on engaging me directly. She asks Alice questions: how old is she, and does she come here a lot. "You look so much like your mommy," she tells her, and smiles at me.

It's not the first time this has happened. Alice and I don't look anything alike, but she does have blond hair—Dirk Hertzberg's genes, presumably. Usually, without missing a beat, Alice just says that I'm not her mommy.

But today she scrambles down off the canary-on-a-spring she's been riding and runs and butts her head against my legs. The first couple times it's sweet, and then it begins to hurt. "Come on, use your words."

"Mommy," she says. She pulls her head back and then swings it toward me, hard.

I catch her before she can butt me again and lift her, kicking, into the air. She's heavier than the last time I picked her up; I stagger a bit, hauling her beneath a Japanese maple. Its rusty leaves cast shifting shadows across her face. The sudden change of venue has surprised her enough to buy me a moment. I pull out what I've packed in the diaper bag: crackers, apples, string cheese beaded with perspiration. Alice is shaking her head and shaking her head, beginning to fuss in that way that means we're one minute from a meltdown.

"Alice!"

She snaps to attention. If I want to keep her interest, I have to do something good. All I can think of is to grab one of our apples and bite as deeply into it as I can. She watches, mouth half open, eyes fixed on mine, as I consume it: the stem, the core, the sharp seed casings that scratch my throat on their way down.

acknowledgments

I am so lucky for the insightful edits and loyal friendship of Molly Breen, Jennifer Noel, Margaret Lea Noel, Malena Watrous, and Laura Wexler, and for the other smart and kind friends who read this book in its early stages: Elisa Albert, Maria Hummel, Matt Iribarne, Greg Martin, Jeff O'Keefe, and Glori Simmons. I've also been very grateful for the support and friendship of Elaine Blair, Meara Daly, Beth Maloney, Loren Mayor, and the M.F.A. Alliance of Greater Baltimore. My father, Gordon Noel, and my friend Laeben Lester helped me a great deal with medical questions. Thank you to the Creative Writing Department at Stanford University, the Continuing Studies program at Stanford, the Literature Department at Claremont McKenna College, and the Writing Seminars at Johns Hopkins University. Thank you to my indomitable agent Kim Witherspoon, to my brilliant and generous editor Corinna Barsan, to Allison Hunter and Elisabeth Schmitz, and to everyone else at Inkwell Management and Grove Atlantic who helped shepherd this book into the world. Thank you to my parents Margaret Wilkins Noel and Gordon Noel, who provided not just emotional support but also very practical support in the form of letting us housesit for them in Portland every summer.

Thanks to Tess and Clem, who never accept easy answers. And thanks most of all to Eric Puchner: I am lucky to have someone of such fierce intelligence, compassion, and humor as my collaborator in work and life.